Duck Lessons

by

James LeCuyer

DARKHOUSE
BOOKS

Accolades for James M. LeCuyer

"Duck Lessons: Great, gut-wrenching story, well told."
     – **Tamim Ansary**, author of *Games Without Rules : The Often-Interrupted History of Afghanistan, Destiny Disrupted, West of Kabul, East of New York,* and more.

"At last! A refreshing blast of political incorrectness from comic writer, Jim LeCuyer. From a hapless high school teacher Harry's confrontation with a "fat, angry purple haired Native American prostitute poet" he's invited to his 10th grade ethnic lit class (*Delta*) to his visitation from a formidable, pissed off Ph.D. mother who won't accept her son's B+ in his AP English class (*Stoned*), LeCuyer's irreverent stories may raise your hackles, but you'll end up cackling."
     – **Judy Wells**, author of *The Glass Ship, Little Lulu Talks to Vincent Van Gogh, Everything Irish,* and many more.

Accolades for James M. LeCuyer

"LeCuyer's stories, all beautifully written, are at once funny and poignant. He writes like an angel with a devilish grin. Get ready for a delightful evening."
    – **Richard Michael Levine**, author of the bestselling nonfiction book, *Bad Blood: A Family Murder in Marin County*, as well as the short story collection, *The Man Who Gave Away His Organs: Tales of Love and Obsession at Midlife.*

"There are so many wonderful things about your stories: humor, interesting characters, intriguing plots, and poetic descriptions. I hope many people will read this book."
    – **Lucy Lang Day**, author of *Married at Fourteen, The curvature of Blue, Dreaming of Sunflowers*, and many more.

Duck Lessons
by
James M. LeCuyer

Duck Lessons

Cover photo by Peter Linenthal

*Copyright © 2018 by James M. LeCuyer
ISBN 978-1-945467-10-3
Published August, 2018
Published in the United States of America*

*Darkhouse Books
160 J Street, #2223
Niles, California 94536*

Table of Contents

Dedication

To the children, to Tezla, Mr. James, and Sophie, and to all those I have loved, to the gallant souls who are trying to alleviate the effects of Global Warming, and to all the adults working for a peaceful future. May the lessons we learn not be ducked.

Acknowledgments

The author would like to thank the following, without whose help and encouragement this book would not exist. Florence Miller, Judy Wells, Lucy Lang Day, Dale Jensen, Angio Batle, Richard Levine, Jon Batle, and Ralph Dranow.

Introduction

These stories are completely true, or, if not factually true, are true emotionally. That phrase sums me up. From my earliest memories I believed that love and adventure were important. I felt abandoned so many times when I was a child of five or ten that I soon realized early how painful and how beautiful love was. As a young adult I was often offered love, but didn't understand what it was, for it didn't fit my expectations. When I did understand, I wasn't prepared or settled enough to make the compromises necessary to have the double life a marriage entails. I had little to offer a partner, neither home nor money nor success. I spent years one step away from being out on the streets homeless. I lived for two years in the laundry room of the burned down Marshall Hotel in Marshall California on the shores of Tomales Bay, and spent another five years living on a fishing boat with a leaky deck. I just adapted. I never felt as if I were a hopeless failure. I always knew I was about to do something of great value. I always felt I was an important person.

These stories are the best I can do right now, and that is something not many people can say, that they have done their best in anything. I admire all who struggle to live up to their own best expectations. I despise the narrow minded, the racists, the selfish, the self important. I admire most writers, and am in awe of the greats, the Tolstoys, the Dostoyevskies, the Thomas Manns, the James Joyces, the Virginia Woolfs. Most of all I admire those whose hearts are kind, however innocent or simple they may feel themselves to be.

I was a lost child whose family was wrecked by The Great Depression, a poor university student, a ridiculous Naval Officer, an unsuccessful commercial fisherman, an English teacher (sometimes a good one), a seeker of truth, and a left of left liberal. I believe in worker's unions, and this probably makes me a disbeliever in our economic system, which some call capitalistic, but which is no such thing, is a monstrous, inhumane parody run by narcissistic mostly very rich assholes.

As far back as I can recall, I scribbled stories and thought that some day I would settle down and just plain write. Finally, after a lifetime of hard struggle against myself, I found the love and support necessary to write. It's not something everyone wants to do, to sit for hours at a time looking into one's own life, dredging up long repressed memories, trying to understand what had happened. I had little else to do when I retired from teaching in 2002, and so I got into a daily routine where if I didn't write I felt I was wasting time. I was almost 70. I might kick off at any time with my stories unwritten.

The modern world with all its computers and facebooks and googles had run over my world. I wanted to write of real people coming together, of my own foolishnesses. I wanted to see in print the stories I'd been telling people for decades, for a lifetime in some cases. It's ironic and quite typical of my life that when I finally started writing seriously, bookstores and books as I'd known them, were nearly extinct.

I've tried to tell how it was in the fifties and sixties before Silicon Valley. How it was to love and work for myself, so I could feel free to make my own mistakes, to say, as my proverbial boat sank, I sank the damned thing myself!

James M. LeCuyer
Fremont, California

Too Soon for Boobies

"You gonna get us in trouble," I whisper, as Jerry kicks the storage room door shut behind us and the space explodes into darkness. He's eleven, almost twelve, I'm nine and a half. He's my best and only friend. I have to follow.

"Shut up," he says. His face is impressively scarred from chicken pox. He tells people he got hit by Nazi shrapnel. I don't believe him, but he outweighs me by twenty pounds or more, and he has muscles where I have spaghetti-thin arms.

"You chicken?" he asks, his voice tight with threat after we crawl a few feet. "You wanna go back?" His voice is so low I can hardly hear him.

What I want to do is cry, but he'd hate me. I shiver with fear and cold. A frightening, high-pitched, rhythmic squeaking rises from somewhere in the room.

"What's that guinea pig noise?" Jerry hisses. It's me. I can't see him, but he's breathing hard just ahead of me. "Knock off that squeaking or I'm gonna bust you one."

The storage area stinks like wet dogs. It's a passageway six or eight feet wide piled with old diving boards, ropes and cork floats on top of thick, still moist, tumbling mats. I've passed the door to this area a hundred times on my way down to the pool, and never gave it a thought. Jerry has not only thought about it, he has opened the door and crawled to the other side before coming back especially for me. So now I owe him and have to go along.

Being here is against every rule of the Pacific Coast Club, and every law I'd ever imagined. But Jerry can't stand babies. He has already shown me how to ditch school, has taken me to the all-day movies at the Strand on The Long Beach Pike to see Sherlock Holmes starring Basil Rathbone, plus a Johnny Weismuller Tarzan and a Charley Chan where we had to crawl inside on our knees past the ticket lady. We had to go inside or we might have been caught in the open by the Truant Officer, and that could have been the end of my life.

"I'm *freezing*." I whine as I clamber slowly over a stack of kickboards. One board slips with a bang against a wall, another knifes into my right knee. "Uhh! Wholaahwwup!" I'm trying to say whoa or stop or hold up and remain silent all at once. For a moment I can't move because of the pain.

"For chrissake!" Jerry whispers. "You're more noise than an elephant. Why am I dragging you along?"

"Because of Uncle Pat," I say as I try not to cry.

"Uncle Pat?" he snickers. "Your Uncle *Pat*. He's just the *Door-man*."

The door to the Women's Locker Room is outlined faintly in a buttery glow. Jerry cracks it open and light floods in so bright I can't see anything else. I imagine a huge woman waiting to capture us as we peer out, two boys in grey, woolen, bathing suits staring up at a descending net. *Caught!*

The door slowly opens wider. My heart pounds so hard my head balloons with blood. Steam envelops us with the smell of coconut soap and mixes with the dog sweat coming from the storage room.

"You go on," I say. "I hurt my knee."

Jerry slides butt backward toward me, reaches around and tugs at me hard by the belt of my itchy woolen trunks. "You don't come right now," he says, "I'll yell."

I'm too afraid to resist as he drags me out into the light of the passageway. I'm dizzy. I get dizzy a lot, from a playground merry go round, or rolling down a hill. In the passageway there's no one, no woman with net or bare breast or raised fist.

"See?" he says, standing and clicking his tongue, something he's taught me to do. I click back. He points up a short passageway to a sharp turn. "Zero. Empty. Didn't I tell you?"

His right hand circles my skinny wrist, and I stay quiet, trying not to look at anything, trying to be invisible. He wants to see naked breasts on naked women. I don't. The only naked woman I ever saw was my grandmother whose flat wrinkled blue breasts sagged past her belly button, a horrible sight. Though I love her and on cold nights I snuggle up like a bug in a rug with her, I always wear my grey duck-footed jammies that protect me from neck to flat pink webbed feet.

The Women's Locker Room passageway lights are soft and cream yellow and recessed into the walls, unlike those in the Men's passageway where glaring white bulbs illuminate the cold walkway from dressing room to pool. Though this is the forbidden women's walkway, it has a familiar rough cement feel on my bare feet, even if it leads up to disaster, enormous breasted women in showers scrubbing themselves purple, mothers and aunts who will catch us and turn us over to my Uncle Pat who stands in his black suit and grey tie at the Front Desk giving orders and correcting and directing with his cigar all who enter.

All the hairs on my body point down away from the showers. If Jerry weren't squeezing the blood out of my left wrist I would instantly race into the warm waters of the pool, even if it would look odd for a boy to explode like a bomb out of the passage from the Women's Locker Room.

Move fast! Run! Maybe the lifeguard wouldn't see where I'd come from. I wouldn't say a word. I learned, from Jerry, if you shut up and look stupid, no adult has the patience to keep talking to you. And you can always cry.

Jerry, holds my wrist. We come to the open, frosted glass door of a shower cubicle the floor tiled in blue and white squares just like the Men's showers, only this is a one person room with a single nozzle while the Men's side is a huge open space with two dozen nozzles side by side on one wall.

This room is empty. "See?" I whisper. "Nothing here. Now we can turn back."

Jerry purses his lips. "We haven't *seen* nothing," he says through his tightly shut teeth.

Around the corner, steamy clouds of light roll out of an open door. A few wet footprints and puddles lead away around a corner. There's a hiss of water from the shower. This is the real thing. I hold back and flatten against the cold wall next to the door, paralyzed, certain we'll be caught.

How could I explain this to my uncle?

"I got lost, Uncle Pat."

"In the *Women's* Locker Room?!"

"Yes, sir."

"And *Jerry*?"

"He got lost there, too."

Jerry peers around through the open door, but I close my eyes. Then, though I'd rather be anywhere else, he yanks me into the stall and says, "Look!"

I can't breathe or open my eyes. There's a sharp slap on my right cheek.

"*See!*"

A little girl, maybe two or three years old, sits alone on the tiled floor, patting puddles of water with both hands. She's naked and peach skinned, and baby fat. She has no breasts. How do they get them, I wonder. When she looks up and sees us, she smiles. I smile back.

"Sheee…it!" Jerry says. He turns his back to her, pulls down his trunks, sticks out his white butt and makes a farting noise by blowing on his forearm. Her wail echoes like an air-raid siren through the Women's Locker Room, arousing, I know, a thousand stampeding mothers.

We race back down the cement walkway and hurl ourselves feet first into the warm, safe, chlorinated waters of the Pacific Coast Club pool. If the lifeguard sitting in his stand were to see us, there might be hell to pay, as Jerry always tells me. I frog-swim underwater as far as I can. When I emerge there are no mothers but plenty of girls and boys who scream and chase each other around the huge sun-lit pool, splashing water, just as always. No Running, the pool sign says. No one has come after me, except Jerry. My chest aches as I inhale and my body shakes with each thump of my heart. I cling to the safety of the gutter at the side of the pool.

"Don't worry," Jerry says, surfacing next to my left shoulder as I take deep breaths. "There's this art class in this hut outside this hotel…" He nods and spits knowingly through his big front teeth into the gutter. His chickenpox scars sit pale against his red cheeks. His blue eyes shine hard as marbles into my unprotected thoughts.

"On Wednesday nights," he says, "you can climb up on a bench and look through a hole in the wall and see a real naked woman. With real boobies."

A Fox Went Out

A fox went out on a chase one night,
Prayed to the moon to give him light,
He'd many a mile to go that night
Before he reached the town…O
      town … O

Bobby sat many minutes at the kitchen table staring at a glass of carrot juice that rose like a pillar before him. He found it interesting because it was the same color as his hair. From its round mouth came a volcanic glow as if sister Mitzi's Baby Jesus Himself had laid hands on it. Ever since Bobby had stayed home with a fake cold to avoid a fight with Ernie Allen at school, Mitzi had been after him to drink this hated carrot juice.

"Drink!" demanded Mitzi. Bobby frowned up at her orangish, radiant, carrot-like face. Just last year he had loved this Mitzi more than anything, had followed her around, watching to see what she might do next. Now…

She tugged at his hair and yanked his head back. "Drink."

"Ow."

"Nobody hurt you, but they will if you don't finish that juice. I have ironing."

"It smells like piss. From Jesus," Bobby added quickly. He tried to include Jesus in all his swearing since Mitzi had forced him to listen to her lecture on how Jesus was the son of God, and was our Big Brother, and how Jesus fed fish "to the multitudes," and we should live pure and eat fish on Fridays in honor of Him. He should be included in all our thoughts. Now Bobby hated Jesus almost more than carrot juice. Who were these people anyway? God and Jesus were robbers who replaced his real sister with a horrible witch. He didn't like carrot juice and he didn't like fish.

"Drink!" With her left thumb and forefinger she squeezed his neck hard enough to fill his eyes with tears. With her right hand she banged the glass to his lips. She was three years older and much stronger. She "worked out" in her gym class at middle school, and had big, flat, gorilla fingers. For months she had made his life miserable.

Bobby took a deep breath and blew a carrot colored cloud over the table and on to Mitzi's pale blue skirt.

"You damned little devil!" She whacked him with the flat of her hand on the back of his head.

Bobby saw whirling stars. He fell sideways off his chair and scooted under the table to avoid a second furious slap aimed at his cheek. Mitzi's arm banged against the chair which toppled the table sending a spray of juice over the kitchen floor followed by the glass that shattered into shards sticking up from a carroty sea on the yellow linoleum.

"*Look what you did, you…!*" Mitzi said. She turned a wonderful shade of purple. Bobby scooted around and cowered behind the overturned table avoiding the juice and the red tennis shoe that kicked down at him. He would get even, if not today, then soon.

"*You* did it," Bobby said from his hiding place. "With your fat arm. And you *swore*. Again."

Muttering a prayer Mitzi righted the table, yanked him up by his wrist and thrust a pan and broom into his hands. For an instant he held them at arm's length as if they were about to attack, before he howled and dropped them in the juice on the floor.

It was turning out so much better than he'd hoped. Mitzi could not stand disorder. She shoved Bobby into a corner and began to sweep up wet shards of glass. Her pimples were about to explode and she was nearly crying. Better and better. He knew he ought to run, but this was all too interesting. He could withstand a slap or two. This was war and he had a plan.

"When I tell him Dad's going to wallop you and ground you until you pray for forgiveness," she said, as she shook the dripping broom at him.

With his face in his hands he faked crying and ran around the kitchen tracking orangish footprints behind him. He was careful not to step on the broken glass.

"Oh, my God!" Mitzi's cheeks once more bloomed into delightful purple blotches. She knelt down in a dry corner, lifted her closed eyes to Heaven and began to pray softly.

"Dear Jesus," her stiff lips muttered. "Help me show my baby brother the light." She turned to Bobby. "Jesus says we must pray together for forgiveness." She leapt up, caught him and dragged him down next to her.

"Dear Baby Jesus, I'm sorry for what Mitzi did," Bobby said, looking innocently at Mitzi. He'd tried Jesus, and found Him not of much use with bullies at school or when Mrs. Wright, his Third Grade teacher, was about to smack his knuckles with a ruler. His parents were of more immediate assistance, for they at least debated the real reasons for the black and blue pinch marks Mitzi left on his skin, about which Bobby complained loudly, while Mitzi explained that she had in no way pinched him, that the marks were due to his lack of good diet, which could only be helped by carrot juice and fish and prayer, according to *The Reader's Digest*.

His parents had been more and more on Mitzi's side since she'd waddled up the aisle to Reverend Moriarti and declared her love for Christ. Mom and Dad did not often go to church, but respected those who did.

"Don't do as we do," his Dad often said. "Do as we say."

With a fierce groan Mitzi stopped praying, rose, pulled Bobby by his neck over to the table, forced him down on the chair, poured more carrot juice, pointed her finger at the new glass and announced in her most holy voice, "DRINK!"

"It's *sour*," Bobby said in a soft and humble tone.

"Oh, lordy me," Mitzi said, glancing up at the ceiling. She shoved the glass against Bobby's lips but he bent his head back, stuck out his chin and gritted his teeth. This time she'd have to pour the juice all over his face.

"Jesus made it *sour*," he insisted between clenched teeth.

"Drink!" she said. "It's not sour. Dad just bought it yesterday. And," she emphasized each word with a neck squeeze, "do… not… spread… blasphemy… about… Jesus!"

"If you like the juice so much," he hissed, "drink it yourself." The glass hovered beneath his nose and emitted an acrid odor.

The secret was to resist but never give in to anger. If he held on to his temper, Mitzi would eventually lose hers and swear one delightful curse after another, despite her Eternal Vow never to use the Lord's Name in vain. At one time she'd been a fairly good sister, but now that she spent so much energy trying to save Bobby through torture she'd become a fat, pimply witch.

There was another little secret that Bobby knew, and that was the carrot juice really *was* sour. He'd poured vinegar into it himself this morning while Mitzi was sitting on the front porch staring at the shirtless, skinny, teen-aged boy painting the Harris' house across the street.

Mitzi raised the glass to her lips and took a mouthful. Her eyes squeezed shut, her head jerked back and a reddish mist sprayed forth like fire from her lips on the just mopped kitchen linoleum. She choked and coughed.

"What did you do, you ratty, horrible, little brat!" She pointed her forefinger at him as he huddled against the far wall. Oh, this was drama beyond his dreams. He sniffled, raised his hands defensively in prayer, and turned his eyes to Heaven, while she gargled tap water at the sink. Her lips set, her face crimson, she came for him and he dashed for the door.

"I was *praying*," he screamed, as she caught him by his left arm and left ear and dragged him howling up the stairs to his room. He pounded his heels on each step and yanked at the banister, shouting as loud as he could, "Dear Jesus, stop Mitzi! My ear! My ear!"

She'd really hurt his ear, but this was all expected. It was too grand.

He was "quarantined." He sat on his bed and stared at his oversized blue sneakers, that used to belong to Mitzi. Theoretically he was locked away, this theory being fact only to Mitzi because he had a key to unlock the door from the inside. He had keys to every door in the house. His feet drummed rapidly against the bedstead. This was the time to act. It only took a little courage.

He waited until he could hear Mitzi's religious radio station booming in the kitchen. She'd must have finished mopping and had started her ironing.

"Let the *CIR*cle be un*BRO*ken," bellowed an old, cracked voice. Mitzi played the music loud enough to echo all over the house because, she said, it would do Bobby good to listen to the Songs of the Lord. She often sang along, though she sounded like a wounded dog.

She obtained her religious ideas from the new young pastor Joseph Moriarti, who she followed around like a poodle, a perfectly fine Mitzi too, until she'd become boy and pastor crazy all at once. Bobby was determined to save her, and himself, from a life of Christian Goodness. Human beings, he thought, should avoid Mitzi like a poisonous snake until she recovered.

From his closet he took a gleaming Penn JigMaster fishing reel, the one dad had given him from Santa last Christmas. And from his ring of secret keys he picked out an old-fashioned skeleton key and quietly unlocked his bedroom door.

He crept along the hallway into his mother's step-in dressing closet and found there, far back in a bottom drawer, a reddish stole made of genuine fox fur, a whole fox in fact, now scabby and almost forgotten, that Mother seldom wore. It was a soft reddish brown with two black button eyes, a bushy tail, six sharp teeth sticking out from a sewn-together mouth, and four little limp paws with black toenails. For years, when he was younger, he'd snuck in and played with it. There were many secrets like this no one knew about him.

He also had a lost key to his Dad's workshop in the basement, from which he was unfairly banned. Mitzi had been warned, at all costs, to keep him out of the workshop. She decided that meant out of the toolshed as well, and out of anything else he might be interested in. But he had a key to the shed too, and had thoroughly explored its once mysterious hoes and shovels and clippers, all very ordinary things he'd seen his mother use many times.

Now he was ready to examine the workshop, which was well guarded by a huge door. If he could open the door without being caught he had no doubt he could work the tools there, for he'd watched his father run the table sander and the whirling lathe on which beautiful round table legs could be formed. There was nothing more he desired than to find a few free minutes alone in the workshop, to set the machines whirring and grinding, chips flying, make the wood dust rise up.

But, for the past few days, it was Mom's backyard shed he'd expressed most obvious interest in, for this was the *misdirection* part of his plan. He loved words such as misdirection. Once you knew a word, you might do something with it.

And he loved to read books about clever animals like Grey Friars Bobby, the little Scotty dog that snuck into Grey Friars Cemetery in Edinburgh every night to sleep under the gravestone where his beloved master lay buried. The tall, skinny, grey-haired lady librarian at school had laughed and said, "It's a book about a Bobby like you."

Grey Friars Bobby led stuffy old gardeners and priests on many a merry chase leading them one way while he escaped another. And who had more right to be in that graveyard than this loyal, true dog?

And there was cunning Lobo the Wolf, one of the greatest wild animals that Ernest Thompson Seton had ever known. As Bobby fell asleep he would often contemplate what he would do if ranchers on horseback hunted him, how he would secretly backtrack through streams and over slippery logs while the men with their hounds followed false paths. He, too, could use misdirection, just as Bobby and Lobo and his Uncle Robert, had.

"Look here," his uncle had said, as he snapped the fingers of his right hand and pulled a quarter out of Bobby's ear with his left. "Very dirty ears. Tsk." And Bobby, who was named after this so-called uncle, would be given the quarter, since it was *found* in his ear, though he knew there were no quarters in his ears, that this was simply another adult lie, a white lie, much as Santa Claus was a lie about a white-bearded fat old man with tiny magic reindeer that flew on to your roof in the snow. It never snowed where he lived. Nor was Uncle Robert a real uncle. He was just an old friend of his Dad's from a time long ago, when both had been "hell raisers."

"Many a beautiful young lady has fallen for that," Uncle Robert said once, as he produced his quarter. When Bobby wanted to know what he meant by that, Mom said seriously, "Uncle Robert means that ladies were surprised to find money in their ears." But Dad and Robert and mom, too, burst out in laughter so Bobby knew there was more to it than ears and quarters and falling ladies.

He'd recently been peeking into the windows of the garden shed, mostly to annoy Mitzi. And he'd dug a hole in back of the shed under the foundation boards and had explored beneath the shed, finding no trapdoor up, such as one might find in any good pirate story, and no good place to hide, except maybe if you were a dog or wolf. Or a fox.

The shed held his mother's mud-stiff work gloves and curved pruning saws and spades and shovels and hoes, all of which he'd examined thoroughly. He'd laughed at the silly story Mitzi had told him about the great spider that hid in a dark corner there. That was another of her lies. She wanted to frighten him until he begged Jesus for help. It was really Mitzi who was afraid of spiders. Bobby and his friend Billy Glass occasionally ate a daddy long legs to prove that spiders didn't frighten them at all.

Mitzi was turning into a holy retard. He would save her. Mom herself had let him in to the garden shed and showed him the tools and even guided him as he trimmed the fuchsias, though he had to use both hands to force the clipping shears shut. Mitzi *knew* this but felt it was her God given job to keep him from having any more fun. She was going to frogmarch him straight to Jesus.

His sights were set much higher than garden tools, or lower, for Dad's workshop could only be entered through a heavy double door that laid flat a foot off the ground on a brick foundation in the yard under the kitchen window. He'd peeked down twice while Dad was working there, but only long enough to see how to push the hidden buttons that started the sander and the lathe.

The great oak door was almost too heavy and noisy for him to lift up on his own. He would need time, and no Mitzi.

He stood holding the fox stole in his Mother's closet and smelled the perfume and the thick body odors that clung to it. Slowly, wondering at himself, he pulled from the fishing reel several feet of monofilament line, tied it securely to the nose of the fox, and added to the tail a tiny lead sinker. He left the fox in the hall outside the door of Mother's bedroom.

Carefully crawling along backwards, his heart beating hard, he stripped off line as he slid on his belly down the stairs. He peered around into the kitchen to see Mitzi ironing away as she listened to her horrible religious music and waggled her fat butt to the boring beat. When he felt sure she wasn't watching and he could sneak past unseen he peeled off more line and led it out the back door, which he wedged open with a brick. He laid line in coils across the back yard to the door of the garden shed, beneath which he tossed his reel through a foot wide hole that led under the shed to the back. This was the dangerous part when Mitzi could easily come outside and see him. But it took less than thirty seconds. He'd timed it before.

He crawled through the large hole at the back of the shed, slid under, found the reel, pulled more line off, wound it until there was just the least resistance, and laid it black handle upright behind the shed, ready for use. Despite his wildly beating heart, he was very focused. This was wonderful fun, though it would take accurate timing of the kind Grey Friars Bobby had used to sleep next to his dead master.

He walked casually around to the front of the shed, took out the key, unlocked the bronze Master Lock and opened the door halfway. *Nearly ready.* He'd thought this out many times, even to diagrams he'd drawn and crumpled up and burned in the fireplace. Not even The Scarlet Pimpernel could be more secretive. When mother and father left, Mitzi would all too often slap his cheeks and pinch his ears to make him do what she wanted, threatening him with much worse if he told. But this time he would turn these hours to his advantage.

His greatest worries had been that Mitzi would catch him as he crept past the kitchen door into the back yard or that she might scream at him as he unlocked the garden shed. Yesterday, he'd taken his Dad's oilcan and squirted the shed door hinges to stop them from groaning with rust. Now the door swung back and forth with barely a squeak. He quietly unlocked it and left it half open.

The workshop doors would be quite another problem, as large and difficult as two great wings. He'd often pulled one door part way from the ground, but it was too heavy for him to easily control. It took all his might just to lift it far enough to put his back under it and push it nearly upright, much less jump around and catch it before it crashed down. All these things formed a puzzle to be solved. The first trick was to trap Mitzi.

He crouched hidden behind the garden shed. With a deep breath, he cranked the reel like mad and shouted as if in fear for his life, "*Mitzzziiii…i!*" He could hear the dead fox with its tiny sinker tapping down the stairs past the kitchen and out the steps to the backyard, followed by a gratifying Mitzi screech. Perfect!

He reeled quickly. This was only the first part of his plan. He pulled the fur through the two holes under the tool shed from which it emerged covered with dirt and cobwebs. He'd have to clean it thoroughly.

A moment later he heard Mitzi clump down the stairs. The back door banged. She said, "Bob…*by*! Did you bring an animal into the house!"

She crashed through the open door of the shed and began to shove tools around, shouting, "Bobby! I know you're in here!"

Bobby raced to the front of the shed, slammed the door shut and dropped the lock into its hasp. Dear Mitzi was locked in. He was breathless with pride. It had worked out as planned, although his plan went just so far and ended in a few unanswered questions.

"BOBBY!" she screamed from inside the shed. The door shook and the lock rattled.

Ah, this was good. She was afraid of the dark shed. Jesus might be on his side after all.

"*Bobby!*" she cried. "There's an animal in here!"

"Who's in there?" Bobby said quietly, placing his ear next to the shaking door.

"Open this door!" The thick wood door threatened to shatter under Mitzi's ferocious pounding, and Bobby pulled away.

"Open this door right now!" she screamed. "Some filthy ratty little animal ran in here."

Amid the rattling of the hinges and Mitzi's grunts he stood back and waited to see if the door *would* give way. When the clamor stopped, Bobby placed his mouth next to the door and asked quietly, "Who's there?"

"WHO'S THERE?!!" she screamed. "Your *sister*, Mitzi, you little shit!"

"Ah. You can't be Mitzi. She would never swear. She loves Jesus."

"God damn you!" came her reply. "Open this door or I'll *kill* you."

"*My* Mitzi is a good, religious Mitzi. She would never kill anyone. And she would never use the Lord's Name in vain."

Mitzi began to cry softly. "Please. *Please.* There's something in here. It looked like a weasel or a big rat. Let me out. I'll buy you a Baby Ruth bar." Her voice sounded far away, exhausted, and for a moment he felt regret for the conquest of his once all-powerful sister, now his defeated enemy. But there had been a year of pinching and slapping and the unresolved issue of carrot juice. And Jesus.

"Baby Ruths cause pimples, my real sister says." He moved back from the shed over to the workshop double doors, unlocked them, and heaved one side up, one great wing unfolding to reveal the dark basement below. He tried to catch hold but the oak door flew past his grip and fell, *Whang!* and the entrance to the workshop was open.

Across the yard Mitzi was screaming and sobbing too hard to hear anything.

The door had long stumped him. He'd never been able to sneak in under Mitzi's gaze, for he knew the crash could bring her running and reveal that he had a spare key.

But, oh, the workshop was a golden storehouse of treasures as wonderful as any Ali Baba might have found, for here was father's lathe and circular power sander, his table saw, and dozens of untouched, unknown magical tools hanging from hooks on the wall, each with an outline in marker pen on the plywood behind them. He didn't understand their use yet, but he could touch them as he wished, and turn the electric machines on and off.

He kept his finger lovingly on the sander switch before he flipped it up and it rose into life. He jumped back and waited until there was a steady whirr. Gingerly, he lifted a four-foot piece of two-by-four onto the table and pushed it forward slowly, into the spinning wheel. Sawdust filled the room, stung his eyes, and made him cough. He pushed harder and the two-by-four ripped out of his hands and flew across the shop on to a wall, shocking him.

Amazing! He did it again, and again the two-by-four flew away. Whack! It was dangerous. He might break something. He turned off the sander, listening to its descending moan, and smiled.

He'd never been so excited. He climbed up on a bench, lifted strange instruments, humped, steel-handled devices strung with wire-thin saw blades, a dozen wooden-handled boat-like devices containing a sharp knife edge in the middle, hammers with rubber heads, drill bits nearly as tall as he was, a long coil of rusty wire like a slinky with a round metal top attached to a large steel handle that only a grown man might turn. He stood on a table and stabbed the air with a huge screwdriver.

"*Zorro! Zut alors!*" He was in a heaven of pleasure that promised much for the future, even if this first time he had to be quick.

He searched under tables and through drawers. He found a disconcerting pile of magazines showing half naked women on the cover. Though tempted he didn't look inside. That could come later, when he decided to return, and he would return, for he now knew himself to be quite clever, at least more than Mitzi, who depended on slaps to get her way, whereas he could plan out a good campaign, be a brave warrior, and perform a bit of magic.

He put everything back in order, dusted away his footprints with a black brush, eliminating all traces behind him as if he were an indian, and leaving the shop quite as if untouched. He'd been there less than ten minutes. It was too overwhelming to take in all at once.

But this was not only a successful first foray into Dad's workshop, he'd won a great victory over Mitzi. She just might think twice about pinching him again, or trying to make him drink carrot juice, especially if he got her agreement this afternoon, sworn on the Word of God, not to say anything about any of this, for it could well be a good two hours until Mom and Dad got home, and darkness might fall, and if Mitzi didn't come to some quick agreement with him, the garden shed would get very cold and dark and full of spiders and foxes. Mitzi was undependable now-a-days, however, and what she might actually say when his parents returned would determine his fate. Even then he saw ways he could bring doubt to her story.

He retrieved the fox stole, looked into its gleaming black button eyes, shook it clean, stroked it, and hid it away back in Mother's closet where no one might think of it. What then would Mitzi say about an animal in the house? God and Jesus might just be useful after all.

Duck Lessons

"Bitchin'," eleven year old Ekkis says, as he and my nephew, Joey, hardcore wannabe street hoods from L.A., poke at their salmon steaks. They stare at tiny, stabbed pieces of fish far out on the end of their forks. They have never eaten completely pink meat before. Fish are, in general, unknown, possibly poisonous.

"Is this shit cooked?" Joey asks. "I mean, man, I dunno."

"Sure," I say. I eat my salmon in four bites. "Tastes good to me. You don't want it?" I reach over with my fork towards Joey's plate. He stabs back with his fork and his piece of salmon falls on a very dirty tablecloth. Our relationship is one where I occasionally imitate a parent, and he and his pal Ekkis occasionally imitate obedient children.

Ekkis says, "Hey. Like fish sticks." And these are key words and they eat.

Both are almost twelve going on twenty-five, not a normal age to be friendly with old uncles like me, but I laugh at their jokes, not because I think them funny, but because I think the whole experience is outrageous, the two boys, quite pimpled from their fried food diet, eager to steal figs from Mr. Berlucci's fig ranch, wanting to catch ducks at Quarry Lakes, and would I show them how to cook a duck?

We all sit on the front porch after the salmon ordeal. Two teenaged girls drive by in a convertible and the boys make stabbing gestures with their fingers, roll their eyes and claim to be hot for females. Fortunately, females have eluded them so far.

Joey says to Ekkis, "Ducks always come for bread. We could lure them with bread and get them to feed out of our hands, and you could grab one."

"*Me?*" Ekkis says, "Ducks are fuckin vicious."

"They don't got teeth."

"They got big beaks. They got claws too."

"They ain't as bad as that seagull you caught on the pier," Joey says. "That was fuckin' gross." Joey looks at me as he catches himself with the f word, and I nod and grin encouragement. He's trying to stop saying fuck in public ever since his mom, my sister-in-law, warned him that she would slap him silly and burn his skateboard if he didn't watch his mouth. She would too, for she believes in direct action and external control. I believe in overfulfillment of desires until it leads to comprehension.

They sit on my front steps and share a plastic bottle of Coca Cola. I often buy them pop and ice cream and Snicker's bars in order to make them as pimply as possible before returning them to Oakland and the dietary laws of their respective mothers, so I'm the good old guy in the family, despite the fact I used to be a high school teacher. Sometimes I even offer a useful idea. For example, I was the one who first turned them on to the figs.

"What did the optimist who jumped from the Empire State Building say to a lady on the way down?" Joey's voice is a little disdainful. He's a slow but insistent talker. He hands the coke to Ekkis. Ekkis says his name means X because his parents, white and working class, sympathized with the Black Muslims, until Malcolm X was assassinated. Or they didn't quite completely sympathize because Ekkis does not exactly mean X, but it is somehow as X as Malcolm X's X.

"Wait a minute," I say to Joey. "Crank up that joke again. Who was on the way down? The lady?"

Joeey explains to me, with a note of impatience, "Duuude… some guy, an optimist see, jumps from the Empire State Building, see? I told you."

I compliment him on knowing the word optimist. They both know it from this joke, they explain.

I say, "This is a joke about an optimist then?"

Joey's stumped. He leans toward Ekkis and and they whisper together and Ekkis hands Joey the last inch of coke.

"Mostly brown spit," Joey says to me, pushing the bottle forward next to my nose. "Want some?"

I lift up my nose and turn down my lips in a teen-age face, and growl, "No, man. I don't need no pimple juice." Their smiles glow. They have argued vehemently against the idea that Coca Cola breeds pimples, but, on a deeper level, they know it's true. Just doesn't apply right now to them, maybe later in life. I'm old but I'm okay. I'm not an adult telling them they can't have a Coke. Who needs teeth? I say. Drink up, I tell them. I can be in their gang.

I *want* to be in their gang. Being a retired teacher can be slow, and a hell of a lot less interesting than their fig stealing gang. Damned good figs too, big, black, and sweet ripe red inside. Turkey figs.

"Okay," Joey says, his expression blank. "Here's the deal. A dude… he's an optimist… jumps from the Empire State Building. See? You say you know what an optimist is." He looks at me from the corners of his eyes, getting back at me.

"Sure," I say. "He's a kid who thinks he can tell a joke and make some old guy laugh."

After a dead moment, Ekkis says quite seriously, "He's right."

Joey has almost lost patience. His joke has strayed from the straight path he had in mind. But he started this joke, and he's going to tell me whether I want it or not. He opens his mouth.

"When you finish this joke," I interrupt and say, "maybe sometime later in the week, I have a good idea about catching ducks."

Ekkis is interested. Joey's face flares up. He has to finish this joke *right now*. I know him and I know if I interrupt him again he's going to stomp off to his room and lock everyone out and play some loud angry rap music. I've thought about ways of destroying his collection of rap, without being held to account. I'm too old to be lumped together with all the racist whites in the world, with the Ku Klux Klan, the police pigs, and Bank Executives. I don't like the word bitches and ho's for girls. What do Joey and Ekkis know of the politics and greed of the world? They know stolen fruit. Ducks.

Joey starts again, "This optimist dude is falling past the 42nd Floor." He drops the coke bottle onto the lawn, thick brown juice spurting up. "Whoomp," he says, his hand slicing down showing me how it is to fall.

"A lady leans out," he says, "and asks the guy, 'Howzit goin'?'"

"Wait," I say. "A lady leans out of what?"

Ekkis smacks Joey on the shoulder, "You're fuckin' it up. You forgot the restaurant."

"Yeah. Okay. A lady leans out of the restaurant there and says, 'Howzit goin'?'"

"Phew," I whistle a little through my teeth. "A restaurant on the 42nd floor and there's a lady eating salad or something, and she sees this guy falling past and she doesn't scream? Instead she asks him how he's doing? Wow!" I can't help myself.

Joey jumps up. Words rise to his twisting lips but don't come fast enough to keep up with his anger.

"*Fuck it, dude*," he says, teeth clenched. Pimples with pale cream centers flare up like tiny volcanoes on his cheeks. Off he races upstairs. His bedroom door slams. Rap music blasts through the house.

Ekkis and I laugh. I've been sarcastic, but in a kid way, and Joey will forgive me and we'll be pals again. He'll hit me as hard as he can on the shoulder and I'll throw him up in the air, something I can still do despite his dignified age of almost twelve. He used to love it when he was two or three, and he still giggles over it, he, a Sixth Grade boy, flying up through the air. Catching him, I'm afraid, is a good bit harder now. I just guide him down gently.

"So, what about the optimist," I say to Ekkis above a rap chorus of

Nobody I know got killed in East Central L.A.

Today was a good day...

Ekkis looks at me, his eyes serious. He's dark where Joey's hair is white blonde. His grey sweat shirt is streaked with what looks like dried blood. Joey's too. They claim it's fig juice. Their jeans are solid dirt, crispy to the touch, and torn. They stink like old meat. They haven't taken a bath since they came a week ago.

"No questions, dude," Ekkis warns. "I just tell the joke straight. Don't say a fuckin' word. Okay?"

"Fuckin' fine with me," I say, imitating his tone. "I'm fuckin' cool with that."

"Okay, then. This optimist jumps off the Empire State Building, and a lady in a restaurant on the 42nd Floor leans out and says, "Howzit goin'?"

I nod silently.

"The guy says, as he falls past, *So o o o o o f f aa rrr so o o o goo oo oo ddd…*"

I laugh a little, politely. It's more of a cough. It's an old joke.

"Get it?" he asks.

"Sort of," I say, pausing as if in deep thought. "A man who believes everything is okay, an official optimist, wants to commit suicide so he jumps off the Empire State Building, and a lady eating a salad or something in a restaurant on the 42nd Floor leans out of a window there and asks him as he falls past how is he doing? And he says he's doing fine because he's an optimist. The only question I have is the guy an optimist because he thinks he won't die when he hits, or is he unable to plan for the future?"

Ekkis shakes his head hopelessly, frowns and stares at me. Am I serious? I smile eyes wide, cock my head, curious as a kitten.

"Sonofabitch," he says. "I gotta go up and see Joe."

The next night at dinner, which is pizza and vanilla ice cream slathered in chocolate syrup, Joey, now recovered, says, "What about that duck deal?"

How far, I think, should I go with this? I am, after all, almost 70, and considered by most adults who don't know me to be a responsible male. I'm in good health and can still do a very slow military roll over the four-foot cement wall that marks the boundary between the Hope of Peace Cemetery and Berlucci's figs. The boys can hurl themselves at the wall right leg over the top and down on their backs onto the dirt of the fig ranch in a flash and rise up running. I try it but very carefully, gracefully. I don't land on my back. I'm proud that, even with a bad left knee, I am able to still do it, just not as fast as I could at Joey's age. My back hurts. My knees shout in agony as I hop up and twist sideways to the wall.

"You gotta do it faster," Joey says, sizing me up after my one attempt. He explains patiently how I have to leap and throw myself at the wall, but I know if I were to miss that five or six inches of thigh cushion between my knee and genitalia it would send me straight past Kaiser Hospital into my own personal plot at Hope of Peace cemetery.

"Yeah," Ekkis says. "Faster, or they get you."

"Who gets me?"

"The cemetery dogs."

I try to imagine a flock of wild cemetery dogs chasing me over the wall.

"Doobermen pinchers," Joey says, harsh eyes gleaming violet. "The worst!"

He wants to train me, but maybe I'm not trainable, maybe I'm too old to hang around with after all. I'm often on trial. There are things he and Ekkis want to do that I might not approve of. Fortunately, so far, these things are also too scary for them without my help. They want to break into Mrs. Vandy's house, for example, and explore it. I tell them Mrs. Vandy has asked me to keep an eye on it while she's visiting her family in Quebec, so I have a conflict of interest. They've heard that phrase.

"It could be great to break into a house," I say. "But Mrs. Vandy is my pal. I couldn't break in to the home of a pal. Besides, I have the key. It wouldn't be the same. You know what I mean?"

If I add *You know what I mean* to a sentence I always get a nod yes from them. They never want to admit they don't know something, a fatal error at almost twelve.

They want to tour the house, sure, but mostly they want to break in. They need to practice breaking in techniques.

"But we won't trash it," Ekkis says. "We just wanna look inside."

I slowly shake my head no, "Can't do it, man," I say. I put my hand on Joey's shoulder and bite my lip. "It's a harsh crime," I tell them. "The cops would put you away."

They know, because I've told them, that kids who get put away automatically get buggered up the ass. Their school friends have said the same thing.

"It wouldn't be the same for me," I explain. "I'd be safe in jail. Too old." I pat my butt softly and look sorrowful.

"Sad, dude," Ekkis says, shaking his head sympathetically and staring at my elderly butt.

"Now," I say to Joey, "You trying to tell me that doing a military roll over this five-foot wall is going to stop some Doobermen Pinchers from ripping my guts out?" Gut ripping is what all Doobermens do.

"Naw," Joey says. "They get you anyway." When cornered he tends to be honest. "But it's good practice."

Now, with pizza and icecream swirling in their bloated bellies, ducks are on the agenda again.

"You up for ducks?" Joey says to me.

"I'm an old duck hand," I say. "From the Rio Grande."

Golden pizza crusts surround us. The Safeway quart of vanilla ice cream sits scraped out, a melted puddle in the bottom of the container. I'll send them home one mass of deadly pimples and they will bless me in their dreams. I have warned them about their dietary habits, about pimples and boils, but while they're beginning to think Coca Cola could cause pimples, they're not convinced of the relationship between ice-cream and pimples. It's probably one of those adult lies meant to torture kids, like coffee stunts your growth. Ice cream and Coca Cola are entirely different, one's white and frozen with a lot of healthy milk or cream, and the other is brown with unknown liquid.

"What's your duck plan?" Joey is persistent, a trait that will do him well if he lives through his teen years.

Okay. They've accepted my restriction on the break-in at Mrs. Vandy's, and maybe I can accept their duck scheme. Am I in this gang or am I just another phoney adult?

"Look," I say. "I love you guys. You're my pals. But there are some age differences between us, and the cops might not take too kindly to an old guy like me grabbing some duck from a park. You know what I mean?"

"Yeah," Ekkis says.

But Joey is impatient. "We want to cook a duck," he says.

"I could buy one," I say. I shift constantly between my role as counselor and follower of the Joey-Ekkis gang.

They look at each other. Do they want to cook a duck or do they want to steal one? They shake their heads. They want to steal a duck and then cook it, and eat it. It's a process. It's a way of ensuring that they will be able to eat for nothing. They could run away and live on ducks. They are willing to do the dirty work of stealing, if they can figure out how to catch a duck. If I will use my special knowledge as an adult to show them how to cook it. I've never cooked a duck, but I've cooked many a chicken.

"Same difference," they both say scornfully.

"Chickens cost dough," Joey adds. "Ducks is free."

They scout around through the house and read one of my old Foxfire magazines, an article about traps made out of wooden boxes baited with corn. A great magazine, they feel. How to dig a pit for bears. How to catch trout without hooks. How, when trapping wild birds, you can prop a box up with a twig and make a little triggering device from a mousetrap. They find a mousetrap in the basement. Where can they get some corn? It's not corn season yet, I tell them.

"Okay. We don't need no fuckin' corn," Joey says. "Bread works good."

They debate the honesty, or realness, as they say, of using bread instead of corn. The old trappers might have used sourdough bread, so they'll go with sourdough.

We discuss a potential flaw in their mousetrap plan. They don't want the duck to get its beak hurt when the trap snaps shut and pulls the string that yanks the twig that drops the tilted box down over the duck. They want to trap the duck, chop off its head painlessly, pluck it, cook it, and then eat it, basically before the duck has realized what's happening. Ducks, after all, according to them, are trusting, like pets.

The boys are not into torture of large creatures, only insects. They would never torture a dog unless it was very mean, like a Doobermen. Then they might have to poison it by putting that rat stuff in a piece of raw steak.

They retire and from their room there's silence for an hour or so. They come down where I'm watching the Giants lose to the Dodgers. This has been my allotted adult hour. They could care less about baseball, a fake, slow game that children are forced to endure so their fathers might feel good about themselves.

"We got a plan here," Joey says, after an inning of respectful silence. He presents me with some crayoned drawings showing a huge box dropping down on a tiny duck which has just pecked at a piece of bread glued to a flat piece of wood tied by string to the fatal mousetrap which snaps and pulls out a twig. It's a series, like a comic strip, and not bad. The duck looks like a duck, and its one eye looks up from the just pecked mousetrap at the falling box with some astonishment.

"But can you glue bread?" Joey asks.

"Good question," I say. "Maybe you can paste it on." I tell them how paste is made from flour. They think that's amazing. They've been pasting textbook pages together for years in school and no one ever told them paste was flour you could eat. Driven by duck schemes, they are willing to learn anything that might add to their plan.

Next day they scour the neighborhood clear to the Freeway for a proper wooden box. Wooden boxes, they discover, hardly exist any more except in old stories, or in shapes that aren't very useful, with too many wires or too small. Safeway had some but they were all smashed up.

"Them Safeway bastids wouldn't give us no whole wooden box," Ekkis says. "They broke them."

"We're gonna set fire to all their damn boxes," Joey says.

"That'll show them," I say. "But you might burn down Safeway and kill someone and get put away, and then you know what'll happen in prison. So you gotta take that into account."

"Ah, dude. They won't catch us," Joey says.

"Didn't you already go in and ask for wooden boxes? Didn't they see your faces?"

They think about it. "Yeah," Joey says.

"So, what're we gonna do?" Ekkis says. I like Ekkis almost as much as I like Joey. His skeletal ribs stick out, but he can eat a large pizza by himself, or a pound of bacon for breakfast. Both boys are revved up all day like zippy little bumper cars.

My general theory is whenever they want something that's bad for them, give them way too much of it. The theory works with bacon and coffee, but not ice cream. That is, after I cooked three pounds of bacon one morning for breakfast, they both stuffed themselves and went to the toilet and vomited, and couldn't be persuaded to eat even one piece of bacon the next day. But ice cream is different. Even a gallon of vanilla ice cream disappears, and, though vomiting may occur, they are willing to try ice cream again almost immediately, maybe a different flavor. Maybe two or three gallons would do the trick, but I don't want to kill them.

"Okay," I say. "Maybe Niles Park is good for ducks. I used to catch them in Westlake Park when I was a kid."

"Yeah?" Joey says. He lives near Westlake Park, now called MacArthur Park. "And you never cooked none?"

"No," I say, "but I cooked a seagull once."

They look at me respectfully. Ekkis had caught his seagull on a hook and line by accident when he was fishing for perch. But they never thought of cooking it.

"How was it?" Joey says.

"Terrible," I say. "Fishy. You might as well cook cat food."

They are really impressed. They can imagine how horrible cat food might be, but this opens up a whole new world. How best to catch a cat?

"I just figured out how to catch a duck," Joey says after a moment of silent contemplation of cats and seagulls. "It came to me."

"Yeah?" Ekkis and I say. Ekkis says it doubtfully, because he has often been a victim of Joey's ideas, but Joey is the plan maker.

"Get a piece of monofilament and a hook and stick on some bread and chum up the ducks until they get excited then throw the bread with the hook into the middle of them and you'll catch one."

The genius of youth. This was the very tactic I'd used at their age. It does work, but I know there are unforeseen problems that I think they ought to experience before they decide to become professional duck catchers.

They scout out Sears and steal a package of Number 6 Eagle-claw hooks and some clear leader material. I warn them about working Sears too obviously, relating my own experience getting caught almost 60 years before by a fat lady with a purse who turned out to be a store detective.

"You wanna steal something there you gotta be really careful," I tell them. "They watch hard for shoplifters."

"Aw, Sears is a cinch," Ekkis says. "We steal from them all the time."

"Yeah," I say. "But now they have overhead cameras. You know how they work?"

"Yeah?" they say. But I explain anyway.

"The cameras record you, and then someone looks at the film when they realize that something has been stolen, and they can see you on film maybe six weeks later, and then they put your photo up everywhere for the employees so they can identify you when you come in. The next time you steal something they catch you. It's cut and dried. They show the film of everything you ever stole there to the jury, and they got you."

"Right. And the jury puts you away and you get butt fucked," Joey says, his voice drifting down to scorn. "Bulllll...*shit*. They're not gonna give no jury trial to no kids."

"Yeah. Right." I shake my head, considering. "Not the first time anyway. But they got all those cameras and all that evidence, so if you get serious about stealing, they can nail you."

They're really nice kids, but one thing leads to another and they could jump in over their heads. Still, that's how you learn, you go too far once or twice, and you never want to do it again. How can we keep them from the worst of it, the sloppy, snuffling justice that follows after minor criminals like a hound.

I could use some advice, here. I remembered my poker pal Buddy, a retired cop now working part time as a ranger at Niles Park. He's perfect.

Ekkis and Joey are too young to join neighborhood gangs, and not into drugs so far as I know, not yet. Here, in Fremont, it's pretty quiet. They're free to roam, to explore the limits of their slowly emerging world, adventurers in a land of endless possibilities. Rebels. Conquistadores. Mountain men. A dog can be a grizzly, a cat can be a mountain lion. They face them down.

Though they listen to rap, they don't want gang bangers telling them what to do. They look to me for adult advice and I try to trick them into following the rules most of the time, not that I necessarily believe in the honesty of our laws and leaders or the wars they lead us into. But that revelation comes later for them. Sadly, not much later.

I love them. I can't force them to be one way or another. I'm not eleven. I'm not with them all the time. I'm something of a coward too, made fearful by my love for them. I want to keep them from pain, an old story that only the old can tell properly.

Joey plans the duck attack. Niles Park Lake has a lot of wild ducks and geese that flock like mad for bread. It's the right season for mallards. The boys decide to lift a couple of loaves of bread from Safeway, and mosey over to the lakes about sundown tomorrow, when it's just dark enough to hide their duck action, and after hours for park rangers.

I suggest they check the dumpsters outside Safeway before they steal bread off the shelves. I explain it would be something of a glitch in their plan if they were busted for theft before they even got to the lake.

"Yeah. Yeah," they say.

"There could be a lot of old thrown away bread there in back of Safeway," I say. "Ducks don't care how old it is. You might get a half dozen loaves."

They discover three slightly moldy loaves of bread in a big dumpster out back of Safeway and come back excited. Free duck bread. All they had to do was climb a fence. They no longer want to burn down the store.

They get their roll of monofilament leader and hooks and we all three take the hour walk to the lakes. It's better to walk, just in case, Joey says. He has watched movies where people spot license plates, and he has my interests at heart.

The sun is setting but the lake is clear enough reflecting a few fleecy clouds rolling in from the bay. A mile or two behind us to the southeast the Fremont hills are purple, verging on red. An energetic black and white Jack Russell terrier drags a tall, dark, bearded man along the lakeside walk. A dozen or more mallards and three coots swim out to the center wary of the dog. Pepper trees and pines rim the edge, and a few small cypress trees grow up through the water from the shallow bottom. The reflected images of the trees hang green with Spanish moss layered with curtained passageways, pepper tree branches in graceful frills touch mirror images in the water, bald cypresses struggle to lift up and fly away, female and male, all beautifully swamp like.

The man with the Jack Russell disappears around a bend. We sit on a bench together and watch everything, the boys discussing possible park rangers, waiting, excited. When they look up at me their faces are very young.

I'm worried. Is what I'm doing right? Am I just encouraging them? I've worked this out, but you never know how the most careful plans might fail. The best lessons often have an edge of uncontrollable danger, as I have learned as a teacher.

But there are no lessons about catching ducks in a public park lake.

When the coast is clear, and the lake is very quiet, the boys rustle up from our bench.

"Are you *down?*" Joey asks me.

"I'll stand back there, under the trees. I'll whistle if I see anyone."

When they nod, I say, "I've got a little plan. A ranger catches you, I'm going to pretend to be one damned angry parent type. Then I'll drag you home. You know what I mean?"

"Perfect," Joey says. "You're backup."

"Right," I say. I thump them both on their wild unwashed heads.

They walk slowly toward the most sheltered corner of the lake, tossing bread out on the water as they go along. Soon they've attracted a crowd of birds, mostly big mallards, some drakes in flashy greens, a larger number of dull brown hens, some pintails, two or three shy buffleheads, two stiff gulls red beaks held high, and a half dozen pesky black coots that grunt like tiny pigs.

I fade into the trees and call Buddy on my cell phone. I feel guilty, but I've talked it over, and this is the game. Buddy's my good old gambling pal. Once in for a hand, he's hard to bluff out.

"Where you at," I say.

"I'm watching now," he says. "I see them."

"Don't overdo it. They're lovely boys."

"Hey, I'm a pro." His gravelly voice is soft.

Joey and Ekkis stop and throw more bread and the ducks dart along the water, quacking eagerly, charging at each other as a chunk comes their way, shaking crusts in their bills, racing off. The boys look behind them.

I'd reminded them to scout the place, just so they wouldn't do anything completely obvious. Joey placed his right hand on his head and stared at me mouth open as if I were crazy. Am I trying to warn them *and* help them catch a duck? What kind of deal is *that?*

Joey slips the hook with the mono from his pocket, pierces a fat piece of crust and throws it out as Ekkis tosses a spread of bread. A glorious, iridescent, blue and green drake mallard races in. But they've discussed how males might be too tough to eat, and Joey yanks the line back. The soggy bread stays behind and is gobbled up. He re-baits and tries again. A plain brown female mallard takes the hooked bread this time, and in her haste to dash away before some other duck can snatch it, gets hooked in a fleshy corner of her beak.

A furor of bright wings and feathers and ducks flying scattering and hurtling wings and orange feet across the lake and into the air dripping water as the female screams and tries to fly straight upward pulling the monofilament with her, the other ducks emitting great blasting quacks of alarm. Up she flies yanking at the line and Joey jumps back but holds on. There are high-energy screams such as two inner-city boys have never imagined might come from a duck.

They don't know ducks. They don't know the way ducks rape each other in spring, or their booming adolescent quacks at night, or that this dull looking female, hooked as she is, might fly at them and beat at them with her wings, that she might understand what was happening to her and want to attack them.

There's an orchestral assault of ducks, the whole lake a cacophony of quacks and shrieks and hoots, a wild, modern operatic explosion, enough screeching to wake every warden in Niles. Most of the birds have settled back forty feet or so. They paddle about calling to their frantic companion. Some fly off and circle the caught hen. Joey pulls her in, but she hurls herself into the air again, squawking hoarsely as he winds her closer. Ekkis falls back, afraid, perhaps, or just astonished.

In the middle of this melee Buddy strides out of a eucalyptus grove directly behind the boys. He's in full regalia, in a khaki Park Security uniform, ranger cap, his .45 pistol in a gleaming black holster on his polished belt. He used to be a full time San Francisco cop. He's a lot beefier now, but still fast on his feet.

Ekkis whoops, "*Pig!*" and runs.

Joey drops the monofilament and turns to run, but Buddy has him by the shoulder and holds him tight. Buddy yells at the fleeing Ekkis, "Halt, you're under arrest," but this doesn't slow Ekkis who vanishes in a puff of leaves.

I hurry up to them just as Buddy pulls out his cuffs and shakes them at Joey who stares up at him. "I let you up, you promise not to try to escape? Or do I have to put the cuffs on you?"

"What's going on officer," I say.

"Stand back, sir," Buddy says. "I caught this boy illegally fishing for ducks."

"What? He's my nephew, officer."

"Stand back, sir, or I will have to arrest you too."

Joey shakes and cries. This is far more than he can handle.

"What were you doing, boy?" Buddy lifts Joey up by his tee shirt and pushes him spread-eagled his back flat on the huge trunk of a cypress. Joey can't move or twist free as Buddy has shoved his belly up against him, the pistol on his belt almost in Joey's teary face.

I yell at Joey. "What were you doing?"

"Fishing," he gasps. "Just fishing."

"You caught a duck," Buddy booms. "What were you going to do with it?"

"Let it go, sir."

"It's illegal to fish in this park. Did you know that, boy?"

"Nosir."

"It's illegal to capture a duck in a public place by any means. Did you know that?"

"Nosir." Joey's voice is so small I can barely hear it from five feet away.

"Do you know that this is a female duck who might have ducklings hidden over there in the reeds? A mother?" Buddy is shaking with apparent rage. "Don't you care?"

"Nosir. I mean… yessir."

"It's kids like you who wreck this park."

"Yessir."

"Officer," I say. "I'm this boy's uncle, and this makes me very very angry. This is a terrible disappointment. Maybe I can help here."

"I'm booking him for a violation of the law against fishing in a restricted area, and for catching a duck on a public lake."

He leans his fat paunch into Joey's face, crushing him against the tree trunk, then stumbles back and swears.

"Damn you boy. You trying to bite me?"

"Nosir," Joey says. "You stuck a button in my mouth, sir." For a moment I see a sly, triumphant gleam in his eyes.

"What's your name, boy."

"Joe, sir. Joseph."

"Joseph what?"

"Wheelock, sir." He nods at me. "That's my uncle, sir."

"I'll get to him later," Buddy says, motioning me back farther.

"Who's your accomplice? That boy who ran away?"

"Nobody. He was just some kid. I don't know him."

"You lying, boy?"

"Nosir."

"Damn you boy, are you contradicting me?"

"Nosir. I mean…"

"Are you going to tell me the truth?"

Joey looks at me and breaks into sobs. He's been trying to keep up a front, but now he sees that I can't help him, and he can't hang on by himself.

"C'mon boy. Will you stop lying to me."

Joey shakes his head. *No. Yes.* It's torture. The last thing any boy wants to do is rat out his pal.

Ekkis reappears from the trees.

"I'm back," he says breathlessly.

Ekkis makes me whoop with joy.

"My name is Ekkis Phelps, officer."

"You fishing for ducks too?"

"Just fishing, officer. We don't want no ducks."

"That's not true, is it, Joseph? You attracted the ducks with bread. You were using the same bread. Weren't you!"

Joey says nothing. He looks down at his feet. There's a stand-off. No one says anything for a minute or two while Buddy stares at them.

"I tell you what," Buddy says. "You tell me the complete, entire truth, and I'll let you both go home to bed."

Buddy, of course, knows the story, even down to the stolen fishing hooks and mono.

Joey says, "I thought once you arrested someone, sir, you got to carry it through."

"You trying to tell me how to do my job? I'm trying to determine what happened here. And I want the whole truth. I'm giving you a chance. Now, *were* you fishing for ducks?"

"Yessir," Joey says at last.

"And was this boy, Ekkis, fishing for ducks too?"

Before Joey can answer, Ekkis says, "I was, officer. I was helping him."

"And what were you going to do with a duck?"

"We were going to eat it, sir." Joey takes a step toward me but Buddy shoves him back against the cypress.

"Eat it?" Buddy says. "You and your accomplice Ekkis were going to eat this duck?"

"Yessir."

"And can you cook, boy?"

"Nosir."

"And you, boy," Buddy says to Ekkis. "Can you cook?"

"Nosir, officer. I ain't old enough."

"Now just who was going to cook this duck for you?" Buddy looks at me sternly, and for a second my heart skips a beat. I'm beginning to feel a little of what Joey and Ekkis must feel. The ducks on the lake have gathered closely around the hooked hen, who is swimming and jerking her bill from side to side trying to break free of the hook and the trailing monofilament.

Buddy follows my eyes. "You boys see that mother duck out there, squawking for her ducklings. That hook can kill her, you know. She's probably a wild, migrating duck who stopped to have babies. In fact, if I can't catch her she'll starve to death, you understand? I'll have to shoot her and let her poor babies die. Do you know what it feels like to be a mother starving to death? Huh?"

We all stare at the flopping hen. Maybe twenty-five feet of mono trails from her beak, and every time she tries to lift off she's dragged back. She doesn't give up.

Buddy hooks a huge finger in Joey's belt and jerks him forward, saying, "The world is filled with billions of people like you who do not give a damn if they kill a mother duck, or if they pollute a nice clean lake, or foul up the water supply for a hundred thousand people. Did you boys know Niles Lake is part of Quarry Lakes which are part of the city water supply?"

"Nosir," they both say.

"We're from Los Angeles," Ekkis adds. "We're just visiting."

"Tough guys from L.A., right? You see how that monofilament trails along across the lake, tough guys?"

"Yessir."

"Well, that monofilament is tied to every damned thing that's wrong with this world, with the cruelty of mean boys, with all that human beings do to mess up this world. Do you understand me?"

"Yessir."

"I don't think you do!"

He suddenly takes Ekkis by the wrist and yanks him next to Joey. Ekkis gasps. I move forward to interfere. This has gone far enough. I don't want the boys scarred for life, or hurt, or vengeful.

"Stand back, sir," Buddy says to me. "I will take action if you interfere in any way. I mean it, sir. Do not test me." I can't tell if he's acting or not, but I have to believe him. He'd always seemed to be a kind man, at least he's told me stories that make me think that, but his face and body language are so aggressive now that I have no idea what he would do if I were to step forward and say, *Game over, Buddy.*

I don't know him well enough, I see. It's not my play any more. What he knows of life is different than what I know. He was a cop. What images are imprinted on his mind, and what drama he now thinks he's playing out, I have no idea. But if he were to reveal my phone calls, my betrayal of the boy's plans, that might be a strong lesson for them about the adult world. They'd never trust me again, and I couldn't bear it.

Of course, there's nothing really to arrest anyone for. A kid's crime.

Buddy's cold, whiskey scarred voice, breaks in. "One or the other of you better tell me the whole truth. Who was going to cook this duck for you?"

They're silent. Joey sneaks a look at me.

"I promise you in front of your uncle," Buddy says, "that if you tell me the whole truth, the whole story, where you got your idea and where you got the fish hooks, and who was in on this game with you, I will let you go. I swear it in the name of the law, and in the name of Almighty God."

Buddy waits and then turns to me and says, "What were you doing here? What's your part in this?"

They're both sweating. Their trapped eyes roll whitely. More than ever they want to run. It's not the boys who can't stand this interrogation, it's me.

I step forward. "I…"

Buddy takes a step back and places his hand on his pistol holster. "I've warned you once, sir. One more step forward or make a single physical gesture, I will have to charge you. These boys belong to me now."

Joey and Ekkis look at me and I nod and mouth, Okay. *Okay. Tell him.*

"We got our fishing stuff from Sears," Joey says. "We stole it."

"And were you going to catch ducks with it?"

"Yessir," Joey says. Ekkis nods. They both look relieved.

"And who was going to help you do this? Who was going to cook this duck?"

"Nobody," Ekkis says. His shoulders hunch up and he tries to wriggle free. "We was gonna do it ourselves."

"At your uncle's?"

"No," Joey says. 'No. That's not it. We were gonna ask my uncle to cook it."

"And did he know what you planned? Was he in on it?"

Ekkis says, "Nosir," while Joey says, "Yessir."

Buddy turns to me and says grimly, "*Were* you in on this?" The way he says it is so filled with threat, I have trouble responding. He doesn't wink or relax his wooden face. I've lost contact with him. I just don't know if it will come out right. Am I an adult or am I an uncle pervert? I didn't expect to be this involved. My heart races. How far will he go?

"I was aware of their plans, officer. I thought they might learn from the experience. About cruelty to animals."

"And you thought they could learn this if they killed a duck?"

"I don't think you learn by theory alone. I wanted them to let the duck go. I think sometimes a small cruelty can stop a much larger one."

"And sometimes it leads to more and more cruelty."

He writes my address in a little black book. "I'm busting you all."

"Yessir," I say, in the exact repressed voice of the boys.

There are tears in both boys' eyes. Joey's voice rises and he sobs at me, "I didn't want to tell him. He promised he'd let us go if I told him all the truth."

"I'm gonna book all of you. You," he says to the boys, "for trying to murder a whole family of ducks. Ducks are living creatures, not experiments. When you kill one thing, it's never just one thing, it always stretches far beyond what you expect. It's called the law of unexpected consequences. You boys get it?"

"Yessir," they respond. But their faces reflect anger and fear.

Buddy turns to me and says in a thoughtful tone, "You, I'm gonna book for playing around with something you know nothing about. For encouraging these kids to be criminals, for not explaining to them in words they could understand what it means to break the law, to let them steal and break park laws, to torture helpless, hungry creatures who merely want to get on with their simple lives."

His voice runs down. His heavy shoulders fall an inch, and he shakes his head slowly. He says to the ground at his feet, "I just don't know. I just don't know what we're all doing. There's too much. Is it hopeless?"

Then he straightens his back and turns to the boys. "When I write this up it will be on permanent record with all your names, all that you've said, your uncle too, the whole thing, and if you give your promise that you will respect ducks and laws and all of nature and promise to help this little lake and its families of ducks, I'll let you off on probation with the record open on file for anyone to see, for the whole world to see and judge until you're eighteen, because I just don't know what will work, what's best in this case, and whether one lesson taught to two boys and an uncle, even if they do straighten up and fly right, will make any difference at all. You have to repay Sears too. I'm calling them and giving them your names, that you will be in to pay for what you've stolen."

His voice is tender. I've underestimated this man, and for a relieved moment I love him as much as I could love anyone. He's fat bellied with a bullfrog voice, and his drooping cheeks and red veins make him seem as if he'd rather spend his hours sucking on a Budweiser, but he's a saint, at least for the moment.

"Okay," he says, after he writes us all up. "You're all on probation. You can go home."

It's dark across the lake now, and there's a small sliver of waning moon over the hills, a semicircle missing on the right side, the unknown. The trees, so fragile and green earlier, blend into the shadows behind them. There are a few unidentifiable sounds, birds, a scream in the underbrush of something entirely alien. The sounds of darkness closing in. Who-whoing of doves, owls. Crows clacking.

"What about *this* duck?" Joey says.

"Not a damned thing I can do about her tonight," Buddy says. "Too dark. I'll get a skiff and we'll try to catch her in the morning. If she hasn't drowned."

"I can do something about it right now," Joey says. He takes off running around the lake, his white sneakers lifting high behind him. If he'd been able to run before, Buddy would never have caught him.

"Hey!" Buddy yells.

Buddy and Ekkis and I stand side-by-side, big and little shoulders wide or narrow, as Joey disappears behind some cattails. The duck has jerked the monofilament across the lake toward the reeds, but the line drags well out behind her. From the other side, beyond the cattails, in the twilight, there's a huge splash reflecting silver moonlight as Joey jumps in. The lake is shallow with stumps. Joey's dark outline slides waist deep against darker night toward the duck, which tries to hurl herself into the air but is yanked down, or not so much yanked as she is towed as Joey takes the mono in his right hand and walks toward shore, wrapping the invisible line around the knuckles of his left hand as he wades back through the water, a shade among shadows, forearms and hands rotating as if grinding an old coffee machine, until, on the bank, he hauls the duck up to him and we hear her furious screams.

Joey shouts in pain across the lake, "Motherfucker!"

There's quiet, and against a few stars and the grey of the sky we see the duck's shadow rise straight up and streak out over the trees and disappear. In a moment Joey stands dripping next to us and wet from the soles of his sneakers up to his waist. He shivers. It's his first near bath in a week. He smells of mud and decayed reeds. His right hand is bleeding.

"You could have drowned," I say, stupidly. I look at Buddy. Will he feel he has to do something?

"Did anyone see what jumped into that lake?" Buddy says to no one, looking up at the moon. "A dog?"

Later on, after a warm bath, as Joe explains once again he's sorry for squealing on me, I tell him, "Knock off the apologies, I'm proud of you, and especially proud because you told the truth."

"But…"

"I tried to tell you to tell him about me," I say.

"I thought so, but I wasn't sure," he says. "I almost chickened out."

To Ekkis he says, "Thanks for coming back, dude."

"Dude," Ekkis says. "I was scared shitless, too. I was way gone from that park when I thought, go back, dude, go back. I couldn't let you both down."

Joe says, "That cop was too smart. He knew we were lying. He knew about the fuckin hooks too."

"But you bit his button off," Ekkis says in awe.

"I wanted to bite his fat belly," Joe says. "He stunk."

We sit in chairs on the porch, Joe in clean, dry clothes. Now, as his warm skin cools, we rehash the cries of the duck and the boys fear of being caught. It will be a story they'll tell years from now, the pig ranger, the duck, and it will continue and be told to grandchildren maybe even great grandchildren when I'm gone, when this story is long over.

"What finally made you believe what he said?" I ask.

"I never did. When he stuffed his button in my mouth, I just figured we had no real choice. He was gonna bust us, you too, if he didn't get all he wanted, so I figured I'd take him at his word and keep telling him what he wanted to know and maybe he really would let us go."

"Smart! I'm proud of you both, boys. You let it all hang out, the whole truth."

"So far as I know it," Joe says. He gives me a long hard look, and it sends a swift jolt through my heart.

"There's something wrong," he says. "Something don't make no sense. What was that pig doing there so late anyway?"

But he grows sleepy and I pick him up like a small child over my shoulder and carry him to bed. In his hand he clutches the button he bit from Buddy's shirt. His fingers open like a flower and he smiles as he shows me.

When Joe's parents return, my brother asks me how it went.

"So… o…o o… fa a aarrrrr so…o o… ggoo…oo oo dddddd," I say, glugging hard on the thick ddd sound, the thudding sound.

"What're you trying to imitate," he says, just a little irritated. "A toilet?"

Well, maybe he doesn't know the joke, but Joe will tell him.

An optimist jumps from the Empire State Building, see?

My Sister and Me and Buffy

"What's this," Cardy said after we got home from grammar school that day. There was a cold cup of coffee and a half eaten tuna sandwich on the kitchen table and a note with a credit card.

"Don't be stupid," I said. "It's mom's Visa card."

"But she was going shopping at Macy's."

"Well, I dunno," I said, reading the note. *Shopping at Macy's. Gone for a few days. Use this Visa. See you later. Love. Mom.*

The credit card was good for three hundred dollars a day and we got excited, but what were two little girls going to do with that much money? I didn't want much more than ballerina shoes and a pet rabbit, and Cardy only wanted a kitten.

It wasn't the first time mom had run off. She hated father, but she never got over finding him a bloody mess in the garage where, according to her, because we never saw it, he "scattered his brains" all over the wall with his shotgun. But by the time we came in from school she'd cleaned up entirely and buried him in back and planted a Big Boy tomato vine from Ace Hardware on him, so it was only a bad story that we were never to tell anyone. We didn't want to tell anyone anyway. What would we say? *Did you know our father took a shotgun and scattered his brains in the garage and mom cleaned up?*

Well, I guess regular people would tell the police, or a detective, or some nice neighbor, or call someone at least and things would get investigated and files kept and all kinds of papers filled out, but not if it was our mother. First place, our mother was certain the CIA and FBI and the police were after us because father had been a physicist for the Lawrence Radiation Lab, and had secrets so secret he said he couldn't even tell anyone he had any secrets.

He'd always said, "Know nothing, see nothing, speak nothing," and put his hands in great big weird movements over his head and over his eyes and over his ears like those monkeys from China. He thought that was funny, imitating people who might do that kind of thing. He was tall and skinny and mean. He hit. He pinched. He would spend a whole afternoon in an argument with himself, waving his arms, talking to a blank screen on the TV.

He said, "I helped invent these spy machines and I know there's someone watching, and I'm giving them plenty."

He was so scarey that when he shot himself we weren't surprised. We were sort of glad we wouldn't have to hide around and avoid the house whenever he was there. But, then, maybe he didn't kill himself. Maybe it was really true what mom hinted, that he'd been murdered because he had secrets. Six of one, half dozen of the other as far as Cardy and I were concerned. Maybe mom killed him. We didn't think so, not even when mom got more nuts, leaving her energy pills and champagne bottles all over the place. We tried to clean up, and also lead a regular life with friends, at least during school hours.

Mom would ask, "Any police in the back yard?"

Cardy said once, "Only three today," and mom ran screaming out the front door. So we learned to say, "No, mom." Or, "See nothing, know nothing, speak nothing." Whatever.

"Fine," mom would say. "Shall I fix some dinner?' And that was usually pizza or canned spaghetti mixed with stewed tomatoes or Colonel Sanders Bucket O' Chicken sometimes with some cole slaw and a piece of fruit, like an apple. If she were really in a cooking mood, she'd make real hamburgers with sliced tomatoes and onions and two pieces of white bread slathered with mayonnaise. Or bring in a ready cooked chicken from Safeway, with fruit salad from their deli. She'd serve it up on a big platter with a smile saying, "Special occasion!"

Sometimes she'd fry potatoes in butter. We'd have to keep our eyes on the frying pan, though, or whatever was cooking would fill the kitchen with smoke and an alarm dad had installed would go off and mom would hit it with a hammer and the pan would burst into flames and she would swear and collapse in her room and sob behind her locked door, while we would run around shouting, turning off everything and pulling out plugs and pouring pots of water on the fire.

We had fire patrol down. Throw wet towels over the flaming pan, pick up the handle with mittens, throw the whole thing in the yard, turn on the hose, open the front and back doors and the windows to the kitchen, let everything air out and wave mom's-at-it-again gestures at the neighbors. If we watched her carefully, we could stop the process before the pan caught fire, and mom was sometimes just fine, so it only happened maybe once or twice a month, which in some ways made it worse because we'd almost forget.

But we ate. Peanut butter sandwiches for breakfast, a hotdog we bought at school for lunch with apple sauce or an orange and milk. Dinty Moore's Beef Stew or a can of Campbell's soup for dinner. We ate sandwiches from Safeway a lot. Mom always gave us a couple of dollars each. She forgot how much, so we could ask twice and share with our friends and be popular at school.

After mom was gone for three months, the longest she'd ever been gone, we began to wonder maybe someone took her away. Maybe the FBI. We went to school, did whatever little amount of schoolwork they offered us, got regular grades, some A's, mostly B's, and came home and watched TV, or I would read a book and Cardy would draw, mostly pictures of cats and horses.

She *found* a kitten complete with a blanket-lined pink basket and named it Buffy after Buffy the Vampire Killer, her heroine. I didn't want a cat around, and said so, because I was still thinking about my rabbit, but she said it was not a cat it was a kitten and would keep it and love it until mom came back. I was going to throw it out over the back fence anyway, but Cardy was ready to scream.

"I'll tell everyone there's no one in charge here," she said.

I said, "No you won't. They'll put us in a home with a witch. You too."

We worked it out. We had to stick together. In less than a week I was in love with Buffy too, though I tried to rename it Cleopatra, since I'd read somewhere every cat contained the soul of Cleopatra, Queen of the Nile. Cardy just ignored me. So, for a few days I called it Cleo and she called it Buffy.

Neither of us wanted anyone involved in our lives, no neighbors, no police, no helpful social workers, and certainly not Uncle Carl Haldani (also known by mom as Uncle Houdini). His big trick was to suddenly appear in our bedrooms at night in the old days when he was visiting mom and try to tuck us into bed with his creepy feely hairy hands. Where mom was thin, Uncle Houdini was fat and sweaty. And full of cornball jokes.

"Oley is dying and says to his wife Lena, 'When I die you have to promise me you will marry my brother Carl.'

'I will, dearest Oley, but I thought you hated Carl."

'I do."

When we first heard it, we thought that was pretty funny, coming as it did from Uncle Carl, an adult, but after the umpteenth telling and many fat finger tuck in fumbles, we locked the door to our bedroom whenever he was in the house. We held our breath when we heard him at the door softly turning the handle, until we learned to scream, "Mom, Uncle Carl is trying to get in and touch us." He'd thump away down the hall, and maybe she would come up to check and see why we were screaming, but she wasn't much help.

"Go to sleep, shitheads," she'd say in a soft voice through the locked door. Still, in those days, Uncle Houdini wasn't going to break down the door, or fool with us while we were screaming. And if we wanted we could shout loud enough out the window to wake up Mr. and Mrs. Gordon next door, the ones we called the pinheads because they had such small heads.

Buffy/Cleo the kitten stayed home during the day. We bought kitty litter and plenty of catfood from Safeway. And this was fine for a while.

Uncle Houdini moved to Alberta Canada a few weeks before dad shot himself and only called us once in a while. I always told him mom and dad were out. That wasn't a lie.

"How you little girls?" he'd slurped the last time on the phone. I could just picture him licking his fat tongue over his puffy red lips.

"I'm fine and Cardy's fine," I said, and hung up hard.

No one else thought to ask us where our parents were. Our family wasn't too popular since every time neighbors had got involved in our weird lives they'd get insulted or disgusted. Maybe they felt sorry for Cardy and me, but they didn't dare do anything like visit.

We played in the street and waved to people we knew and smiled and things went along until one very hot afternoon Buffy raced outside to play with us on the weedy lawn and the first thing I knew Cardy and Buffy had disappeared around Mrs. Pinhead's house and I heard a loud barking and Buffy and a poodle ran out into the street and Buffy dashed into a curbside sewer entrance in front of our house, and Cardy ran out with a wet mop and a furious expression on her face, and I screamed at the dog and Cardy splashed the mop down on it and it ran off. I'd never seen the dog before. It wasn't a neighbor dog.

We called down in the sewer for the kitty but couldn't see her. There was a rusty iron ladder down and it was scarey dark.

"You have to get her back," Cardy said.

"*Me?* Why me? Cleo's your cat."

"Buffy! You said you love her. She's all we got. And you're the mom."

I hadn't thought about being the mom, but it was true. I was the one who used the ATM, who got the groceries, who pushed them home in the Safeway carts that we'd stolen. I even paid the bills with mom's checks. I'd watched her enough, and before she left she'd shown me how she did it, how to make out the checks, how to include the account numbers, how to address the envelopes, put on the stamps, all of it. So I was the mom, and dad too.

But I was afraid of the sewer, though I'd seen how Seymour Giller had climbed down one day after a baseball. It could be done. But I'd thought Seymour was an idiot for going down there, and it made my heart beat hard when he slipped in and then reappeared. I didn't know what to expect when he came back, be covered in sludge made of old vegetables and excrement and pee, or half dead from rat rot.

He only smiled same as ever when he climbed out with two baseballs instead of just one.

"*You* have to climb down," Cardy said. "Buffy will die. She can't climb up a ladder."

"*I* will di*e*."

"But you can climb a ladder."

"Cleo," I called through the sewer entrance.

"She's used to Buffy," Cardy hissed.

"Buffffffff*eeeee*." Nothing. Darkness. It didn't smell too bad. Seymour had said it only had a few leaves on the floor, nothing awful. You just had to wait until your eyes adjusted.

We compromised. I was okay as mom and dad, but no good at sewers. I would go down if Cardy went with me. It wasn't hard to squeeze in, so, with Cardy snuffling behind me, down the ladder we went. It really wasn't bad. It didn't have poison sewer gas. We kept calling for Cleo or Buffy, but not one mew came from the tunnel, which was large enough to stand up in. We stood in the dim light under the entrance for a few moments, then I led Cardy around a wall, an odd wall that slanted away from the side of the sewer tunnel instead of being perpendicular to it. On the other side of the wall above us was a grate.

As we stood there staring about a rumbling began and a hard breeze or suction began from a machine behind the grate drawing leaves and whatever was in the tunnel upward making them swirl like dust devils. Our hair flew up. The noise and suction grew in strength. We were afraid.

"Buffffff eeeeee," Cardy shouted.

We thought we heard a mew up behind the grate. We got close and looked inside and could see some flashing lights, some black buttons, strange greens and reds, and some letters and numbers that ran underneath. It looked something like a stock market machine you might see on TV. A shadow appeared and then there was a shriek and a flash of fire like an electrical wire had shorted and smoke and a horrible stink. The machine went dark. Cardy and I grabbed each other, both of us crying, though I tried not to. We backed away to the ladder.

"What *was* it," she said, her lips quivering, her skinny body shaking. "Did it eat Buffy?"

"I don't know," I said with as calm a voice as I could manage. "Must be something to clean the sewer, that's all." Saying that's all made it less frightening.

"It wasn't Buffy,"I said firmly. I was shaking inside. I wanted to reassure Cardy but I knew it was the kitten. I was trying to stay cool, yet scared worse than I'd ever been before. I wanted out of this black horrible sewer. It was creepy, and it stank of horrible things like toilets and dried out worms that you could find on streets after rains. You want to gag, smell a lot of dead worms some day.

I wanted a real mother and father. I was tired of hiding from the world and pretending we were okay. We'd be found out, maybe the police would get us and we'd be sent to a horrible home with a mean old lady who would beat us. Maybe that stock market machine was dad's Secret Service. My knees wouldn't stop quivering. We just couldn't live the rest of our lives without someone to take care of us. I was only twelve and Cardy was only eight. We'd done pretty well on our own as long as no one knew about us, but I'd read about orphans. Oliver Twist. Candy Man Can. Greyfriars Bobby, a dog orphan. We couldn't stay home alone until we were all grown up. Children need at least one parent, even a nutty one. I had to type and sign notes from parents. I was the parent of Cardy. And me.

Far down the sewer in the darkness where we stared came a deep hissing, like a huge snake slithering our way.

"Come on!" I said, grabbing Cardy's right wrist and dragging her back to the ladder.

"*Buffy*," she screamed and held back. I was mad but proud of her too. She was scared out of her tough little mind, still she wanted to save our kitten. But I was too wild to think much about what I was thinking. "Get out," I shouted. "Get out!"

Buffy's fried! I almost said. The hissing sound got louder and rumbled, and I could see a thin stream of oily water running like black blood down the center of the sewer. I climbed up on the ladder and tried to pull Cardy up, but she wouldn't come. She was stuck.

Oh, my God! She wouldn't come. I imagined her drowned in the sewer, or sucked into some giant fan, or pulled along with sewage and toilet paper into the sea. Or electrocuted. What would I do if Cardy refused? If she stayed and got swept away to the sea where there were giant albino alligators. I couldn't leave her, and she wouldn't leave without her Buffy.

I hung there one leg out of the sewer. The noise built up until it sounded like what we'd heard on the TV news when they'd shown a hurricane in Florida hurling breakers up a cement wall onto palms bent over like old ladies.

"We'll *drown*!" I screamed. "There's water coming."

"*Bufffffeeee.*"

"Carrdeeeee!" I shouted down at her at the bottom of the ladder.

Cardy was so afraid she was trembling on the rungs. I tried to think. I pretended to look out. All I could see was brilliant blinking sunlight.

"Come on, " I said. "Come on. Oh. Hey! Come look! I see Buffy up here."

Cardy stopped crying.

"She's over by the house. She's waiting for us."

I got out and squeezed through and reached back and Cardy scrambled up even if she did tremble. I pulled her through. Of course there was no Buffy. I explained I'd seen a cat like Buffy, but she didn't believe me. She only cried for a few hours and stopped talking to me.

In fact she said almost nothing to anyone for weeks. It took a long time for her to forgive me for not saving Buffy and lying, and it wasn't fair. She was only in the Second Grade, so she didn't understand I had no choice.

Cardy. Cardigan. I love her. I have to. There's no one else. I saved her life. Mine, too. At night we snuggled up together in one bed, but she still wouldn't talk. Or couldn't. She could nod or shake her head. I cried myself to sleep every night. But I don't know how I would have survived if Cardy's knees hadn't been shoved sharp against my back.

What would anyone have done? Adults might understand these things, but at twelve, it was too hard.

And for almost a year we've only had each other, no Buffy, no new cat. All we really have left from our mother is her ATM card. And from our father some fat, ripe, shiny, gross, Big Boy tomatoes in the back yard, which we can't even think about eating. We're not cannibals.

Perch Fishing in Tomales Bay

It's like this. You wait for an early incoming tide, preferably five or six a.m., and then, from Marconi Cove – named for wireless inventor Guglielmo Marconi, who never visited this tiny harbor named after him – you might row across the bay two miles to Heart's Desire Beach where the eelgrass is thick. There's a sandy cove bordered with rocks covered with oysters and bay mussels, the thin shelled almost flat variety, and a beach of golden sand sliding down into murky water where perch love to hide within long waving green fronds, where they feed on tiny crabs and shrimp, and so you head there hoping the afternoon wind stays down. Keep the wake of the skiff straight behind you and keep your eye on just the right angle of the dock at Marconi, and put your back into each stroke of the oars, the oar heads digging into the water, not splashing, just dipping in softly and then you pull with arms and feet and legs and back and finish with forearms sliding into your chest, relax, stroke, relax, not too fast, don't burn out, that's how you do it for two, sometimes three or four miles, ten fifteen feet a stroke, say 400 strokes a mile, stroke after stroke steady the skiff built heavy for hard work, and when you turn and look over your shoulder, there it is, Heart's Desire.

Stop rowing, slide up silently the last thirty yards to the beach. On dry sand drop in your net anchor, an eight pound window sash, and start laying out net straight out until you reach ten or fifteen foot depth of water just off the beach, and turn and row slow slow, down-current, trying to curve out into the tide parallel to the shoreline, helping the monofilament gill net drop soundlessly from the stern net-board over a muffled well-oiled roller, no clanking or splashing of floats or lead-line, just the soft hiss of net into these shallow waters, until the whole shackle, 300 feet, sits on the bottom in the eelgrass like a huge, curved underwater tennis net, almost invisible, hooked at the end back toward the beach, waiting for perch to swarm in to hunt through the green forest. When both shackles of nets are out, some 600 feet total, two football fields in length altogether, each shackle set one after the other weighted at either end with the weights found at junk yards, just enough weight to keep the two nets from drifting away in the easy back current of the bay, jaunty red flags one at either end of each net, there's nothing more to do for three or four hours. Hop off and drag the bow of the boat ashore up far past the waterline lapping in with its sticks and leaves and bits of plastic and discarded crab shells, and tie your painter off on a tree. You were up early, and the rowing work was good and the sun has fought through the morning mist and grown warm and now you're thirsty. Drink the bottled water you brought. Eat the fine tuna sandwich you packed last night, thick with lots of onions and mayonnaise and lettuce and tomatoes, and take off your shirt, tan up a bit, and doze and wait for the perch, hoping they come today. Sometimes they don't. They might swarm into a different cove, one time Heart's Desire, another, Indian Beach, or glide in along the flats north of White's Gulch. Hog Island used to be a good spot, but the herring fleet attracted hungry seal cows with pups, and now the likelihood of a seal tearing up your net is far greater than catching a perch there. There were never any hogs there, just seals. And the pups look so hopeless and innocent when they get tangled in the net that you are sorry and let them go, except they and their mothers have ruined two hundred dollars worth of netting and have set you back three days mending work and they will do it again each time you fish the island and the season is whizzing by, and they have captured the island. Where are white sharks when you need them? They stay outside the mouth of the bay, along Dillon Beach, waiting for the delicious mothers and pups to emerge.

The mid-waters of the bay are seal heaven but the back bay is still seal free, uncomfortably shallow perhaps, too murky to see, so it's still possible to catch perch there. That's where you have to go.

This is fishing not for riches but for basics. Food. Gas. Kerosene for the Aladdin Blue Flame Heater that warms your shack. Money for an occasional trip to the Western Saloon in Point Reyes for a beer, or to wash the stink of old fish off your clothes out of your hair. A hot shower. The simplest things.

And you fish for the absurd and ridiculous pleasure of making a living from Nature, from the diminishing treasures of the ocean, every year a little less to catch, but a simple life still possible, with hard hard good work, rowing, fishing, and you set the hours, you are your own sometimes terrible boss. The work is prehistoric. It ties you to the Mediterranean, to the shores of Africa, to those fishing on the Sea of Galilee. To Jesus. A religious experience.

The nets wave, shimmering in their eelgrass lair. You almost sleep. It's warm and your body feels good. You sit on the beach and hold your knees, you ponder life. It's a sunny fine morning ticking on down to mid day, the sun and sand fine, heat waves dancing upward and if you do catch fish you'll have to keep them wet and cool under a burlap. It would be fine to have ice, but there's no ice anywhere along Marshall, and no good place to store ice overnight.

In Point Reyes, if Jim the Butcher is feeling magnanimous, you might get ice for a night's storage of fish. He's a player though, and extracts a pound of flesh for any "gift." Without ice you must keep the perch, dead or alive, in a cage in the chill water next to the dock at Marconi, only that's dangerous with seals around for they will tear right through any flimsy netting or light wire, even go up on the dock and rip down and steal away a whole day's catch, and you will curse them, curse them, admire their intelligence but hate and want to shotgun them, for they are not the fisherman's friends, are as wild as wild dogs, eyes rolling white in their brown dog faces as they plead for understanding. *We eat fish.*

The net floats sit on calm waters. Two long lines of them like one-foot red tubes bobbing on the surface. You walk back into the bushes and pee, and climb up onto the ridge where you can look down into the water to see if there are little flashes of silver in the net, only the light is not right to see into the water. Looking is just something you do while you wait and wait you must until the tide begins to change, until the water recedes a few inches and the wet sand remains behind, no longer pale dry sand at the water's rising edge but dark wet sand as the bay falls back into itself. Drink the thermos of coffee you made this morning before dawn. Lift your warm bones. Wake up! Drag the skiff into the water. Make all the noise you want now. Splash! Clatter! Kick up the mud. Stay inside the hook of the net. Create watery havoc. Drive any remaining perch back into the net.

And now the joy of it, the great thrill of it. You push off and row to one end of the first shackle, beating on the side of the boat and splashing with an oar to panic the last few perch that might be slinking away in the eelgrass. Last chance to be caught, dear fellows. Last chance to prove your worth. Be bold, you sneaky perch! Entangle yourselves, and I will love and caress you and place you in a nice wet box and take you to meet some Chinese.

With a boathook you snag the outer end of your net, marked by two extra fat red corks and a little red flag, a red piece of highway warning flag, the waterproof plastic kind that you look for whenever you drive along Highway One, or anywhere, the flags being of great worth to you, a real find, free too. You've attached them to short bamboo poles marking the net and have put your commercial number on the buoys and the flags too. That's the law.

And now haul in, sing, *"Come ye fish of the waters. Come ye fish, heigh ho!"* Pull the buoy line and the sash weight up over the roller, and begin to drag the boat forward, under the anchored net, laying float line and lead line and monofilament down nice and easy in figure eights back and forth in the skiff midships and untangled so it will go out next time freely, without sound without crossovers, but now you mostly care about those silver dollars coming up along in the net, up from the opaque brown waters roiled up by a first breath of breeze, the normal back bay breeze warning of afternoon wind, and now you know you were a little too relaxed on that beach, waited a half hour too long thinking of love maybe, or all the fish you're going to catch, or the eternal wonder and why you are here working at something as silly and unprofitable and fine as fishing.

Poor fish. They are born to be eaten. They come in to feed and spawn and are caught and feed us instead. I am sorry, dear little fish. But this is the way it is.

The net shakes quicksilver and down in the water at the edge of visibility you can see a fine fresh perch maybe a two or three pound fish slashing back and forth, three dollars for this fish, and your heart goes a little faster as it does with every fish, each fish lovely, and the rubberlip perch strong, twisting away trying to break free where it's caught by its gills in the webbing so it can't back out and you even feel a bit of sorrow for it strangling there but it's beautiful in its struggles and over it comes, fat golden lips working as if asking what is this terrible unimagineable fate, dark silver body pounding on the deck, a line of muscle and power along its back, eyes rolling gills flashing, wanting to dive back from an incomprehensible nightmare. You, a great dimly seen beast, have come and you are death for this fish it is your time fish as it has been and will be for all living things some day. Did you think your life was eternal? Your little chewing swimming life?

You need gloves now to protect your hands, for these fish have nasty spines that can, over a day's work, make your fingers swell until uselessly infected, the small vengeance of fish surrendering their lives. And now more and more fish, a fat redtail, a half dozen barred surf perch, unusual so far back in the bay, more rubber lips, some rainbow, and a dozen slim splittails coming up all at once from a little school that went by an hour or so ago, and the fish keep coming one after the other like round fat silver dollars, a great set, as good as it gets, and maybe a hundred or so fish in the first shackle, two hundred pounds maybe, just fine, almost makes up for all the fishless days, and another net to go.

You place the perch in the fish box, and cover them with a wet burlap, some fish still complaining kicking looking at you accusingly but you are their God, an unjust God who kills for survival, who shouts for glee when a fish comes up in the net, and who curses when one does wriggle back into the bay from the net.

Here you are wanting to catch fish and here the damned things are trying not to be caught. You can't blame them. All the blame is yours, but you need them so you can sell them so you can continue to fish. Only you have a little guilt, you are the murderer, not the fish. They fear you maybe hate you but they are only perch, and fishing is a noble life, an ancient life found wherever there was water and hungry people. Animals fish. Bears fish. It's in you this fishing blueprint, imprinted on your soul. A thousand generations of fishermen. That ancient feeling of catching for survival is why you are here. Haul away! *Heigh ho!*

The second shackle comes over the roller and there are 40 or 50 more nice perch, but halfway along there's a damned snag, a heaviness, and the net is caught somewhere, really caught, hooked on some sunken branches, and to get free you have to pull with all your back and shoulders your legs straining until the skiff almost tips under and there's a rip and up comes a heavy piece of Bishop Pine recently fallen into the bay its tangle of branches dark green black and water logged green leafed wood wrapped like the claws of death into your ragged net.

It had to be, it was all going too well. All you can do is pull and rip until the webbing breaks free and breaks your heart a long section of net ripping on the snag. Almost free but there's something more too, a living heaviness, and something big begins to jerk powerfully at the net. Up it comes jerking hard a dark brown body and instantly recognizable as a bat ray, a big one, over a hundred pounds, and you slide it over the roller into the boat where it pounds the deck with its wings and you do not want it or like it or feel anything but irritated because it is the culprit that swept the net under that snag and even now is tearing huge holes in the flimsy monofilament netting, a day's repairs, not that expensive, except the net will take time and be out of action and it was a new net too, just hung last week, and when will you have time to do it? You want to kill the ray, you could with a single stab between the eyes, but it's too big too alive, a being bigger than a big dog.

Now you must work out this big grim beast with it tail lashing upwards stinger stabbing up toward your foot, a sting ray. And beware that stinger. Spines from normal fish are poisonous enough, but this stinger is loaded, and its multi-serrated arrow head once stuck into you stays and can only be ripped or cut out, will drive right through a rubber boot into an ankle, or through a glove into a thumb and create a paralyzing shock, and it has happened to you before careful as you might be, even more careful after it happens once. But this ray is one big black-hooded seal-brown slick-skinned monster with its great wings flapping its nostrils opening closing its eyes rolling, tail jabbing upward toward you whenever you move. It watches, it knows you are there. Now you put a heavy boot on the tail and press it to the deck while bat-like fins whack against the floorboards, and with handy pliers you ever so carefully grasp the stinger, a double stinger this time, and rip one then the other free, now it's defenseless ready to be eaten, as if anything but a Great White Shark would consider a sting ray good to eat. Stingerless it is easy, or at least possible, to untangle and you grasp forefinger and thumb by the operculum with its delicate gills and slide the beast up over gunnel and back into the water, hoping, of course, it won't swim right back into the net, though if it does it won't get caught now for the stinger is gone, that stinger, or double stinger in this case, the only thing that traps it as it slides past the webbing the stinger that jabs into the net and gathers more and more mesh around the serrations the one hard catchy thing on its slimy slippery body, a great spearhead turned backwards, a rear turret stabber.

Goodbye ye monster from fifty million years ago come to haunt humans, swim on eat on live on forever, the least a fisherman can do is let a ray go back, if stingerless, to grow another and be just as jabbing as ever in a year or so. Life is good for creatures like rays if no human wants to eat you, but not so good for the fisherman, if only stingrays were worth even a quarter a pound, they're so big and numerous, four stingrays and a hundred dollars, maybe more, for they grow to two hundred pounds, not really big compared to manta rays of course, which might reach 3000 pounds, though it would be sad to catch something so large, as sad and against Nature as those whalers who harpooned the great whales and flensed the blubber from the carcass and boiled it down for oil and dog food. Candle oil! Pet food! Foof!

You see, you are a hopeless man and will never have a girlfriend or get married with that attitude, the attitude not of a killer but of a curious observer a lover of beautiful sea creatures, and not aggressive enough competitive enough to make a real living, and all the other fishermen intent on catching all they can, but will sea-life survive the constant combing and destruction of its resources by six or seven billion hungry people? A good question you haven't time to answer today, or any day you go fishing for there are fish to catch, nets to pull, a boat to row back home with the days's catch, and a little breeze stiffening down the bay and you have to work against it and with the weight of the wet net and fish not quite centered forcing the bow down so you must start over go back to shore and redistribute the net in the skiff, and then you can row home, a few tiny windcaps fluttering across the bay now each pull a little harder than the last, tough rowing but still possible, and thinking of all the times you wound up blown back to the Golden Hinde, and added two or three hours to an already long day, and all the days when the fog came in so thick you could barely tell where you were, or when it rained or when it was so cold your hands almost froze to the oars and you could hardly row with or without gloves, cold cold cold so count your blessings this warm day with not too much wind. And for once you caught good fish, maybe two hundred and fifty pounds, two fish boxes full, good money too, maybe five hundred bucks, if only you can find some ice because the day is already too late to run these fish to San Francisco Chinatown. Jim the butcher at the Palace can give you ice, dammit he owes you for fish and won't pay and what can you do about it, he has the upper hand, the ice you need, and you never signed a bill of sale, just a handshake until you realized he was a cheat, a humorous bastard, a con artist from New York.

It takes an hour and a half for you to row to Marconi against the growing breeze and lucky at that for if you had waited another hour it would have been the Golden Hinde for you, where you might stop for an espresso at the Knave of Hearts Bakery at the edge of town, and a delicious tart before you hitchhike the extra hour around to the truck at Marconi Cove, an hour back to Inverness, load the fish, an hour back to Marshall, three hours added on to a long day.

Oh, the comfort and sophistication of espresso! Strawberry tarts! Always always snatch pleasure from defeat. Imagine. Create. Get all the life you can get. There are more rewards in poverty than your philosophy can imagine, dear Horatio.

This time the wind is kind and at Marconi you tie up and offload bucket after bucket of perch into your old Dodge pickup bed and pour them carefully into two fish boxes, and then take the oars from the skiff so no one will borrow it for an outing, and off you fly, tired as hell, down Highway One straight to The Palace Market for ice and a bit of sarcasm from Butcher Jim.

Coffee. Any coffee. Only the Station House Coffee Shop has any coffee in Point Reyes and it's weak Farmers Bothers coffee. American coffee. On a skiff fisherman's income you've developed a taste for espresso, something elegant in the midst of gore. Oh, what an opportunity for a businessman, an espresso coffee shop in the middle of Point Reyes Station, but no business entrepreneur thinks espresso will sell in this country town yet so only the Knave of Hearts has it, and your throat aches for it, you are tired, but ice comes first.

Jim is huge, maybe three hundred pounds of blackness, a street wise but witty black man from Queens who runs the finest butcher shop on the Northern California Coast from Marin to Eureka. He's always busy, but mostly busy talking and making jokes, and it gives him a kick to put one over on you, if you let him, and he will use jokes and the promise of friendship as a way to suck you in, so watch yourself. You're tired. All you need is ice.

"Hey," you say. You are in your hip boots rolled down and a Levi Strauss trucker jacket, and you are really tired now.

"Hi guy," he says to you. "You got halibut for me?" He has nerve since he owes you three hundred dollars for past halibut, and it will get worse, you fear.

"Nothing for you today," you say, thinking nothing except a bill. But you can't say it because he's got what you need. "I only got perch and need ice. Can you help me here?'

"Maybe," he says. "Busy." He wants to know if there's something in it for him. He turns and starts chopping a huge pork leg. He won't talk. Five minutes go by. Eight. Chops get wrapped for delivery. You wait. It's his power over you.

"Ice," you remind him. "Ice for perch."

"How many perch?"

"Two boxes."

He thinks for a long time. Turns his back to you. Cuts a lamb shank.

"Four perch for ice," you say at last into his silence. He can filet and eat them and they are delicious. How well he knows you.

"Six" he says, and you sigh and agree to five. A game for him, but fifteen dollars worth of perch for five dollars worth of ice.

"A deal," he says, proud of himself and now friendly. "I'll get the ice."

And you can't help yourself, you think better of him. Business is business.

"Pull your truck in back," he says. And without more trouble you get ice, enough to cover your two boxes of perch, and they will hold for a night in your truck under wet burlap. He gives you a cold beer too, and you uncurse him. And then you drive around to Inverness to the Knave of Hearts and get that longed for espresso and a croissant, and fill your truck with gas in Inverness Texaco —75 cents a gallon, and going up —and go home, or maybe go to Linda's for a hot shower, or maybe to Diane's for a dinner, just offer her a half dozen perch for the family. And then, when unlucky in your choice of possible bed partners, to bed alone in your little laundry room shack, the last unburned remnant of the once famous Marshall Hotel, and in the morning up again at three-thirty, make a pancake on the Aladdin Blue Flame or boil an egg, and by four-thirty truck off to Chinatown with the perch to be there by six to bargain with Chinese butchers who make you feel innocent and foolish and knock the price down a nickel or ten cents a pound because they insist the fish are "too old," but you sell the fish anyway and you take a half day off and it all starts over again, another morning, another row across the bay, maybe up past White's Cove this time, through pea-soup fog, but you hope for the best, all great as long you stay young and healthy forever. Forever.

Hell, when you get a lucky break and strike it rich this life or next, maybe you can buy an outboard motor. Hell. Life is damned good. Bring on the beer. Light up the joints. Life is a blast. There's hard work. Fresh sea air. Fish. And the whole world is young and strong and full of adventure and almost perfect.

Wild!

Sharks Ahead

From a twenty-four foot Oregon Dory tied alongside Marconi Cove dock Harry and Greg tossed their catch, fifty or so soupfin sharks, into the back of Harry's rusted out 1960 Dodge Ram truck, covered the fish with a couple of wet woolen army blankets and headed for Barber's Saltwater Grotto in Berkeley. Not a bad load all in all.

Harry, forty-five and unshaven, felt a hundred-years-old after the day's fishing. It wasn't hot yet, but he was soaked in sweat while Greg, at twenty-seven, was still zooming along, humming, his feet dancing on the rusting floorboards. They'd set nets yesterday early and had worked the rest of the day on a misfiring boat engine until ten that night. Harry managed to find a couple hours sleep, while Greg partied at The Marshall Tavern until it closed. Then up at three in the dark, out through the fog at the mouth of the Bay, and back by eleven a.m., before the weather picked up. Day after day much like this. Still, today's catch was decent, and the morning had been sweet and calm.

They had a steady fifty-cent a pound market for leopard and soupfin sharks when Daddy Barber was buying, but today Harry couldn't verify the sale by phone from Point Reyes Station because son and heir Cuddy Barber wasn't up yet, it merely being noon. Harry's sometime fishing partner Daddy, Cuddy's father, had been hauled off to the hospital to dry out, with only Baby, Daddy's wife, still answering the Barber fish phone.

In her good-natured, whiskey-rough voice she said, "I know Daddy wanted to take 'em from you, Harry, but Cuddy's buying today, and he was out late, so I can't say. Try again in an hour."

"Jesus. You know how it is Baby, we gotta take 'em somewhere before they cook."

"No ice?"

"Not yet."

"They're still good? They don't stink? For sure Cuddy won't take 'em if they stink. Not after that white shark fiasco."

"Baby, that wasn't my fault. Cuddy didn't want to buy and he needed an excuse. That shark was fine. I sold it fine in Bodega."

"He said it smelled like last year's piss."

"Ah, Baby. You been trucking for me and Daddy for years. Did I ever try to sell you bad fish?"

"Not to me. But just take my advice and put 'em on ice."

"I got over a ton of soupfin. We'll pile on the ice. Then maybe I'll treat you to a cocktail at the bar."

"Forget it Harry. No cocktails today. Maybe none for the rest of our lives. Daddy's sick with the booze, and we both got to dry out this time for sure. He can't drink no more. I can't be no bad example."

"Mother of God. Daddy will frizzle up and die of thirst."

"I know it," she said, her voice small. "Me too." Harry could hear how worried she was.

Harry said, "Baby, you tell Cuddy that Daddy already said okay on these fish." Before she could say anything, he hung up.

Sharks weren't rightly fish. They had no backbone, just cartilage. But soupfins were plentiful because they hadn't been fished for twenty-five years or more, not since the war before they synthesized vitamin A. What most people didn't know was that sharks were damned good meat, and properly smoked and flavored, could be delicious. Daddy Barber knew his fish. He was the last of a line of San Francisco Bay fish pirates.

Cuddy, Antony Barber IV, was too hung over to be jollied along when they arrived in Berkeley. Unshaven, eyes hollow, he stared at the sharks like they were about to attack him. Harry wheedled his best, told a couple emergency jokes, but Cuddy didn't give a damn. He was a businessman, a businessman with a bleeding headache, and no expert on fresh fish. If he'd had his way, he'd have never bought another fish from a fisherman. Fish companies only, everything on the phone, then back to the bar. Those who had established Barber's, Cuddy's father, Daddy, otherwise named Antony Barber III, and Cuddy's grandfather, Antony Barber II, and his great grandfather Antony Barber, formerly Barbieri, the first, had been fishermen foremost, and restaurateurs last. Well, drinkers first and party givers second, but always interested in fresh fish. Daddy had lived a long, happy, boozy life. He liked fish fresh off the boat. He was an avid shark fisherman.

He liked to look at them. He liked to pick them up and smell them. He didn't drink as much as Cuddy, Antony number IV, a Stanford trained MBA. Cuddy liked martinis and money and women, and hated fish and fishermen. He'd gotten seasick whenever he'd been dragged out to sea. Harry quietly thought Cuddy was a jerk, and vice versa.

Harry and Greg found Baby inside Barber's at the bar chatting to old Dave, the ancient bartender. They complained to her about Cuddy's refusal.

"Jesus, Harry," Baby said. "You know how it is. You been out with Daddy on his boat enough. You can only go fishing if you're sure of a market." Baby had still been a knockout when Daddy had first introduced them, was it ten or fifteen years ago? Now the glasses she wore on a gold chain and the lines on her neck and face made her look owlish.

"Daddy promised to take them," Harry said forcefully, nodding toward the kitchen door where Cuddy stood. "Barber's *is* my market."

"I know," she said, shaking her head, and sucking in a little wistful slurp through her pursed lips. "But I ain't got much say. Not since Daddy retired and dumped the business on Cuddy." Her hair was perfectly coiffed with shades of silver and red. She still retained her youthful shape, though her sad, florid face made her look old. Harry could imagine what she'd look like later on.

"Two day's hard work and some real money and he don't want 'em," Harry pled. Baby was his last hope. "Cuddy'd make out and so would we."

"He don't want 'em, he don't take 'em. And Daddy's under sedation, so he don't know or care. But you got my sympathy."

"Ah, I know it, Baby." Harry leaned from his stool over to hers and gave her an awkward hug. She pecked him on his cheek.

"You stink good," she said. "Like fish."

"Christ!" Harry said to Greg. "We gotta take 'em to Bodega for ten cents a pound, and that don't even pay expenses. It's a damn shame."

Harry bought Baby a Bloody Mary. She said no, but then lifted the glass with two dainty fingers and bought them one. Old Dave hovered proudly over them grinning a toothless smile. He loaded their drinks. Pretty soon they each had three dead or dying Bloody Marys lined up, tomato red and green with droopy celery stalks. Drink, yes, she would drink with Harry and Greg, but she couldn't persuade her son Cuddy to buy the sharks.

Greg said, "Hell. We ain't off to a particularly good start here, but I got a plan. I know a guy at a bar in Oakland will trade beer for shark."

Harry wanted to get rid of the sharks first, but didn't know where. It was already noon, and not everyone bought sharks. He called Bodega for a possible sale early tomorrow then tried to get through to the guys at Pier 45. He couldn't think of much else. Maybe the Three Captains in Half Moon Bay. He and Greg had killed almost fifty living creatures, and they had to respect them at least enough to sell them. Soupfin weren't beer cans or pogo sticks. In the realm of the sea they were similar to dogs. They were sniffing, thinking animals, dangerous, self-contained, with alien eyes, carrion eaters, devourers of every lesser thing that swam or crawled along the ocean floor. Larger sharks ate humans, but not these soupfins. They furnished meat and fins for soup.

Harry occasionally wondered, if you ate a shark that ate a human were you a cannibal? Greg said to that, "You ain't cut out to be no bullshit philosopher."

Once Harry sold them they were someone else's problem.

He was dead sick of trucking fish all over the Bay Area and trying to peddle them. He needed the money, sure, and he liked the fishing part, but working from early in the morning until sometimes late at night, and then hauling the fish around for no money was not a life he'd ever imagined for himself. He was healthy, and he could work night and day, true, but it was tiring and he wouldn't be forty-five forever. Often enough, they caught no fish, or so few it wasn't worth the hundred-mile roundtrip into Berkeley. Then they might try to sell them pound by pound locally. That took forever. Sometimes he could offload directly from the dory onto Daddy and Baby's dock on the west side of Tomales Bay, where the Barber family had their big, beautiful, million-dollar home. Daddy had a chiller there, and Baby liked to drive the big Barber's fish truck into Berkeley, to take a vacation from their vacation and schmooze around with the bartenders and drunks at the bar, or to shop. Baby was a good, tough gal, and Harry liked her. She and Daddy had all the money they might ever need, since Barber's grossed eight million dollars a year, so Daddy said.

"Why don't you travel around?" Harry had once asked Daddy. "Go to London. Paris."

"Ain't no sharks in Paris," Daddy had said. "Just the human kind."

It was a pain Daddy being in that hospital.

"He got bad last night," Baby said. "Green people was sneakin' around in the shadows. I was scared until I realized it was just the DTs. But you know how isolated that place is. There *could* be people sneakin' around. Anyway, the sonuvabitch got his shotgun out and started shooting up the bushes. *Criminy!* Good thing there *weren't* any people, there'd be dead bodies all over. He must have blasted twenty bushes before I could stop him. You know what that feels like? Your own dear hubby shooting away at everything you own? He blew the goddamn apples off my apple tree. I hid behind the couch for a while. He coulda killed me and never known no difference until he sobered up. I never swore so hard in my life. I was hoping he'd hear me and realize who I was."

Harry and Greg drove the Ram down Broadway toward Jack's East, the little bar in Oakland where Greg's friend worked.

"How do you know this guy will take a shark?" Harry said. "Anyway, only one shark. This is crazy."

"You got a better idea?"

"I'm pert near out," Harry said. "Maybe we can steal some ice from Sea-K on the way back and keep them chilled until tomorrow and try Bodega for a dime."

"We still got nets out," Greg reminded him.

"Oyy vehhhh." Harry gave a deep sigh, straight from the old country.

"Where did that Jewish crap come from?'"

"My grandparents on my mother's side were German Jews from Minneapolis. Had to flee the Nazis."

They sat in the dark bar while Greg shook hands all around. This was one of his old hangouts, a dark, sleazy little place with a big mirror, a jukebox, and a TV up over the Men's Room door. It had a dozen seats at an unpolished bar and some booths. Jack's East Bay. A joke.

After a couple of beers, Greg staggered in and flopped a fifty pound soupfin on the bar, and Greg's bartender pal Benny, a skinny little guy in a stained apron said, "Fer chrissake. What's this?"

"Soupfin," Greg said. "You said you'd take a shark for some beers."

"Not no goddamn huge whole thousand pound shark like this. Hell, what do I do with it?"

"It's fifty pounds," Greg said flatly. "Thirty pounds of meat dressed." He offered to filet it out and Benny shrugged. "Okay. Not in here." Benny looked like a defeated little worm as Greg towered over him and patted him on his slumped shoulders.

Greg cut a shark on the tailgate with a crowd of black guys in suits and porkpie hats looking on and laughing as he dumped guts and carcasses down a sewer. The fillets came out in sweet one-pound steaks that Harry bagged up and gave to Benny for freezing. He gave some to the black guys too.

"It'll take me six months to get rid of the stink," Benny said.

"Nah, if you use baking soda it won't," Greg said. "And you got six months worth of good meals there."

"What does shark taste like anyway?"

"Dee…fucking…licious. Eat it and find out."

"Thirty pounds of shark. *Jesus.* What'm I gonna do?" Benny was almost crying. He tried to give most of it back but Greg shook his head no and wouldn't take it. "A deal's a deal," he said, crossing his arms over his chest.

"Give it to your friends," Harry said. "We don't mind. That shark don't care no more either."

They drove across the Bay Bridge over to Pier 49 on the off chance there might be someone who would buy the catch, but no luck, just a Mexican maintenance guy scrubbing up around some dumped ice, which they shoveled up on the sharks. Old used bloody ice. Fishermen made do with whatever they could beg borrow or steal. The ice would melt next morning, and sharks didn't last long once the sun got them and they warmed up. If they got too hot they'd stink like piss. They urinated through the pores in their skin, and the greasy sweat came out in whiffs of ammonia when they heated up. Otherwise, they were fine. On ice they'd last two days, then they had to be frozen or smoked. Something. They were just fine frozen as long as they didn't defrost.

The pressure to sell was getting to him. Pretty soon it would be dark. A wasted day. Harry really needed someone to run fish to market while he spent his time fishing. Hell, he needed a mechanic too, not to mention a new boat, and a girlfriend who didn't mind the smell of fish. But right now he had to get rid of these fish.

"Let's try the Buena Vista," Greg said. He was grinning, red faced.

"They won't buy no sharks. Anyway, we stink."

"Ah, loosen up. It's on our way home and we ain't gonna sell these sharks tonight."

In their fishy clothes and rubber boots they strode in among the elegant crowd at the Buena Vista. It was crowded. They bumped into people, most of them young and very well dressed. Some backed away when they noticed how smelly Harry and Greg were, how bloody their clothes were. One guy smiled and held his nose. Harry smiled back and held his nose too. He'd been in the Buena Vista when it was first famous for its Irish coffee, when he was working at the post office and had spare cash. He'd better go back to work at the post office. Right now he had to take a piss.

He gave Greg his last twenty. "Order a couple Irish coffees. I'll be right back."

Greg ordered two Irish coffees each, which used up the twenty.

"Christ," Harry said. "That was expensive."

"Hey, everything is everything, right? We'll sell the load in Bodega tomorrow on the cheap and we'll have some dough."

"Sure, there's a whole lot of great things might happen yet," Harry said. "An earthquake, say? Maybe run into a cow on Sir Francis Drake. We might even need money for food. I'm not like you. I like to have food with my alcohol."

"Why worry about food when we can get a pizza, and we can't worry about what hasn't happened, so to hell with it. Right?"

They went out smiling, an Irish coffee in each hand, and sat on a low, rock wall across from the Buena Vista. The saloon looked great, like Christmas, lots of red and green and white lights, the roar of young people trying to get laid. Sure. But what was he doing, stinking like a garbage dump most of the time, worried about a few bucks, never knowing if there was enough money to fill the boat with fuel, or even buy a meal. He rubbed his bristly face. Hell, his beard was turning grey.

He and Greg teetered on a precipice each day they fished. One little failure, one mistake, and… It wasn't easy work either. One dumb miscue at sea and they could eat it. He better try to think of some plan for the future. All he knew was fishing and the post office and milking cows. He remembered leaving high school thinking, "I'm gonna do something great." But nothing so far.

He sipped his Irish, a bittersweet elegance topped with whipped cream, a rich man's delicacy in the midst of fish guts. The day's alcohol caught up with him and he laughed. Fuck it.

"I got an idea," Harry said after maybe five minutes on the wall. His eyes teared up with excitement. He pulled Greg over to the truck and handed him a soupfin that weighed maybe forty pounds, dragging another out from the covering of ice and wet blankets. They cradled them carefully in their arms like precious babies, little pieces of ice crumbling off the chilled bodies. They placed the sharks side by side, as if pals, on the sidewalk in front of the Buena Vista.

Harry and Greg sat across the street on the wall to watch. They sipped their second Irish, now cold but still tasty. For a moment Harry felt rich.

Couples walked in and out of the bar, men in dark suits, women in white nearly-see-through dresses or expensive, butt hugging jeans. Beautiful people. Some stopped and goggled in amazement at the two sharks. Some just stepped around or over, ignoring them in an exaggerated manner, as if not at all surprised by anything. The sharks lay there, flat and greyish-brown and very dead, their cream white bellies blooping out on either side, eyes blank as paper. Harry and Greg sat and giggled from across the street. How would these fancy people explain this to themselves?

"Them poor saps," Greg said. "They can't say nothin'. They never even seen a real shark face-to-face before."

A cop roared up on a motorcycle. He looked at the sharks, then wheeled around them staring down at them as if they might be a mirage that would go away. He parked on the sidewalk next to the sharks and strode to a nearby phone booth. As soon as the cop turned his back to dial, Harry and Greg ran over and grabbed the two sharks and threw them in the truck and took off. Thirty seconds and they were gone. It was a thrill, a crazy adventure where no adventure seemed possible. The cop never saw them. He was still waving his hand and chatting on the phone as they zoomed away.

"Let him try to explain *that* at the station," Harry said. Greg punched him lightly on the shoulder as they started across the Golden Gate Bridge.

"Hey, Sarge," Greg said in a falsetto voice. "You'll never guess what's at the Buena Vista."

"Big bad sharks that disappeared," Harry said.

"He'll lose his cop job," Greg said. "They'll think he's drunk."

Halfway across the Bridge they were still laughing like crazy and feeling no pain when some red lights flashed on behind them.

Harry went cold. How had they found him? He groaned. His Dodge Ram was a backwoods monster, with a broken windshield wiper and headlights that shorted off and on. It was filled with sharks. He tried to think if he had any outstanding tickets. Maybe someone at the Buena Vista told the cop their license plate.

"Our night of fun ain't over," Greg said, reaching behind him. From his jacket he pulled out a baggy of weed.

"We're screwed," Harry said as he parked on the shoulder on the Marin side of the Golden Gate. As soon as they stopped Greg kicked a hole in the rotted floorboard and dropped the baggy through.

"Hi guys," a cop said, shining his flashlight through the open window. Another cop came up on Greg's side. "Come on out, boys, and lean against the car."

"Yessir," Harry said, but Greg took his sweet time.

Flashing a light into Harry's eyes his cop said, "Where you headed? You boys been drinking, it seems."

"No sir," Harry said. "We're tired fishermen headed home with some sharks."

Greg began to sidle away from the car. "We ain't boys, Mr. Officer. And we ain't done nothin'. You got to have a reason to stop us."

"Get back against the truck, sir!" He shoved Greg face down across the hood of the truck. "Spread wide." He tapped each thigh with his flashlight. "Legs wide. Sir."

"You own this truck?" Harry's cop said.

"Yes sir," Harry said. "Such as it is."

"You know why I stopped you?"

"No sir. I thought I was driving carefully."

"Your headlights were cutting out."

"What is this heap?" the other cop yelled at Harry. "A wreck from the junkyard?"

Harry, spread-eagled, looked out across the hood over the bay to Berkeley and its merry lights, where they'd been earlier that day. Why had he driven in anyway, when he didn't have a sure sale? He was sunk. He could see the outcome, seventy-two hours in the can on a hold, a towed truck, a rotten fly-blown pile of dead sharks, nets still set at Ten Mile Beach, abandoned, still loading up with fish, a half dozen tickets, a series of appearances in court, a DUI, maybe six months in jail. Maybe they'd find Greg's weed.

Fucked! Anyway, they'd have to feed him. Hell. Prison might be better than the low life he'd been leading, no girlfriends, smelling like a park toilet all the time.

Behind them the red and blue lights of the police car winked neon explosions.

They were in a pile of trouble. Greg, red-faced and bloodshot from sun and booze, his sharp face hosting several days of stubble, cursed softly as he yanked on the wallet stuck in his back pocket, when they heard the radio whistle in the police car behind them. Harry's cop rushed back and picked up a mike. Harry couldn't hear what was said.

"Come on, Jack. A 211 ongoing at the Quick Stop in Sausalito." Officer Jack pushed Greg on the back of the head so his forehead bounced off the hood of the truck. "Here's your wallet, sir, you dumb punk."

Harry's cop stood up broad-shouldered and very tall and said, "Take it easy, boys. We got a call. There's a whole lot more sharks ahead." He laughed at his little joke.

They whirred off, tail lights growing smaller fast and disappearing as they turned down Alexander Road into Sausalito.

Saved, Harry thought. It happened so fast he hardly had time to understand it.

Greg scrambled under the truck and retrieved his baggy and waved it at Harry smiling.

"Hey, hey," Greg said, "With dope there's hope." When that didn't get a smile, he added, "At least we're still alive."

Harry shook his head. "Yeah." But his tone dropped and his lips flattened in disgust. It was a joke they often repeated as they were coming in after a miserable day's fishing. They were still alive. He was sick of hearing it. It was a ridiculous life.

They drove in silence. A cold wind flowed up through the floorboards. When they got to Rodeo Drive, Greg said, *"Turn here!"*

Harry hesitated but Greg grabbed the steering wheel and pulled right and Harry finished the turn.

"Jesus Christ! What now! You're gonna tip us over."

"We'll hit Gatsby's in Sausalito. We ain't had no dinner. I know a guy there. We'll get a pizza for a shark."

"You been knowing a guy all day."

"Ain't it grand? What would you do without me?"

At Gatsby's Harry went in, sat at the bar, ordered an Irish coffee and asked for a shark pizza. He couldn't help himself. Greg had talked him into it. He'd said it would give his pal at the bar a good laugh and set them right up.

Harry was tired, half swacked, and depressed. But he could use a good laugh and a pizza. The load of sharks piled up in the back of the Ram was growing more monstrous by the minute. They needed more ice.

If he'd piled the truck with cow shit, he could have sold it easier.

The bartender said, "Shark pizza? What the hell. I never heard of no shark pizza."

Greg came in then, on cue, with a sixty-pound soupfin over his shoulder. He flopped it hard on the bar and glasses rattled. "Somebody called for a shark?"

Well-dressed customers stared at the carcass. Harry stared at it. Leaning over and lifting its sagging lips to see the teeth, a fat drunk in a white shirt patted the shark on its very dead head. "Hey," he said to the shark." You don't look so good. You wanna drink?"

The bartender pointed his finger and said to Greg, "I remember you. We eighty-sixed you last year." He motioned over a square shouldered Asian bouncer in a nice pearl grey suit, who told the two politely to leave and never come back. Carefully, smiling, with Teddy Roosevelt buckteeth, the bouncer put his hand on Harry's shoulder and began to gently urge him toward the door. His arms were as thick and muscled as Harry's legs.

"You come here again," he said to Greg, still smiling, "I'll break your fuckin' arms and legs and *then* I'll call the cops."

Greg said, "Excuse us for living." He farted loudly, hoisted the shark on his shoulder, and reached out and gulped Harry's Bloody Mary while the large man's face screwed up dark as the dark cold night outside. "Out. Out."

With the last of their money, Harry and Greg bought two packages of jerky and three quarts of Miller's from the nearby 7-11. It was cheaper by the quart. Sure enough, the clerk said there had been a robbery earlier and the cops had come.

"People shouldn't steal," Harry said sympathetically.

"Ah, no big deal," the clerk, a tall blonde kid with furtive eyes, said. "We get robbed a couple times a month by some strung out freak. I push a button, the cops show up, and that particular freak don't shop here no more."

Then they drove just across the highway and swiped two hundred pounds of leftover crushed ice from Sea K dock and drove back on Sir Francis Drake to Tomales Bay. Harry told Greg to hold the quart bottles of beer down below the window. Who knew what shark was going to try to devour them next, what cop or beast or act of nature? And the days were running past, the years speeding up, Baby and Daddy unreliable. Growing old. Hell.

There remained the sharks to sell for ten cents in Bodega at six tomorrow morning. Harry and Greg looked at each other as they pulled back in to Marconi. A half moon sparkled on the bay. Midnight.

"This glorious life." Harry began. "At least…"

"We're still alive," Greg finished.

Ascension of Jackie

There are strange things done
In the Midnight Sun
By the men who moil for gold;
The Arctic trails have their secret tales
*   That would make your blood run cold...*

The Cremation of Sam McGee
by Robert Service

Conk Widmark and Harry Selke had already spent a month in Dillingham, Alaska, refitting the Tortuga, cutting away the fire scarred forward cabin with a chainsaw and bolting it aft to make the 32-foot gillnetter into a tidy little bowpicker. Conk was a demon for chainsaws. And he was Harry's hero. Conk was forty-two, Harry twenty-three. They were both trying to make enough money to get through the year. Harry had followed Conk all the way from California with the promise of a good payday. In Harry's opinion, Conk was hippest of the hip, in jeans and leather vest and a sly, wide smile for all.

"I should've done this ten years ago," Conk said, slashing away at the boat. "But too damned much else to do just to get ready each season."

Harry was astonished at the fine work Conk performed with a chainsaw. He moved the deckhouse aft and rounded off the gunnels so completely it took only a few swipes of a plane, a bit of sandpaper and some epoxy to smooth everything off. On top of the tiny cabin Conk added an Hawaiian tiki, a foot-high grinning tortoise head chainsawed and carved lovingly out of a stump.

"What's that turtle for," Harry said.

"Well, it's a slow boat and that's for good luck. Tortuga means turtle."

"Not in Hawaiian."

"Spanish. Never hear of the Far Tortugas?"

"What? In Spain?"

"No. In the Caribbean."

"Jesus," Harry said. He was too young to know as much as Conk.

Conk loved tropical Hawaii, though he'd grown up in Alaska. He'd learned a little bit of everything in his youth fishing and hunting along Cook Inlet. He'd gone to UC Berkeley too, and ran his own little engineering company, Redskin Engines, back home in Marshall.

"I'm sailing off to nice warm Kauai with my nice warm Nancy after this season," Conk said. He had built a great long trimaran out of of logs back in California, and he was ready to sail off with his new wife, Nancy. All he needed was a chunk of money and he was ready to go.

"Nancy's never been sailing," Conk said. He grinned. He had a peculiarly wide mouth with flat lips and he looked a little like a friendly monkey when he grinned. Women flocked to him anyway, and Harry was trying to pick up some pointers. Harry knew his own baby face was against him. But he could see that Conk was tricky, and you'd better be careful when you went somewhere with him or you'd be involved in something way out of your league.

Alaska in May was plenty cold, with days and nights well below freezing. When the tide ebbed, the Tortuga would sit locked in the frozen muck of Dillingham Harbor. There was one hell of a tide too, not the six or seven foot change Harry was used to in California but as much as a 30-foot change from low to high, a delta change, accompanied by a two-foot bore that roiled up the Wood River Delta from the distant ocean past Dillingham itself.

At river's edge, from the low-water mark, a long expanse of soft mud rose slowly to far off, dull yellow, sandstone cliffs, the tops of which held a treeless expanse of dwarf shrubs and moss and lichen, a dark grey-green tundra that seemed barren except for mosquitoes and flying insects of all kinds, while the delta waters were, during the season, wildly alive, filled with immense runs of king salmon and the largest sockeye run in the world, and, every other year, a fabled pink run.

"Christ!" Harry had said when they got off the little two propeller plane that brought them over from Anchorage. "This place is the biggest pile of garbage I ever saw." Maybe two or three hundred homes and shacks lined a few dirt streets. In the distance, along Main, lay the brown shack that declared itself to be the N and N supermarket. Rusty machinery and skeletons of wood boats lay here and there. The air was thick with tiny gnats. No-see-ums the natives called them.

"A number one great place," Conk said. "You'll grow to love it."

Conk had grown up in Alaska on the Kenai Peninsula with various families that included fishermen and whores, and, he said, if you looked far enough back to a time even before whores, his ancestral history included French gold miners, Scottish trappers, Eskimos and a few murderers. He might have been part Yu'pik.

"Mom worked the camps," he said. "My father coulda been anybody." He shrugged and widened his lips and opened his eyes wide. "Any male on the Kenai. I keep looking for older men who look like me." His face radiated amusement. He pointed at a passing fisherman, a huge lumbering, red-faced ox. "Who knows."

He had thinning blonde hair and blue eyes that belied his native blood. His mother was Scotch-Irish and she and her sister had been fish cleaners and cooks. and prostitutes. Whatever made money. Sometimes they hooked up with miners and panned for gold. Conk was raised in various honky-tonks on The Kenai by some of the best whore-aunties a boy could have. People do what they have to do, he explained with a shrug.

Conk was smart as they come, Harry knew, maybe a near genius. He had a Master's in Mechanical Engineering from UC Berkeley. His struggle to rise from fish camps to a university was a story in itself.

His face was round, open, with that honest smile that flashed into instant friendliness. He looked right into your eyes and listened, and remembered. He wore a yellow mackinaw, though it was stained and its color had faded under the sun and dirt and blood of many fishing seasons.

Harry, on the other hand, thought of himself as reserved. Shy. It took him forever to open up. He felt he looked like a hillbilly in his Farmer Brown coveralls, but he worked hard and eventually made a few friends with those who took time to know him.

Back home on Bolinas Mesa, over a joint and a jug of Gallo red, Conk had told exotic Alaska stories of near disaster, great stories most of his young audience in California had never imagined, a snowed in winter with wolves, murder of an old trapper, a fishing boat on the rocks 500 miles out of Dutch Harbor.

"This is Channel 16 Coast Guard Station Dutch Harbor to fishing vessel on rocks. Is this an emergency, skipper?"

"Valll…" Conk would say, his voice taking on the calm Swedish accent of the skipper, "Ya might say ve are shloooow…ly sink…in'…"

Great stories, but if you hung around him you'd better watch your wallet, Harry learned. Conk could grin you out of a thousand dollars you didn't even know you had. He'd persuade you of some outrageous scheme or trick that would always take just a touch more cash to make it work, a chance-of-a-lifetime investment, of course, and it-couldn't-go-wrong.

Conk would invest time and money in his own schemes, though, so they were not exactly cons then, except Conk promoted them more than they deserved, and even if they succeeded you'd be lucky to break even. He'd give you a warm hug, and a sweet sales pitch on his newest invention, a new type of outboard engine, or some automatic Swedish machine for catching rockfish. He had his prestigious Berkeley M.A. so his ideas were believable, and he himself seemed to believe in what he told you, and that made those who loved him, like Harry, believe too. You just had to keep tabs on your investment. He wasn't going to do it for you.

"In Alaska," he explained with his grin, "you take everything you can get because you never know when you'll need it. Anyway, we're pals. We take care of each other here, right?" Such a winning glow of intelligence and empathy and affection, a wide, ready smile, Conk being just another guy like anyone, filled with excitement and life and new ways to get rich. Go for it. Life's an adventure. Forget the money. It's just money.

He could be distant sometimes, lost in some important plan, eyes narrow, thin, fine hair flowing up untamed, a memory full of stories of Alaskan gold, millions, billions of salmon. You might be able to buy a farm with the profit from one season, he claimed, or do anything you wish, and this season the run was predicted to be especially good.

"One year," Conk said, "a bunch a whores came up to NakNek and leased a fish tender, a nice big barge, about as big as they come. And they set up a hot water shower and a galley and some beds down below and put a piano on deck, and went cruising up and down through the drift net fleet during the sockeye runs. Those crusty old Swedes and Italians never seen nothing like it. Bee… yoo…tiful women in long black stockings and push up bras with a piano playing nasty, and a sign saying, *Food and Services for Fish*. It was a fisherman's glimpse of Heaven. Oh, yeah…"

We drank his good wine, ate what Nancy set up, cheese sandwiches often, or a nice fish soup as Conk sat back telling us…

"You take a week drifting up and down in boats stinking of salmon and those old bastards would have sold their boats and their families for a hot meal and a piece of ass. Food and sex for fish. Couldn't beat it. Whores with Oars, some fishermen called them, just because it rhymed. Didn't have oars. Only thing, the poor old fucks had to take a shower, and some of them never took more than one or two wash-ups every year, the Yu'piks and the rest of the natives there, and the Swedes and Finns no better, old hermits from upriver.

They would shovel their sockeye or pinks over on to the barge, get washed, fed, and laid until they couldn't wiggle, and leave a tip, sometimes a thousand dollars worth of fish all in all. Fish is just fish, but a good whore is a joyful memory forever. Happy men."

As Conk described the scene, he turned in slow circles and showed off a hairy leg and played an imaginary piano with his fingers.

"End of the season, these ladies made themselves nearly a million dollars, according to Bumblebee where they sold the fish."

Pack up my saddle, Harry said to himself, I wanna go. Still, on reflection, he thought twice and held off. He'd been to Alaska when he was twenty, not in the same area but farther north, seining for herring with a cousin in Togiak Bay, and he'd barely escaped with his life, much less any profit. It wasn't a story he was proud of.

He'd flown in to work on a leased boat in Togiak, and the boat had broken up in a storm and he and the skipper had to wade ashore in ice-cold water. Then he had to borrow enough money to fly home. A disgrace. Wasn't his fault, though, he told everyone. He'd been a twenty-year-old greenhorn, a Chechakwa, an idiot who thought he knew everything and was immortal. The skipper of his wrecked boat, a local halfbreed Yu'pik, was eventually shotgunned by the boat owner, a Swede named Willy, who wanted to have a little talk with Harry, too.

"I might get shotgunned if I go back," Harry said.

"Forget it," laughed Conk. "Old news. That Willy Swede is dead. Yu'piks got him."

"You knew him," Harry said in some astonishment.

"I know every fisherman in Southeast Alaska," Conk said. "We know each other."

Bristol Bay. Just the sound of it. There was hardly any other place in the world an honest working man could make so much money in three months. Harry was now experienced, broken in, Conk explained He'd earned his sea legs. Now he was ready to make his fortune. A smart fisherman who worked hard could make a hundred thousand dollars in a good season, and this season had a great prediction. The sockeye escapement three years previously had been terrific, according to Alaska Fish and Game. And this was the right year for pink salmon as well. Harry, as deckhand, could easily pull in fifty grand.

Harry tried to imagine so much money, what he'd do. Buy a good fishing boat. A farm. Travel to Spain. Get laid by those Anchorage whores in their black stockings. He was ready to work 48 hours a day.

In California Conk had told him what a fine boat the Tortuga was. Harry would have to pay for their travel expenses, that was all, and cover what little they might need until the season opened. They might need a permit, but they could fish without one and still make a bundle of dough, if Harry was willing to push a few limits. Hell, it was a damn wilderness. Not much law to speak of.

Harry was ready, heart and soul, whatever it took.

"This is the first year they ever required a permit," Conk explained. "Up to now it's been wide open. All you needed to do before was be alive, apply, find a boat, and throw out some nets."

Harry mentioned the gale that wrecked his first trip. "It blew ninety mile gusts," he said. He still felt amazed he'd lived, huge waves breaking over his small boat until he had run her ashore.

"Oh, yeah," Conk said. "We get a little blow from time to time. Now you know what to expect. You got your sea legs."

The list of needed supplies grew longer as they readied the Tortuga. It had been a decent boat in the past, but Conk hadn't used it in five or six years, and it was something of a wreck, the cabin burned, the old engine frozen up. Pretty soon Harry was two thousand dollars in debt. He'd borrowed and borrowed. This time he'd have to make good money to pay his friends back. He had friends and family who had trusted him.

The boat needed marine plywood, an expensive thing in Dillingham. Then they needed wiring, which had to come from Anchorage. Then they needed a special propeller, which had to come from Oakland. Harry's pal Charley had it flown up. Harry borrowed five hundred more for it from Charley. Conk had located a barely used gas-driven Atomic Four. He installed it himself, but Harry paid for accessories.

Conk was a helluva boat mechanic and carpenter, highly respected in Dillingham. He'd built and rebuilt boats many times, often under pressure with a season looming. He did the skilled work and Harry did the grunt work, and they raced against the light, starting early and working late, a 14-hour day followed by plenty of beer at The Willow Tree, every day a step by step battle. Harry liked the sweat of it. This was what real men did. It was all working as planned.

"Can't miss opening day," Conk said. The opening was the big deal, when the most money could be made. You might make twenty or thirty thousand that first day, if you could hit the boundary line just right.

"Listen," Harry said to Conk one morning after he wrote another check, "I'm going broke here. I keep handing out money, and there's always more needed, and I'm running out of friends."

"Well, here we are," Conk said. "We're here and if we stop now, all we get is shit on from seagulls."

"I'm not saying stop. I'm saying skeptical. What about the permit? Can we fish without one?"

"Sure," Conk said, "but we might get caught."

"And…?"

"Just a fine. They hardly ever throw you in jail."

"Jail! And what *kind* of fine?"

"Hard to say."

"But you must have some idea. Don't the Fish and Game say?"

"Well, yeah."

"What then?" Harry said.

"Depends," Conk said. "Anyway, you're young. You'll get out after a few years." Conk laughed, yanked on the chainsaw cord, and whatever else he said was lost in the chatter of metal teeth chewing through plywood, hair flying, shoulders shaking and jerking.

Harry went into the local Fish and Game Office, asked for the regulations and read that fishing commercially without a permit was a felony punishable by a minimum of a year and a day in prison, plus a fine. He went back to Conk more than a little pissed off.

"Goddammit. I don't wanna spend a year in prison for some goddam felonious fish."

Conk laughed at him. "I see your point. Anyway, I found someone with a permit. A woman whose husband died. She don't know how to fish."

"So, what does that mean?"

"We fish her permit and give her 20 percent."

"That legal?"

"Sort of. We keep it undercover."

Sort of? Harry groaned. Here he was 2000 miles from California and nearly three thousand dollars in debt, with no round ticket home, and his so-called true pal Conk pulling him under by the shorthairs every day. There wasn't much use in even thinking about California. Once in, you played the game out. No fish and he'd have to borrow the money to get back and he was borrowed out. It was too cold and far off and wet to catch a boat ride back to Anchorage and to try to hitch down across Alaska to Canada. And across Canada too! 1200 miles from civilization.

He'd put his trust in Conk, and had come thousands of miles north with him, and found himself completely dependent on him. Well, Harry had to depend on Conk. But every day was some new obstacle, and every day they had to move forward, anyway. Opening Day was creeping up.

"You'll see," Conk said. "I'll make it work. Think of it as another Alaskan adventure."

They finally met the woman with the permit, Jackie, a forty-year old female built like a pie with legs. She'd dressed up for the meeting, and had gone to the local Dillingham beauty salon and got a beehive hairdo. It sat piled over her thick neck and beefsteak face like a melting rocket.

Jackie stared at Conk and Harry suspiciously. "Guys. I don't know neither one a you, but I hear this guy Conk is a helluva fisherman." She looked at Conk. Then at Harry. "Which is which?"

"Conk," Conk said, holding out his hand and smiling broadly.

"Deckhand," Harry said, quietly, backing away. Jackie shook her head at him, her beehive bobbing.

"We don't need no deckhand." She nodded up at the two big boys behind her, both over six-two or three, and broad, but very young, in their teens. "I already got 'em." Harry flushed angrily. He half turned away. Not only was he deeply in debt and far from home, but he was about to be fired before he began. He looked at Conk, who winked.

"Harry's my partner," Conk said coolly. "I fish with him."

"One of my boys will deckhand," Jackie said, looking up at the two young men next to her. But she hadn't talked this over with them apparently, because they both took a step back and vehemently shook their heads.

"I'm workin' the cannery," one said.

The other said, "I aint goin' out in no crappy wood boat like this with a turtle on top. I aint riskin' *my* goddam neck!"

"You will if I say so!" she said, her voice rising. "I'm your ma!" She swelled up, lips tight and broad, her face set hard and red, beehive waggling as if ready to topple over. "I brung you up. The law says you got to treat me like I am the Holy Mother herself."

"Fuck you," said the youngest. "Fuck God," said the other. They spun around and walked off.

Conk pointed at Harry and said in a firm but comforting tone, "The two of us are a team." Harry felt relieved.

Jackie looked Harry up and down. "No deal," she said. She yelled after her boys. "Better come back here, shitheads!"

"I told you when I called I had a partner," Conk added. "We'll have to take another offer." That seemed to catch her attention.

Harry couldn't look straight into her eyes. A short woman, she was stomach from neck to knees. From a hundred feet away, she looked like a kid's top, small at the top of the beehive, swollen in the middle, and stick skinny in the ankles. Up close her eyes were cold, a thoroughly dumpy female, though Harry knew from his last time in Togiak that a woman you ordinarily wouldn't even notice at home might begin to look damned good after a month or two in Alaska.

Harry climbed back on the boat. Maybe he should have stayed to try and charm Jackie up a bit, but her face chased him right into the cabin of the Tortuga. She looked like she was ready to bite and hang on.

He tried to think about it from her side. She was going to sign over a permit that might be worth a small fortune, and she didn't know Conk or Harry. This was business, not friendship. Someone had got close enough to her at least twice to pump out two big boys, and she must have her good points. She might have been better looking when she was thirteen, say. But now… Harry knew a couple of four-hundred pound plus red-neck fishermen back home in Bolinas who might like to meet her, or possibly cook her for dinner. Yet here she lived under her hair, Conk buttering her up, making her laugh. What Conk said to her, Harry couldn't hear, but she smiled at Harry, looking up through lowered eyes. Harry gave her a quick wave from the safety of the boat.

"Hey," Conk called to Harry, turning from her. "We worked it out. You're on board again." His broad gorilla grin said he'd pulled off a very fast deal. "Harry, meet our new partner, Jackie." She came up on the first rung of the boat ladder and reached thick fingers up past the gunnel and Harry reached down. He shook her hand and she held his a moment too long. When her middle finger tickled his palm, he jerked back and nearly tore her arm off. A wave of despair shivered like an electric shock down his back and into his legs. She grinned at him, a squashed, toothy smile, her cheeks flat, her eyes opened wide. Harry ducked back down into the cabin.

Conk teased Harry about her whenever she came around, which was a daily visit *just to be friendly*.

"Hey, Harry. Here's your *Jackie*."

She was after him, smiling, sliding her hands over him when she got close enough. He dodged away, left the boat on an errand, ran. She reeked of whiskey. Harry didn't want to insult her directly, or slug her. They needed that permit.

"What in hell did you tell her, anyway?" Harry finally said.

Conk shook his head and smacked his lips. "Harry and Jackie went up a hill," he said with a far off dreamy grin. "Don't forget she's a rich widow. The thing men's dreams are built on."

"Dreams?" Harry said, "When you fall asleep at night in our comfy cabin do you ever dream of someone standing over your knee with a hammer?"

Conk laughed.

One thing Harry quickly learned about Dillingham was that the law was not much use. If drunks got into a fight and smashed each other, no one was going to arrest anyone. People disappeared forever off boats and nothing was ever done about it. One especially cold night a drunk fishermen passed out and fell off his boat and into the mud and froze solid. Knifings weren't even newsworthy, not that there was a newspaper. A lot of life, a lot of blood.

There was one tiny medical center. There was a Sheriff's Office, but only three sheriffs during the sockeye season. If people couldn't handle their own affairs, tough titty. Once in a while, if a brawl got out of hand at the Willow Tree or the Sea Inn say, two pissed-off sheriffs might get rousted out of bed and eventually show up and bust everyone still there, their idea being that if someone hadn't fled they'd either been in the fight or were too drunk to move and ought to be locked up anyway.

The sheriffs made money with that theory. If an arrestee wanted to protest, he could pay a hefty fine on the spot, or fly to Anchorage to plead his case. But there wasn't much mercy from Alaska courts, once they booked you.

"Guilty until proven innocent," Conk explained. It was better to pay a fine and get the whole thing over with. Locals protected locals, but outsiders watched out for themselves. Men died, and nothing much was said. You took it as it came. It was the Wild West, the last shadowy battle line of civilization. Beyond was anything you made of it, fueled by a gold rush of salmon.

There were another two weeks until Opening Day and Harry and Conk had to get everything together, finish the boat, hang gear, clear the boat license and Jackie's permit with the Fish and Wildlife, and load the old Tortuga with supplies for the opening. They had no icebox, only a couple of big plastic chests strapped on the top of the cabin on either side of the turtle tiki, each chest half filled with crushed ice. They didn't take much fresh food: twenty-five packages of Top Ramen, twenty pounds of rice, two dozen packs of spaghetti, dehydrated mashed potato flakes, oatmeal, peanut butter, a half dozen packages of ballpark hotdogs pre-cooked, canned milk, some oranges, some apples, three dozen eggs. Not much for the one or two months they'd be gone. They'd eat salmon, or whatever they caught. They could replenish from Fish Buyers. They'd built two bunk beds, one on each cabin wall where they could stuff cook pans and spare clothes and anything else into boxes bolted under the bunks.

Jackie would take twenty percent of the net profit, the going rate this year for a permit. In exchange, she would agree to sign it over to Conk, who planned to motor off the day before the opening, just to be out waiting at Protection Point and to get to the Line ready for the first fish in the first minute of the season. Sounded good to Harry, Protection Point, with its hint of hiding from open swells, its whisper of danger around the corner. It marked the limit of inland waters. Conk talked a lot about the opening, what to do, how to outmaneuver the others to be right on the line the exact moment the season began.

"Hundreds of boats'll be out there ready to drop in. Miss that line when the season opens and you might miss your whole season."

They were just finishing last minute chores and waiting for Jackie to hand over the permit when she appeared at the boat with a sleeping bag and some clothes stuffed into a pillowcase. The pillow-case had a painting of a leaping king salmon with sideburns and a guitar that made the fish look like Elvis Presley. *The King*, it read.

"I am," she said, "going along. It's my permit." Her hair was braided carefully and coiled on her head in a bun. She stood next to the boat in tan khaki shorts from which bulged her cream-white thighs. She seemed almost human, not too sober, but not completely drunk yet. She had occasionally insisted she was going with us, even though Conk had explained to her why she couldn't. He'd told Harry she had eventually agreed with his argument, but here she was. Harry shook his head in disgust. Somehow everything Conk promised had dark corners and back alleys. Harry couldn't imagine even one night on the boat with Jackie, much less a season.

Conk stood his ground. He spoke slowly and carefully as he argued with her. They didn't have room, only two bunks, not enough food or foul weather gear, but she sucked on her bottle of Jack Daniels as she stood on the dock above the Tortuga.

"Fuck you," she said. "Fuck the Tortuga." She tossed her bag on board with a thunk, climbed in and staggered into the cabin. She splayed out cold on her back, huge thighs spread, a mound of pasty flesh oozing over a fragile plywood bunk. In a moment or two she was snoring and spluttering like a volcano.

Conk and Harry looked at each other. Conk laughed and called it a *coup de main*, but Harry was ready for more of a *coup de grâce*, for the opening was next day, and they were headed out to the Line fifty miles away and he could imagine what it would be like on this small boat for a month or two with drunken, amorous Jackie. His feelings sank right down into the black muck of the harbor.

When they tried to drag her dead weight off the Tortuga and dump her ashore, she awoke and fought free, and slipped back face down on the deck, grunting. She began to snore again. She weighed close to 200 pounds. She kicked like a kangaroo.

"Now what, Mr. Captain," Harry said.

"Holy macaroni, Andy," Conk winked. "Leave it to Conkie." But he offered no immediate solution.

They did have an extra day to form a plan. They might be able to convince her to go back if and when she sobered up. It wasn't reasonable to try to fit three on the Tortuga. They didn't have extra food. She didn't know a damned thing about fishing. She'd be in the way. It would cost a lot of lost time and money. Women on boats meant trouble, and Jackie would be trouble times trouble.

They'd have to do something. For a starter, Harry emptied her fifth of Jack Daniels over the side.

Against Harry's protests, Conk headed out for a practice drift. They plowed over to the North Side to lay some nets, just to get them wet and make sure all the equipment worked. The season didn't open until early next morning, so they'd check gear then figure out what to do, and maybe run most of the night.

Harry was desperate. Trapped. His stomach was tight. When he took the wheel, Jackie crept up and tried to grab him from behind by the crotch. He knocked her hands away. He might have felt sorry for her in the abstract, if she hadn't been after him all the time, for she was, after all, a mother, even if a fat, stupid, ugly one with two redneck sons. He wondered what chance did such a woman have? He also wondered what would happen if she accidentally fell overboard.

Again and again she came up on him. "C'mon Harry, baby," she whispered in his right ear. "I hear you're a real cocksman." She pressed against his back and felt again for his crotch with her right hand while in the approximate area of his left ear she waved another fifth of Jack Daniels. He twisted free and elbowed her in the shoulder and she plopped with a howl on the cabin floor. Conk pulled her up and screamed at her to stay in the bunk or she'd get us all killed.

"Killed?" She seemed to wake up. "Don't hurt me."

Harry plowed Tortuga across the bay, slamming hard enough and turning sharp across the chop to keep Jackie falling back into a bunk her feet in the air, giggling. Each time she raised her Jack Daniels high, holy as a crucifix. They'd made a big mistake not searching through the rest of her gear while she was passed out.

As they turned seaward and ran down the south side the cabin filled with smoke. Conk shouted, "Fire!"

"Fire!" Jackie ran around through the cabin smoke shouting. "Wheresa fire?"

The four-inch thick plywood transom holding the Atomic Four exhaust pipe had begun to smolder. This had happened once before in the harbor when they'd run the engine for a half hour, but it wasn't anything, just another messy Alaskan detail, the reason for a good shakedown, all it took was a cup of water to put it out, and a few more wraps of aluminum foil around the exhaust, all smoke no fire. But Conk played it up.

"Christ, Harry. We're on fire! We're gonna *burn up*," Conk shouted, his voice deep and fake. "Where's the fire extinguisher? Where's *the fucking fire extinguisher?*" Jackie bounced drunkenly from bunk to wall, bending over, falling as the boat leapt and swayed. She threw boxes of canned food around searching frantically. *"Don't you fools have no fire extinguisher?"*

Conk shouted, "Head for Bumblebee across the bay, Harry. We might make it." His voice took on a matter of fact tone. He pushed her back into a bunk. "Hang on, Jackie. We might make it yet."

Five miles away, the aluminum building that was Bumblebee Cannery sat glowing like a great church high on top of a hill.

"Call the Coast Guard!" Jackie shouted. She swayed forward and snatched at the VHF mike, but Harry yanked it away.

The Tortuga crashed along through the chop, smoke trailing aft. Conk and Harry took turns screaming, *"We might die."* Harry crossed himself, "Jesus help us." He raised his hands in prayer. "We need help, Lord. Help us get to Bumblebee."

Jackie shouted out over the troubled waters of the bay, "GODDAMMIT, I'M THE BOSS. I COMMAND YOU TO CALL THE COAST GUARD!"

Harry lifted the mike to his lips but didn't switch it on. He shouted, *"Hey! Coast Guard! May Day! May Day! Tortuga on fire. Mayday."*

The Tortuga jerked and bounced against the breeze through the broken waters. Jackie stood, tried to go on deck, fell back through the door on to a bunk and tried to suck on her Jack Daniels bottle. Her lips and gums bled as the bottle rattled against her teeth. Her face dripped with whiskey. Acrid smoke from the exhaust filled the cabin, blew through the door and dissolved. Conk opened and closed the door, alternately filling the cabin with fumes and clearing it.

"Call a goddam Coast Guard," she mumbled. Her blouse shifted sideways, the fly of her enormous shorts unzipped revealing a curly mass of greying pubic hair.

She muttered a string of curses, interrupted only by a short pause for a gulp of whiskey. "I want off, goddammit. I want off." She began to cry. Occasionally she staggered forward against Harry, and he butted her back. Conk dabbed a wet rag at the smoking plywood just enough to keep it from breaking into flames. He shook with repressed laughter. There was no mercy.

It took twenty minutes to cut across and slide The Tortuga up onto the mud below Bumblebee.

It was low in-coming tide. Forty yards of black sewage led up to the first building, one hell of a slippery incline up to the high water mark, hard enough to get there if you were sober. A football sized field of crab shells and hundreds of rotting, fileted salmon bodies spread their bony carcasses all the way down to the water's edge. Fish heads poked out stiffly from the sludge, eyeballs plucked into holes by ravens and gulls. Wide open fish snouts curved up stiff as sticks from lifted tails buried in the ground as if the dead salmon were screaming and still trying to leap free. Rusted remains of cast off engines and pipes and the ribs of wooden hulls lay scattered about, like the remnants of a fishing war.

On top of the hill lay Bumblebee cannery gleaming in the sunlight, a 200-foot-long, two story, unpainted aluminum shed.

Conk said in his most dramatic voice, "Hoist her up there, Harry. I'll fight the fire." He waved Jackie's permit. He winked. When Jackie looked at Conk for reassurance, his face shifted into a mask of open-mouthed fear.

"Jump, Jackie," he shouted. "It's gonna blow any time. I'm gonna try to save her."

Harry wanted to debate about who should stay and fight the imaginary fire and who should haul Jackie up that garbage littered muck to Bumblebee.

But Jackie didn't wait. She lifted one heavy leg over the starboard gunwale and did an awkward roll, falling the length of her body onto her back six inches into the mud. Her fifth of Jack Daniels flew up and slipped upright with a bloop into the sludge. She felt around for the bottle, both arms windmilling in an absurd backstroke. She held the bottle up like a prize. It was coated with shit-brown slime.

Harry didn't want to get near her, much less jump in, but if he didn't lift her up she'd sink in and suffocate. Not a bad idea, he thought for an instant. Might be hard to explain, though.

He slid over the side until he was knee deep, hauled her up, her back dripping black, her slimy breasts showing blotches of egg white flesh. He held her by the wrist and dragged her upward.

She fell back. "What the motherfucking fuck you trying to do to me, you motherfuckers?"

With Harry's help she stood. The whole area reeked with ammonia from decaying salmon and crab carcasses. This was the eleventh circle of Hell, plenty cold too, the surface of the sludge still frozen over in places with a silvery frost.

"God," Jackie muttered. "Goddam." She struggled forward, wiped her face with a mucky hand, waved her bottle in circles and cursed some more. She was the Black Lagoon itself. She half rose and fell back again, trying to pull Harry by his wrist down on top of her. She laughed. "Baby, ba…a…by," she said, "Send me to Heaven."

He placed his boot in her belly and heaved back to break free of her grip, pulled her up by her hair, and lifted her under her armpit to keep her from collapsing. She roared and waved her arms and fell again, and then again. Harry heaved her up hard each time thinking, *Let her go.*

Her teeshirt and bra ripped off after a number of falls, and her rubbery breasts flopped out. She fell. Again. Harry lifted. She fell. She couldn't have got up the incline on her own. A few steps forward, another fall. Her boots had long ago disappeared in the slime. Her shorts filled, slipped down to her knees and vanished. Harry reached down into the ooze and handed them to her. She waved them in circles like a flag in her left hand, the mud coated whiskey bottle in the other.

She tried to kiss him. "Ooooh. Baby," she said. "Sock it to me."

It took twenty minutes to climb up to the aluminum door in the cannery. Harry opened it, gave her a shove, slammed it, placed a stick in the hasp, and fled, breathing heavily. Jesus Christ!

A screaming voice muffled inside the cannery flowed down the hill after him: "Where am I, motherfuckers! God damn you. You got to obey me! I am your owner!" She pounded on the door. "I am your God!"

And what a God. Harry wondered what the Bumblebee Cannery workers, a mixture of natives and college girls, might think when they found her, her eyes glowing white through the black muck, naked, shorts in one hand, a bottle of slime in the other, staggering, cursing, reeking of dead salmon, as if the bottom of the bay had sent an emissary.

Strange things do happen in this land, Harry thought as he slid back down to the boat, and Alaskans know to expect them, but Jackie's sudden appearance might well start a new religion.

An icy bucket of water doused him as he climbed aboard. Conk grinned from ear to ear. "You are one holy mess," he said. "Now let's go get some salmon."

"Amen," Harry said. "Amen. Amen. And Amen."

Rooster Flying Close to the Ground

Once, a long time ago, in the Sixties, on a run-down farm in
Tomales, California, in a different world before computers, there
lived Banty the Rooster. He weighed about a pound, a beautiful
fluff of pheasant like feathers in fluorescent reds, velvets, golds,
shades of brown and blue tending to purple. Proud as a bouquet
of roses, he strode king of the backyard not only of the hens and
geese there, but also of eleven sheep, one goat and any wander-
ing humans. Even the nine starving cats in the basement quickly
learned not to stalk him. A rainbow whirl, a flutter of vibrant
wings, rapid stabs with thorn sharp spurs and deadly beak, and
off each cat would yowl bloody and much bowed. They were not
used to birds that fought back.

Hens that pecked properly chicken-like at corn or leftovers
thrown to them by Jean or the kids would suddenly find themselves
at the viral end of a small tornado. A flurry of dust formed by
whirring feet and Banty would flatten a terrified hen. Three pumps
and a tail shake later and off he would go up to the roof or the
nearest branch to crow his conquest of the known world. A simple,
fierce life.

If an innocent sheep wandered from field to yard, Banty would
whirr up and strike at the eyes of the bewildered animal. Molly,
the goat, a nearly indestructible force in herself, found, after many

a confrontation, reasons to visit elsewhere than in the backyard. Banty, a true drawback to the days of feathered dinosaurs, was far too quick even for her.

At night Banty ignored the chicken coop and roosted on the fence on the side of the road, or in the open, paneless, bedroom window of Jean's old farmhouse. He awoke and crowed lustily at every passing headlamp from a car or whenever anyone in the house dared turn on a light.

"He's driving me crazy," Harry said to Jean. "I gotta sleep. I gotta get up to fish at four."

"We cherish all creatures," said Jean, his beautiful Buddhist love, blonde hair flowing down to her waist, emerald green eyes, Rapunzel in gold, figure firm as a young tree even after three children and fifteen years of marriage to a mad artist. "Banty is only doing what roosters are supposed to do."

Harry had met Jean one morning while she sat sobbing bent forward on a curb in front of Diekmann's, the one market and general merchandise store in the tiny town of Tomales, Pop. 175. He sat down beside her as she looked up and tried to smile, a bundle of radiant hair.

"Can I help?" he'd said. The cement was warm, the day hot.

"No," she said. "I'm fine." But her body continued to shake.

Though he didn't know her more than a passing hello he put his arm around her and she leaned into him and let her tears flow. After a few minutes she began to tell him how she cleaned houses to earn money to keep her three children fed and in school, and how her husband, Jack, who had set up his studio in the center hallway, demanded absolute quiet while he painted his ancestral ghosts.

"He had an inheritance, but it's gone. He's not skilled at anything, so… now… he paints his dead family," she explained, wiping her cheeks and nose. "They all died in a plane crash in Mexico when he was a teen." She snuggled against Harry on the curb. "I'm so sorry." Her breast against his right arm took almost his entire attention. He felt a delectable mix of lust and pity.

Soon Harry pulled her over to sit on his lap and rubbed her shoulders and kissed her hair. This seemed to help both of them. Her tears slowed.

"I went in to buy food, just oatmeal and milk," she said, "but they refused me any more credit."

She owed Diekmann's sixty five dollars.

Harry said, "Stay here. I'll talk to them."

"No!" she said, holding on to his arm, but he went in anyway.

He paid her bill, bought two loaves of bread, some peanut butter, a gallon of milk, three containers of Old Fashioned Quaker Oats, five pounds of brown rice, some vegetables and six pounds of chicken for a good healthy stew.

"You've got credit now," he said, placing three large sacks of food next to her on the sidewalk. "And plenty of oatmeal."

She kissed him on the lobe of his left ear. He fell madly in love.

He wasn't rich. He gill-netted commercially for sharks and halibut from a 24-foot Oregon Dory for survival wages. He lived in the 10-by-20-foot laundry room of the otherwise burned down Marshall Hotel, on the two hundred by two hundred foot square of thick, charred, twelve by twelve Douglas fir timbers that, until 1971, had formed the foundation deck for what had been the loveliest old wooden hotel in Northern California.

The Marshall volunteer fire department had, unfortunately, been able to save only the support timbers, deck, and pilings. And the laundry room which had been full of wet sheets. On the deck lay the remnants of the hotel in shards of broken china, the keys and strings of an upright piano that played eerie notes in the wind, charred chair legs, puddles of melted window glass. Muddy bay waters now could be seen lapping peacefully beneath the timbers where decking had partly burned through.

Harry's laundry room featured a picture-window view of pine trees and hills across the one mile wide bay. He was caretaker, and so paid nothing for rent. It was, all in all, beautiful, green hills, drifting clouds. He was lucky to have it, the view, the shack, scorched though it was.

After meeting Jean he realized how miserably lonely he'd been. They became lovers, despite the limits of motherhood and the mad husband. Harry made sure the family had enough money for food. He paid their bills. Fortunately, the fishing was exceptionally good for a while.

Jean and Harry made love on the sly in his shack on Tuesday afternoons. Jean said she was about to dump Jack. She'd made a lifelong vow to remain with him, and didn't want to break her vow and leave, but the children came first.

"The death of his family made him crazy," she said one day as they stared out at the bay. "He was exciting, a real artist, and I understood his suffering, but he's abusive toward the kids." Her shoulders shook with the strength of her words. She leaned in to his ear and whispered, "And I do not love him any more."

She urged Jack out. Harry wondered how she did it but didn't ask. Soon Harry moved into Jean's ancient bed in the ancient three bedroom farmhouse on eleven acres of Scotch broom, sawgrass and blackberry, all of which she leased for $75 a month. Harry fished harder and fed the family and paid the bills. Jack, now free to paint all day, and all night too, settled into a garage a mile away. How he got enough money to eat and pay rent, Jean didn't know, or care. She was finished with him.

"I'm sorry I don't have more money for us," Harry said. "I never planned on love."

"I bet you never made love with anyone as beautiful as me," Jean said. She stood naked before him, breasts high, body firm.

"Absolutely not," Harry said. "But I also want to make you more beautiful and buy you things."

"Why buy anything extra? Food is enough. Love is beautiful. What we have is very beautiful."

But along with this beautiful life came three unhappy children, Andy, twelve, Mimi nine, and Star, five. They weren't adjusting well to the loss of their father, irrational though he'd been. The replacement in their mother's bed by Harry was unacceptable. And Star screamed and was unappeasable when separated even for two minutes from Jean.

And there were the farm animals, the chickens and sheep as well as the cats that lived in the basement and ate anything small that moved or stayed still long enough to be snatched up, mice, rats, songbirds, crickets, flies, food left on a plate, attacking everything, except fierce Banty.

Jean gathered eggs from the nesting hens, but killed none of her creatures. She forgave Banty his irritating aggressiveness. "He's part of nature," she said. "He's a rooster."

Harry soon realized he was more than a rooster. He was a one-pound feathered demon. He danced and fluttered around and stabbed at Harry's ankles whenever they met.

Jean cared for the children, cooked vegetarian stews for them, sang them to sleep. Her vibrant contralto voice was quite professional, it seemed to Harry.

If you had not fallen
then I would not have found you
Angel flying too close to the ground...

Star, five, clung to her Mama's skirts as she scurried from one household task to another. Each night Star and sometimes Mimi, would creep into Jean's bed and lie next to her snuggled up. Andy used to do this too, Jean said, but wouldn't if Harry were there. Her three kids made it difficult for them to make love. Such a new, lusty relationship required free space and a door that would lock.

Harry had never lived with a mother and children, and his ability to adapt was sorely tested. He loved deeply, but was sometimes filled with bitterness at the children's demands. He never complained, but Jean knew. She expected him to understand and give way.

"They're only children," she said. "And this is all hard for them." He did understand. But it was still difficult for him to meet their desires. They'd exclude him if they could.

Jean knew the hearts of all around her, animals as well as humans. She tried to keep everything, Harry, Jack, children, even the two old horses Royce and Pone, in delicate balance. The world, as she saw it through her Buddhist eyes, sat balanced on a pin and it was the duty of all good people to keep it from tumbling over into darkness. One must care for all living creatures.

But Star wanted Harry gone, and her daddy back. It became her duty to turn Harry in. If he swore, Jean heard about it from Star, and she would patiently tell Harry not to swear in front of the children.

"Right," he explained. "But I wasn't swearing in front of the children. I was swearing in front of the house." A joke, right? Dumb, yes, but he had to keep some personal respect. Jean didn't see any humor in anyone swearing anywhere the children might hear.

What made him swear most was Banty. He'd never been harassed by a chicken before. As Harry returned from collecting eggs, or as he carried a pail of milk from Molly the goat into the house, a hidden Banty might suddenly crow from a branch or a bush next to his head, and the milk bucket slosh, or eggs splatter, and Harry swear. Star, ever on the alert in her campaign to eliminate Harry, would run in shouting, "Mama! He's swearing!"

Star and Harry had at first liked each other. He'd played with her, carried her around on his shoulders._She would laugh and pound happily on his head. But she hated him from the moment he'd first taken Jean out of the house on a dinner date, and from that point on her anger was unrelenting.

"Don't go, mama." Star had screamed as she'd clung to Jean's skirt. Jean's friend Ethel, babysitting for the night, pulled on Star's arm.

"Shush, shssssh," Ethel had said. Star fought and wailed and kicked at Ethel, though she'd often claimed that Ethel was her favorite friend. The two other children tried to shush Star, to distract her. They were older and they understood when Jean explained she needed to spend time talking to Harry. They pulled on the tiny girl, but her body was filled with superhuman strength, and she bit Andy on the thumb.

"I can't go," Jean had said. She was so helpless, so lovely in her beautiful dark blue skirt and light blue cashmere sweater. She looked twenty, but here were her three children.

Harry, disappointed, had said, "Will we never be able to spend an evening together?" He felt if he gave in to Star now he would lose Jean. Even mothers had the right to go out to dinner, or did they?

"She's never been separated from me," Jean said, her eyes wide and rolling. "She's only five."

Harry nodded grimly. He stepped back from the door. Jean moved with him. Star screamed at a higher pitch as the door closed and Ethel carried her back into the depths of the house. It wasn't until Jean sat safely in Harry's station wagon with the window rolled up that the cries of Star had faded. But it was awful. Harry began to relent. He pressed his forehead down on the steering wheel. This had to be terrible for Jean. She had tears in her eyes.

"Go back in," he'd said. "I can't break her heart like this."

"No! Let's go on," Jean said. "I'll bring her a piece of apple pie. She likes pie. I'll say it came from you." And so Harry had become a part of the family, but not an especially welcome part.

Jean, Buddhist that she was, wanted no loud voices or outward show of anger of any kind in her house. She would ever so slowly explain each time a child in fury swore or punched that God demanded we be peaceful. Harry was supposed to model a calm adult presence. At sea, fishing alone on his dory, he could freely curse the weather, the fish, God. But he was in love, and so he listened to Jean and at home tried his best to practice the eight-fold path. He tried to curb any frustration, to understand and reflect on it.

But when he finally let go he exploded. He could only contain a certain amount of anger, and it had to come out one way or another. He was careful around the farm, around the kids, and especially around Jean. It wasn't a big thing she had to have from him, just that he show self control. Be gentle, speak softly. That was reasonable. When the children fought among themselves, as even a Buddhist's children must, Harry could see the need for a firm hand, yet he held back. And when they openly turned their anger on him and yelled at him, he felt helpless, for Jean allowed no other authority over the children. She didn't trust anyone with them, except Ethel.

She led Harry to Easwaran's Blue Mountain Center for Meditation. But Harry was no good at meditating. He was not a believer. He could, with effort, cross his legs, fold his hands as if in prayer, and sit quietly for five minutes concentrating on breathing until he began to snore. Sometimes he fell over.

"I didn't realize I snored," Harry said. "I'm so sorry."

"You also snore whenever you sleep on your back. And you have an annoying way of puffing when you breathe out. I punch you sometimes."

"I'm sorry," Harry said. But he got a small thrill out of the thought of beautiful peaceful Jean punching him as he slept. He was so much larger. He could imagine her grim smile and her tiny Buddhist fists striking him. Wasn't everyone human, then, even Jean? Not just an angel, but a real life person. Well, she might yet descend to a level where he, fish-bloody Harry, waited, wounded by storms and children and roosters and love, hoping.

He'd never felt this deeply in love. He'd been in lust before, or had been in half love with someone who didn't quite love him back, but Jean had come to him, clasped him full on, despite all the other things she'd had to juggle, such as her religious friends at Blue Mountain who complained that Harry killed fish for a living. There were the children, the animals, and, of course, Jack, who was now filling the children with hostility for Harry.

Harry didn't fit in. He liked Ethel and her husband Spann, the pig farmer. He liked most of Jean's friends, the neighbors, even the people at Blue Mountain, as individuals. But the Blue Mountain people suspected him. He was an outsider because of his fish killing work. He wasn't religious, accepted neither the Catholicism of the local ranchers, nor the peaceful breathing of the Buddhists. True, the ranchers hated the Buddhists, who they thought of as a bunch of tree hugging hippies from Berkeley. But the ranchers didn't like Harry either, with his long hair. He was an outsider, neither Portuguese nor Italian.

The Buddhists irritated the ranchers even more by greeting them with smiles and words of love. If Blue Mountain were a commune, so the inhabitants must be communists, and all communists were the enemies of free enterprise, which included ranching.

But Harry's love for Jean was solid. It could survive any impediment, despite the children who played one parent against the other, who refused to do anything Harry suggested, except when Jean laid down the law. When husband Jack babysat, he gave the kids free reign over the town, so long as they left him in peace to paint. But Jean, and, by extension, Harry, never allowed them to wander freely, or cross Highway One, next to which sat the farmhouse hidden behind a ten foot hedge.

Andy, nine, said to Harry, "Dad allows us to cross over to see our friends."

Harry told them he'd ask their mother. "Meanwhile, no." He explained that cars driven by unwary vacationers zoomed past at 70 or 80 miles an hour and could crush people. But they didn't believe or respect him, so across they went anyway. They dared him to turn them in. If he told Jean, the children would scream their hatred of him, and even she would look askance at him. Why had he let them go across in the first place?

Mostly Harry tried to stay out of the way, to remain outside of the ongoing struggle between mother and children. But he became the main source of the trouble. He offered the kids little gifts, candy, or ice cream, which they took eagerly, but the deeper hostility they felt for him was unassuaged. Andy and Mimi wanted to run free, to stay out with friends well past dark. Not Star, though. She wanted to cleave as close to Jean as possible.

One evening late, Jean sat next to the old wood-fire stove in the kitchen, its warmth sweet. It was well into November, and cold and wet enough outside for them all to wear heavy jackets and boots. The back yard was slick with mud thickened by chicken manure. Cats prowled the dinner table and floor.

"Star's afraid she'll lose me," Jean said to Harry as she poked at the stove fire.

"Of course. I know," Harry said. He had sympathy for the kids. They were trying to understand too many changes, a replacement father for one thing, himself, Harry. They'd formed a pact against him, though he often took them to the movies in Petaluma, or for a fat Chicago style pizza. Such momentary pleasures were quickly forgotten, and Harry received little credit for his best efforts.

But he was patient and liked kids, and had been friends with all of them for the months before he'd moved in. He considered himself to be a good person. Fitting in to the family was a struggle, a contest, and Jean was the prize, and he could put up with anything. They'd see he was okay in the long run. He kept his temper, even when pushed hard, but the kids noticed the tightening of his jaw. They were super sensitive to the angry moods of adults. When Jack had been angry he'd been the bad father, and now Harry was the bad father no matter what he did.

Harry and Jean sometimes kissed before the wood fire. But Star, ever watchful, would come in and push Harry away and Jean would pick her up and hold her close. "She's too young to understand," Jean said. "I'm sorry."

"I know. I know," Harry said, hunching down on the couch as the other two came for their hugs. He couldn't see any way to resolve any of this except over time. But he would wait for Jean, forever.

All the children snuggled against her as she embraced them in her wide open arms, and they looked up at Harry with cold faces as if to say we have her and you don't. But Harry felt how beautiful she and the children were together in the soft firelight from the open oven. A real family sat there, almost his, something he longed for. How fine it all smelled too, the burning wood,, a pot of soup for dinner from vegetables they'd grown, and home-made bread still warm next to a pot of freshly churned butter.

Jean began a front room weaving business with two hand looms she'd purchased. Harry gave her money for a beautiful wooden loom. It took all his savings. She would make a weaving business, and pay him back. Harry encouraged her, was amazed by her energy.

Still, they argued over the kids and the Banty rooster crowing and all the cats, and the fishing, and Buddhism, and many other small things, not so small that they didn't stab into Harry's heart. Six months along into the relationship everything was getting bogged down.

"I can sell angora jackets for a lot of money. I'll pay you back every penny for the looms." She suggested that Harry might learn to weave. He could be a weaver and work at home and give up fishing.

"Well, I'd like to help you out more, but fishing is what I know. I'm paying the bills with it." From spring perch through fall halibut and winter herring Harry fished or repaired gear or sold his catch, every day filled with hard effort, weather permitting, from early morning to dark. It had the thrill of sudden winds, breaking surf. He could die, he could overcome. He made just enough for the family to get by on, but he loved his work. On the ocean he was his own master, just the water and the fish and the wind, the simple demands of boat and gear, and during that time he was free as a shearwater on a fresh breeze. Who but fishermen knew this ancient pleasure? To make your own life, to farm the sea, to bring food for many, the gamble of it.

"You could quit fishing," Jean suggested. "It's not a good thing to do anyway." She meant he killed God's own creatures.

Fishing had beautiful as well as harsh edges. He was out in all kinds of wind and weather, fighting Nature, feeling every muscle, struggling in a very old profession, wet, cold. Alive. What he didn't sell could be eaten or traded with neighbors. In return they gave him cheese, fresh whole milk, cuts of meat, home repairs, the loan of a tractor.

Some of the catch, the halibut for example, sold easily, though he had to take an extra day off from fishing to peddle them in San Francisco. Sometimes he tried to retail them pound by pound in Point Reyes from the back of his truck, but it was a lot of work and not enough customers.

Jean had helped sell them from the back of his truck two or three times, but it disgusted her. Too many dead fish, and not enough money. Not worth the effort. The butcher at The Palace market complained they were unlicensed.

He often had to drive his catch in to China Town, or into Berkeley to Spenger's Restaurant, maybe a hundred and fifty miles round trip. Sometimes he caught too few fish to be worth such a trip, and sometimes nothing. Occasionally a net was lost or ruined. On bad days where he might be blown off the water he thought seriously about quitting, but if he gave up fishing, then what? Help weave, Jean urged. But all day in front of a hand loom seemed very tame after his tumultuous life as a fisherman.

"I couldn't do it," he said.

But Jean kept after him. "You don't need to kill fish for money. The looms can make enough for both of us. Anyway, I always fear for you every day. You might drown."

Harry had unwittingly told her of the dangers that he loved, of the huge sneaker waves at the mouth of Tomales Bay, of the gusty winds from the offshore fog belt. He tried to get her to feel what he felt, to see the water rising up ready to strike as he waited to power through to the open sea. The absolute thrill of bursting like a rocket through a swell just before it broke. The timing and experience it took. But she saw it as frightening. The one time she went with him, she began to cross herself and pray as they left the bay into the ocean. He turned back, and she never went again.

"So, you don't have to do it," she'd said. "But you keep doing it. You choose to do it. So why should I have any sympathy for you?"

But he didn't want sympathy. He wanted her love. He could accept her life, most of it, why couldn't she accept his? But she was so strong in her ways, and if he wanted her, then he had to acquiesce. She'd been exhausted by Jack's refusal to see beyond his paintings, to even notice her friends, by Jack's failure to see the beauty of trees and fields and animals around them, the plumed quail families that paraded through in the early mornings, the amazing coordinated flights of redwing blackbirds, thousands lifting and circling over a field, and then down hidden in grass and bushes as if never there. He continued to paint ghosts.

"As if a shadow came to life only to vanish in an instant," she'd explained. "As if each black wing flashed a warning flag of red."

She wanted Harry to love what she loved, and she demanded that the children grow up breathing the love of life she felt. She was on the right path. Harry, too, could be nurtured by Buddhist beliefs. Couldn't he see that all living things had good souls according to their kind? But Harry thought the souls of fish were narrow, more centered on food, on eating and avoiding being eaten. Souls. Did fleas have souls? If so, he wished they'd have them in some other house.

Jean set up four looms in the front room, a regular handcraft factory, and put her friends Ethel and the others working day after day weaving lovely designs into woolen cloth that she cut and sewed into *Jackets By Jean*. They sold for 200 dollars each, but it took a lot of work to make one, for she sheared her own sheep, and she carded and spun her own wool, and the amount of overhead she had to pay out for help took most of it. There was little profit even though her friends worked at first almost for free until they would have to draw back, and Jean would make promises, feel sorry, and search for others to help. She'd get involved in their lives. She was a fixer, a helper. She tried to pay them back if not with money then with love and support or eggs, or gifts of fish that Harry caught.

Besides struggling with the children and cats and sheep and Banty, Harry fought mechanical problems too. He was dependent on his old Chevy station wagon to get to his boat docked at Marconi Cove. He also used the wagon to haul fish to market. The Tomales farm was an hour's drive from the nearest fish buyers in Petaluma, Point Reyes, or Bodega. Other markets in Berkeley and San Francisco were even farther. If his wagon went belly up he'd have to roust around and borrow a truck, and not many neighbors would loan out their precious trucks. It was hard on any vehicle to carry a thousand or so pounds of fish and ice into Berkeley or in to San Francisco, and then Harry couldn't always sell all his fish in one day, and he might have to keep them under ice over night, so borrowing a truck was a dilemma. Farmers and ranchers needed their vehicles.

The boat engine would break down, the outdrive freeze. Fishing, upkeep on the boat, all of it was complicated, though he found ways to do it, even if there was waste at times. He had plenty of energy and hopes for a real killing. But sometimes the markets were jammed with fish and he would have to dump them in Bodega for pennies on the pound.

Jean looked at him and held him so her lips were on his mouth, her face so close it was a double image, two noses, four eyes. "Quit! Quit! Quit!" she said to his lips. She shook him hard with each forceful word. She kissed him.

"I love you! Quit!" She licked his ear. She threw her thighs against his.

He took deep breaths. Maybe he *would* quit fishing. Then the day would go smooth and clear, the fishing and selling would be just right. In the summer he could fish three or four days a week and make a fair amount of money when everything went well. But just as suddenly a storm would come up or the fish disappear, or the market get flooded or the boat steering come loose, or the truck might throw a rod, or a flat tire cause him to swear, and the world turn bleak as he sweated to fix something. Money. It rang through the house.

Money. Money. Money. It was a ghost, a shadow that lifted and vanished into the house, into the cries of the cats.

On a sunny Friday early in December, the carburetor on his truck gave out, and Harry had to take it out and go into Santa Rosa for a replacement. Fortunately, he had no fish to deliver. He'd borrowed his neighbor Al Wilson's old Ford for the trip, and he had to return it as soon as he could, but the bolts holding his ancient carburetor to his engine were rusted on tight. His station wagon had coughed and died right in front of their farmhouse, next to the big hedge there, a few feet off Highway One, not exactly a safe place with the coming weekend traffic and a lot of drunken ranch kids driving half blind during Friday and Saturday nights, so it was best to fix it right away.

He buried his head deep under the hood, trying with a crescent wrench and a vise grip to break out the bolts. He'd soaked them with WD 40 and it was a question of patience and a little bit of time. Jean was shopping with the kids so he swore freely as he dropped nuts and and bolts and wrenches down under the car or into the engine.

Harry wasn't a good mechanic. He could change carburetors or spark plugs or charge a battery or replace a head gasket. Beyond the simple stuff, he needed a professional. Though he liked the ocean rough as it could be, admired each fish as it came up, liked hanging nets, the grease of a malfunctioning vehicle or a boat engine was dirty and frustrating. Some people loved working on engines, but not Harry. And repairs were half of the fishing game.

It was ungodly hot for November. His hands dripped sweat, his knuckles bled. He swore. The sun beat through the raised hood.

Without warning, from the high, thick hedge next to the wagon, Banty crowed so loud it seemed to come from inside Harry's ear.

"ROOK A ROOK A ROO!"

Banty was, in fact, two or three feet away hidden in the green leaves of the hedge. Harry's head jerked automatically upward, the hood fell and jammed him in the back of the head, and it hurt like bloody hell. His wrench dropped into the bowels of the engine.

God damned little son of a bitch! He'd strangle Banty right there, bite its head off, rip it into a pile of feathers, spurs, beak and all. The last straw.

"ROOK A ROO!"

Harry plunged both hands into the hedge to catch Banty by the throat and shut it up for good, but it screamed in fury and flew down to a corner of the yard on the other side of the hedge where it strode back and forth its neck feathers ruffled. Who was in charge here? He could see the damned thing all puffed up through the breaks in the hedge.

Harry's hands bled. His head and back were bruised. Furious, cursing violently, he grabbed the shotgun he carried beneath the seat of the truck. He was crazy. He stalked Banty and drove it behind a thick stemmed ancient rose bush filled with thorns where it had once before avoided capture.

He could see the rooster peering at him mocking him ready to flee. Harry blasted the bush and the bird into a cloud of smoke and pink petals and lovely floating feathers. Banty died immediately.

Its body was still warm when he picked it up. For a moment life felt so good.

He plucked the amazingly small rat-sized body and wrapped it in paper and shoved it far back in the freezer where he kept fish steaks. He'd eat him later, the little fucker. He'd stew Banty's iron hard little body, and eat him, and grind his feet and beak into chicken feed. It was what cannibals did to their enemies. Let the hens run free now. Let the sheep come into the yard, the goat, the cats. Freedom for all, especially Harry. Afterwards he swept up feathers and petals, and rearranged what was left of the bush. He thought it best not to say a word about Banty to Jean, just let its absence drift slowly into everyone's consciousness.

But as soon as he returned from Santa Rosa, even as he was replacing the carburetor, Jean came out and asked about Banty.

At first, still a little angry, he said from under the hood, "Haven't seen him."

She waited, standing directly behind him.

He stood, wiped the grease from his hands, and faced her, hoping she would let it go, but she gave him a withering look. "I found some feathers in the yard, and I found this." She held up the unwrapped package that held Banty's plucked body, now a tiny frozen lump of pale grey, goose bumped flesh that looked as if it were formed of candle wax.

Her voice shook. "What do you call this?"

A dead chicken, Harry was about to say, but she stopped him. "It doesn't matter. You lied to me. I'm not talking to you for at least two weeks. You have something to say, write me a letter." Her voice quivered with fury, vast armies of Buddhists behind her glaring at Harry.

He watched the swing of her slim hips, her exquisite long blonde braided pony tail swaying as she strode back into her looms. The ladies were on their way over for the afternoon's work. Most likely they wouldn't talk to him either. He dropped off the truck and told Al what happened. Together they drove to Point Reyes Station to have a beer at The Old Western Saloon.

"Best thing to do," Al said, "when attacked by women, is to drink beer." A half dozen beers later they drove home laughing. It was great to have a friend.

He fell asleep on a pile of hay next to the sheep pen. When he awoke it was dark and icy cold, and the ammonia smell of the sheep was overpowering. He went in to the house, where everyone was in bed, and tried to talk to Jean. He was still loaded. He smelled like beer and sheep shit, and she kicked at him and would not talk to him. He slept in the front room on the couch next to the looms. They hadn't slept apart for six months or more.

That was how it remained for ten days, though Harry was soon allowed to sleep on the far side of the bed away from Jean. They didn't have another bed. If he touched her she shook him off. If he insisted on talking to her she would get up and sleep on the front room floor among the looms, where cats snuggled in next to her, and a pet white chicken looked down from its roost on top of a loom. This chicken had been nearly decapitated by Banty.

No one in the family spoke to him. Any word he said to the children was met by silence, hardly even anger, though Star stuck out her tongue at him.

Two weeks and then another went by. He set up gear for herring. He came home. He cooked his own meals, in silence. He couldn't stand it. He could stay excommunicated, or he could leave. If he were a man, he'd leave. To hell with the whole thing. But he couldn't leave. He couldn't quite believe that the love they'd had for so many months had gone up in a blast of feathers and roses. He kept trying to elicit a word, to charm Jean, to turn her towards him and make her see that he still loved her and was suffering.

"Look, how sorry I am." He held his arms out. Nothing.

"What do you want of me," he said.

"Quit fishing," she said, the only two words she'd given him for three weeks. But it was the middle of herring season, the best season for making money. He had to wait it out. He explained, for the umptieth time, what happened with Banty, and she listened for a moment or two and then turned coldly away to sit back turned to him a grey blanket over her head silent on a chair next to the dying fire in the stove. More days went by. Nothing.

Then he came in from fishing one rain-swept night after a terrible day at sea and found his old friend David kissing Jean passionately in the kitchen. It took his breath away. Jean opened her eyes and looked over David's shoulder at Harry but didn't stop. He understood everything. He'd become Jack. This must have been how she'd gotten rid of her husband. Silence. Indifference. He was out permanently. He was the ghost haunting the family.

Harry stuffed his clothes into a canvas bag. It was very hard to leave, to look around at the bed, the familiar things he was leaving. But he had a little bit of pride left. He stood for a moment before the kitchen door, the warm stove, and looked out into the rain. He had on his orange Helly Hanson rubberized fishing gear, his yellow sou'wester hat, his black hip boots. He carried a huge canvas navy bag over his shoulder. He looked absurd, like a cartoon. This relationship was dead, all the trust and love, as strong as it had seemed, broken at last by a god damned bantam rooster. And by his friend David. And there wasn't much he could do about it. It was his fault, he knew, his inability to adapt to Buddhism, to love, if it had been love. The last two weeks had been agony.

He wanted to kill David, his own good friend who had so many times congratulated him on his beautiful Jean. Why didn't he challenge him? He wanted to hurt Jean, as she had hurt him. A chicken had destroyed them, but that wasn't it, not half of it. Would a fight with David bring her back? Wouldn't he fight for her? Nothing could bring her back where she had been in his mind, trusting, loving, willing.

Love? Where does it go? Up in steam like Jack's ghosts. Dissolving as it rose. And this love had seemed so vibrant, so strong and real, at least more real than a banty rooster.

"See you," he said sullenly to the two who stood arms around each other's waist. They looked at him, their faces expressionless, but he looked away. He couldn't look at their faces for fear of attacking them both. He let the door slam behind him in the wind. He was sorry he didn't have another rooster to blast. He didn't think he would hurt Jean but as he got into his truck he felt for the shotgun beneath the seat. He could go back in. He could hold up the gun and say, "Don't mind me." Then he would shoot the stove.

He was glad he'd learned something from Jean, to control his breathing, to take a deep breath and hold it and let it go all at once, let tension drift through his toes and fingers. To contain. To let go. To relax. Maybe something Buddhist had rubbed off. He hadn't killed anyone, or burned down the house. Not yet. What was the use? What was the use of anything at all, of violence, of peace, of hate? Of life as a fisherman? There wasn't much love in it.

Stop thinking, he thought. He took another deep breath and held it for a slow count of ten. Then he exhaled, let it take the pain away, sensed the pain oozing out through fingers and toes. He felt better, but the feeling didn't last. Breathe. Exhale. A moment's peace.

But what *could* he do? The night was too dark, and the slick, rainy highway demanded attention. He'd shot it out with a rooster, and lost. He drove slowly toward his cold shack. Familiar places passed by. Northshore Boats. The Tavern. Mark's house over the water. He could survive a hell of a lot. The ocean had taught him that.

He laughed a few sharp sounds, more like grunting or cackling.

"I'm better than a chicken," he said to himself. "But not much better."

Salvation

When Ruth Rosenstein agreed to marry Harry Selke she said, "My parents are Orthodox."

Harry tried to forget about religion entirely. He was mad for her with her shoulder length blonde hair, eyes green as new grass, shapely yet strong arms, a slender, long, lovely nose that made her seem as if she were looking down humbly at the world. Five foot seven, and a figure and warm smile that made men, and women, stare. And a perfect klutz, so she often said.

Things fell on her from shelves. One afternoon, as she'd sat on their single bed in their tiny studio, a pot lifted itself off its perch above her, took aim and threw itself at her head. Another time, while they were searching for her forever lost wallet, Harry heard a crunch, and, of course, there beneath her shoe were the shards of her brand new and very expensive glasses last seen on a table on the other side of the room. They had crawled under her foot and sacrificed themselves.

These things happened daily, and she even blamed herself when bad things happened to other people. As they were waiting to cross the busy intersection of College and Ashby, a truck towing a two-wheeled trailer/kettle filled with boiling tar turned suddenly south. The trailer holding the hot kettle disconnected and went hurtling tongue scraping forward up Ashby fifty yards or so until it dumped its smoking load on what had been a fine new Chrysler parked there, pastel blue turning to black goo. Harry shouted in disbelief.

Ruth pulled his sleeve and whispered, "Let's get out of here."

"What?"

"It's my fault," she said, tugging on him harder, the tip of her nose white.

The little upward flip the tar trailer took as its tongue slid under the Chrysler was still vivid in Harry's mind.

"What?" he said again, his voice rising as he began to move toward the accident. What could she have done?

"The driver was looking at me."

Everybody looked at her, Harry thought. Did that make her responsible for anyone who chanced to see her?

But she took her effect on the world seriously, so he tried to make her feel better. "No one in their right mind would hold you responsible for that tar truck."

"No. No. It's too weird," she said. "It's too big a thing."

Too big a thing. He couldn't see the logic. "But how do you think this is your fault? Rather than the driver's or that bum on the corner over there?"

"Because these things happen to me all the time. An old black dog fell down an open manhole the other day while it was barking at me. He was terribly hurt."

"Look. I've been with you every day for almost a year, and nothing has happened to me."

"Not yet," she said, her voice low and slightly fearful. She pulled him by his shirt fast down Ashby, while the rest of the world ran toward the tar covered Chrysler. He couldn't help looking back and laughing. All the Chrysler lacked was feathers.

After months of living with her in marvelous sin Harry noticed that her accent changed whenever she talked on the telephone with her mother or father. She spoke to them in a questioning, Yiddish whine, her perfect English suddenly ghettoized. She came away from these phone conversations pale. She'd sit speechlessly next to him and sometimes cry while he held her shoulders and hummed. He'd pet her silken hair until she calmed. He began to dislike her unknown, distant parents. Fortunately, they lived 400 miles south in Los Angeles and seemed to have as little desire to meet him as he had to meet them.

"What's up?" he insisted, after a particularly long phone call from her mother, but her lips pressed into a narrow smile and she said, "Oh, they're getting so old. It makes me sad. And I'm not helping." Then she wrapped her strong arms around him and they undressed each other and made love, and who cared about faraway parents anyway?

She still had a year to go at UC Berkeley before she got her Bachelor's in Physical Therapy. To prove her independence of her parents, she worked nights at the box-office of the Telegraph Repertory Theater. That's where Harry first met her. She was so big and beautiful and glowing she filled up the tiny cubicle. Harry showed up nearly every night about a half hour before she got off, and went inside and watched whatever was on, which, for weeks, was Bergman's The Seventh Seal. He memorized the dialogue between the knight crusader, Block, and Death as they played chess for the souls of two innocent circus performers who were in love.

Death: I am Death.
Block: Wait a moment.
Death: You all say that.

Ah, Ruth and Harry were breathless in love and Death was far away, much farther than Los Angeles, and the world was young and Harry was in school, a whole life before him, working on his Teaching Credential. Twice a week he took care of one-year-old Florence, his daughter from a defeated marriage.

So here he was in heaven, Florence smiling and waving in her playpen in the middle of the room, he and Ruth cuddled up on the bed babbling away enthusiastically, an infinity of blissful happiness, blackbirds yodeling as they strutted through the yard, pansies blooming their lovely smiles, a trellis of purple bougainvillea over the doorway, and not a breath of argument or disagreement. Harry sometimes expected something bad to happen, but apart from the Empire State Building traveling cross country to Berkeley and falling on Ruth, he couldn't imagine what it might be.

She put up a Christmas tree and they gave each other presents. Harry gave her the most expensive string of cultured pearls with matching earrings he could afford. She gave him frog socks and an Orvis fly rod. They would have a dozen Florences, or Benjamins, or Judiths, Jews, Gentiles, whatever. Harry would name every girl child Ruth, Ruth Junior, Ruth the Third. He would teach, she would get her degree in Physical Therapy and become, until there were too many children, a terrific and highly paid therapist.

Still, eventually, they had to face the father and mother.

"They're really nice people," Ruth said, "but they're worried about me marrying a non Jew."

"Goys," Harry said. "Us goys is everywhere."

They drove down to L.A. in Harry's rusty Volkswagen Camper. On the way Ruth said, "They won't let us sleep together, you know."

It made sense, but Harry wasn't going to let that stop him. "In*to* your *bed* I'll cre…ee…*eep*," he sang, The Sheik of Araby, an off-key Rudolph Valentino stealing sex from the forbidden tent of the forbidding parents.

"We better not," she said, drawing back from him. "I love my parents. I don't want to hurt them."

"For God's sake," Harry burst out, suddenly and really deprived. She was regressing back to babyhood from her role as competent UC Berkeley Physical Therapist. "Don't they know anything about the world? The pill? The sexual revolution?" He hadn't spent a night apart from her for almost a year. "We're from Berkeley. What do they expect?"

"They're not stupid," she said. "They're Orthodox. They know about Berkeley, but my mother rules, and we're visiting them in their house in L.A. They expect me to still be their good, pure daughter. It's only three days. Can't you hold off?"

"Me? Three whole nights, you mean?" Harry moaned and tightened his lips in dismay, but thought the parents would have to be pretty vigilant to keep him from their good, pure, very passionate Ruth in the middle of the night.

When they arrived the parents were waiting at the door nervously, both of them taller than Harry. The father, Ben, a bent-over man wearing a brown sport coat and tie and yarmulke, was charming as he nodded and beamed, and his warm hugs and obvious relief in meeting a normal looking Harry revealed that he certainly loved Ruth, their only child. Almost the first thing he said was, "Will you keep our daughter happy?"

Ruth and Harry together breathed an emphatic, "Yes!" and Ben and Harry smiled at each other, two men, Harry an unashamed atheist, Ben an Orthodox Jew, a psychiatrist who loved baseball it turned out, and had, at one time, played semi-pro ball and tried out for the old Hollywood Stars. Harry, too, had played a year of ball for San Francisco State.

"You maybe heard of the great Luke Easter?" Ben asked. "Nuh?" He bent even lower and smiled and rose up, all very friendly. "Luke Easter was hero supreme of the Pacific Coast League when I played. A black man, one of the first when baseball was integrated, hit fifty home runs one year. I was good. I played shortstop. Comes the war, and so I join the army to fight the Nazis, but Judith insists I marry her traditionally before I go and get killed. No more baseball. She is Orthodox, and very beautiful, you know. Our Ruthie is like her. See it?"

Ben smiled lovingly at Judith and Ruth who sat hunched together head to head, old and young, chattering away over the dining room table, a huge, round, polished mahogany affair that only lacked a few knights in armor to make it even more impressive.

Harry nodded in sympathy, though he thought Orthodox Judaism, baseball and psychiatry an odd mix. The Torah, Luke Easter, and Freud. Well, made sense to Ben. But these things seemed to belong to some distant era.

The mother, Judith, a tall, handsome woman with an impressive bosom of her own, asked Harry bluntly, "And what have you done to deserve our Ruth?"

She smiled warmly but there was a sharp edge to her voice. She wasn't to be so easily charmed as Ben.

Ruth had warned Harry to be extra careful with the Mama. "She has a good heart," she'd said, with a sigh. "But Orthodox to the bone."

"He was a Navy Officer, Mama," Ruth said, answering for Harry. It was a little minor white lie. True, he had been a very junior officer in the Navy, but wanted nothing more to do with following orders or freezing at sea.

"So, where's the battleship," Judith said. Her lips smiled but her eyes stayed hard.

"I was only in for three years," Harry said. "Not long enough to earn a battleship." He chuckled to show he was joking.

"And why did you leave?" Judith's voice slid polished through the room.

A plate crashed from the table as Ruth stood up, an anxious smile on her face. She hadn't touched the plate, it just took off as if on marbles and shattered on the polished hardwood floor. She bent down and began to pick up the pieces. Harry had been watching her face, hoping for some support, and hadn't seen her near the plate. How did she do it?

Ben interrupted, holding up his hand. "Oy vey. Enough inquisition already. Look, the plates are falling already, and the kids just got here."

Judith threw up her hands and pulled out a broom and plastic pink dustpan from a kitchen closet. She pushed them at Ruth.

Harry had been prepared to defend himself, feeling he was a pretty good catch for anyone, not a young fellow with no future, but an almost finished product. He'd passed some difficult tests to get into the Navy, though he hadn't liked his time there, the gung-ho suck up to senior officers quality of it. After getting out, he'd become a respected Berkeley Free Speech activist, a member of Students for a Democratic Society, was about to get his Master's in Education, and not yet thirty. He'd climbed up out of poverty and was about to be someone, a teacher, maybe get a Ph.D. But here he was under inspection like some downy teen, suspect because he wanted to marry their daughter, his Ruthie, who he knew much better than they, his little klutz, his goddess responsible for the world.

The parents had mezuzahs and seven-branched candelabras and a kosher kitchen, all the food properly blessed, little of which Harry truly understood. He thought he understood, of course. They smiled, Harry smiled, and Ruth sank back into a Yiddish accent. It was catching. Even Harry said "Oy, vey" once, at which all three laughed, while he blushed like a child.

The mother grew more and more motherly, treating Harry and Ruth as if they didn't quite know how to feed themselves. She was an overwhelmingly perfect hostess. When she was a little too direct in her questioning, Harry tried to forgive her. She was the mother of Ruth. She was still very striking. She looked into every detail with almost obsessive forethought. Harry was given his own washcloth and towel and sole access to the lower bathroom, while Ruth and her parents shared the upper. He was to sleep in the guest room downstairs, while Ruth slept once again among stuffed dolls and animals in her childhood room upstairs next to the parents. They were to sleep this way for three nights. During the day they were free, except for dinner at five. If they went out later, Judith wanted them in by eleven, in her opinion a reasonable time.

Alone with Ruth, Harry complained, "This is more difficult than I expected."

"When I was eighteen curfew was eight," Ruth said. "She's getting better."

Harry was prepared to be thoroughly examined, even prepared to be kept from Ruth at night, but hadn't planned on curfew. He hadn't been on curfew since he was thirteen, and he tried hard not to show he was irritated. There wasn't much he could do. Judith was in charge of the house, the captain of the ship, and he, a junior officer under tight inspection.

"It's just that they go to bed early," Ruth said. "And Mama worries."

"We should have stayed in a motel," Harry said.

"They'd feel hurt if we didn't stay here."

"I know. I know." He'd heard of such situations. You get engaged, and the parents of your fiancée critique you until you jump ship. Harry was going to bear up, no matter what, for he had a really good thing.

But here he was squirming uncomfortably, an irreligious, non-Jewish bug under an Orthodox microscope. He blamed the whole predicament on the lack of culture in L.A. In Berkeley, Jews and Muslims and goys and blacks and everyone else got along on the basis of intelligence or shared politics, not whether they belonged to the same religion or ate the same food. They could be themselves. In L.A., one had to explain, defend, examine, justify, give in, join.

The first night at dinner, which was a nice veal roast with potatoes and gravy —nothing strange at all —Harry responded to Judith's question about a glass of wine by saying he'd prefer milk.

An electric shock spread through all the Rosenstein faces. *Milk*. With dinner. *Oy vey*.

Ruth put her hand on her mother's hand and hurriedly said, "He doesn't know, Mama." Her fork slipped to the floor and clattered and hid under the stove.

Mama nodded slowly with a heavy frown, but tried to smile, apparently torn between politeness and the desire to pour the contents of her wine pitcher over Harry's head.

"So why doesn't he know," Judith demanded.

Ben and Ruth interrupted each other to explain to Harry that in kosher families one did not use the milk of the mother with the meat of the offspring. Unfair to babies and mothers. Unclean. Harry imagined the taboo went back before Old Testament days when fresh squeezed milk turned immediately bad and carried disease. True, veal with cow's milk did suggest something similar to cannibalism, like drinking breast milk while chewing slices of baby.

"So Ruth was raised Orthodox," Ben reminded Harry, his voice friendly, full of baseball tones. "As long as you're here as our guest, we all keep kosher together. It's a good way to eat."

'It's the way of our belief," Judith said, glaring at Ruth, who shrank all five foot seven back into childhood.

The next day, for lunch, Harry cleansed his system with a Snug Harbor hamburger and a vanilla shake. Ruth had a hotdog. They laughed at each other. Her hotdog made Harry realize that this ordeal was as bad for her as for him. Worse. He could be an ignoramus, a dumb goy, but she had to balance parental expectations against her irreligious life with him. To distract everyone, Ruth had perfected some completely mysterious kind of magic act, a sleight of hand that made plates fall, doorknobs come off in a person's hand. The parents didn't openly criticize her, but if she hummed to herself thoughtlessly or placed a knife or fork wrong, or contradicted Papa, the eyes of the Mama grew chilly.

Harry had never seen Ruth so nervous. Her sensuality disappeared. Her breasts collapsed beneath heavy blouses and tight bras. She said Oy a lot.

But Harry managed to crawl up the stairs silently into her bed the second night, so quietly that if he hadn't placed his hand over her mouth she might have cried out. There were her familiar breasts again. There's nothing like forbidden sex. Jacob sneaking into Rachel's tent. Love. What Harry wished to do was almost too daring for Ruth, but after a certain marbled stiffness she melted and they had a terrific if muffled time. To eliminate bed squeaks, they laid the mattress on the floor, and repressed even their heavy breathing.

Ruth giggled. "Shush," she said to herself, and giggled some more as they did things the mother might never have imagined. Ruth's childhood stuffed animals watched in amazement.

On the second day at dinner Judith put her hand on Harry's cheek and said she thought he was a decent man and that he might make a good convert to Judaism. Not Orthodox Judaism, just Reformed would be fine. Her eyes softened, not green like

Ruth's, but a light tan. When her face softened in a smile she was a great beauty, even at fifty five.

Ruth had warned him this might be coming, and he'd vehemently opposed it. "Just agree," she'd said. "You go to a few Rabbis and a few classes and we'll have a Jewish wedding. Otherwise Mama will yip at us forever."

She could oppose the Mama only so much. Harry's parents died when he was a teen, so, except for being baptized a Lutheran as a defenseless baby, and except for the half dozen times his mother had bribed him into going to Sunday School, he not only knew nothing about Judaism, he knew almost nothing about religion.

Or about family, he realized. He'd thought of Ruth as his, but she wasn't all his, he began to see. She was the result of a lot of training and religious pressure. She was the valued only child of upper middle-class Jewish parents. But she was as beautiful as a Pacific sunset, an angel who offered herself to him for the rest of her life. It was like being offered the ocean.

At home they made love two, sometimes three times a night. No one had ever been more his.

"It's good we can't sleep together all the time at my parents'," she'd whispered after they'd put the mattress back. "We'll appreciate it more later." Harry didn't know about that, but he was at that stage where everything she said was straight from Heaven. He would have pounded nails into his own hands and climbed on that proverbial cross for her, built a temple, or torn it down, blown a shofar. Converting to Judaism seemed like a comparatively small thing.

The Mama was anxious to know Harry's plans about becoming a Jew.

"I'll give it a try," Harry said doubtfully, just before they left. Mama's lips set hard. Harry looked at the papa who was smiling beneficently as he chewed a toasted onion bagel slathered with cream cheese for lunch. A little jar of pike gefilte fish sat open before him, and he waved a fork at it.

"So, give a try with this," Ben said, with a big grin. "Irresistible."

Harry gave a smell and resisted.

Against some pressure, Ruth and Harry declined food saying they'd eat on the road. Dame Judith wasn't pleased with the meagerness of Harry's acquiescence to Judaism, but the father gave him a wink.

"So, let the youngsters do for themselves," he said, and Harry smiled gratefully, glad to get in the car and wave goodbye. All in all, Harry thought, it hadn't been a bad three days, though Ruth did not immediately respond. In fact, she said nothing at all for some time. Then all she said was, "Can we eat?"

They stopped at Bob's Big Boy on La Cienega on the way home. The waitresses wore short skirts and roller-skated to the car door balancing trays of dishes and glasses, swooping and bending low to expose cleavage. Very clever, very fast, very sexy, and delightfully non-kosher. Chili dogs. Onion rings. Coffee to go, and milk.

"I love hot dogs," Judith said. "I love those ball park dogs." Then her mouth opened to add something else but she caught herself and said nothing, and for a long time as they drove north on Highway Five she was quiet.

Harry's sense of self had been wounded but not fatally during the three days with Ben and Judith. Harry knew a thing or two, and was ready to take care of a family. He was, for one thing, an experienced father. He was well on his way as a teacher. Judith, it turned out, would have preferred not only that Harry be a Jew but also a doctor or a lawyer or business executive. Teachers were fine, but of little importance in the real world. No money in it, for one thing.

But Harry was going places. He had energy and will. He'd never been so loved before, and as the miles flashed by and he thought of their safe little nest, their tiny bed filled with joy, he began to perk up. He tried to make a joke or two with Ruth about what had happened, but she didn't respond.

"Do you know the one about the Rabbi, the Minister and the Priest on the sinking ship?" he said. Silence. He wanted to tell her the joke.

She dozed and stared out her window. He drove. Visiting had been harder on her than on him, he reasoned, though he was worn out too, and the driving made him depressed. Ruth wouldn't share the driving. She was afraid of freeways and never drove faster than thirty five.

"What are you thinking," he said, as they sped through the desert. He thought that she might be crying, her hair hiding her face as she pressed her head to her window. A breeze rippled her golden hair.

She turned to smile distantly at Harry. It was a little smile, but a smile. "Just enjoying the scenery," she said. The scenery featured a flat, hot, sandy desert mixed with gas stations, and every so often a lovely oil derrick. Another hour of silence followed, accompanied by country western music that faded in and out. Preachers raved about Jesus. American wasteland.

"C'mon, Ruthie. Let me know. Are you sad? I'm your goy here." Her silence made him more and more nervous. She smiled very quickly, and put her hand on his thigh. "I love you," she said. "It will make my parents so happy if you even become a little bit Jewish. They're just worried about me, you know."

"Hey, hey!" Harry said, glad she said anything. "I promised I'd do it. I'll join up. I'll be really Jewish. I love you too."

But how does one become a little bit Jewish? The words were English, and it was proper syntax, but it didn't make sense. Maybe it made sense in Yiddish.

It was a relief to get home. He felt like he'd traveled in time to Czarist Russia, kidnapped a bride, tied her up, and driven her a thousand years back to the present. They climbed into bed and snuggled up. Harry wanted to make love, but Ruth resisted.

"Car lagged," she said.

"Me too. Koshered out," he said. He could wait. And everything was just fine again in an hour or so.

He'd been taking weekend and evening education classes at the University of California in the Graduate Internship Program, and was student teaching a summer class for kids at Harry Ells High. By autumn he was to be on display at what teachers called a slave auction for principals to cross-examine and hire. What with Ruth's PT classes and homework, their schedules cut holes into their loving relationship. How was he to find extra time for classes in Judaism?

"Find it for *me*," she explained after they made love and he was weak, as if the conversation hadn't lagged, as if he hadn't understood the situation. He knew.

"You can do it if you really want," she said. "I try to please them myself."

Harry was offered a position at Albany High, which was less than two miles from their little cottage, and, as September approached, he began to get more and more anxious, imagining academic disaster, feeling captured, with little idea how or what to teach. Albany offered five hundred a month, not enough to support a family, but he was told he was lucky at that, since many student teachers worked for less, or even nothing.

"We'll get by," Ruth said. From time to time Harry brought up the trip to L.A., asking what Ruth felt her parents really expected of him, but this was a subject about which Ruthie had little to say except, "Go to Schul."

They sought some way for Harry to convert to Judaism. A buck-toothed, red-lipped, hard eyed Orthodox Rabbi sat at a small desk under a dim light glancing up once at Harry as if he were something forbidden, said hello only to Ruth, and shook his head and refused to listen as they explained what they wanted Using all the fingers of both hands, he flicked them out of his chamber.

Screw you, you arrogant little twit, Harry thought. If you added a "t" to Rabbi, you'd have a damned Rabbit.

A Conservative Rabbi explained, after patiently listening, "I'm sorry. We Conservatives believe you're either Jewish in your soul or you aren't. There's no way to convert."

A Reformed Rabbi said, with a shrug, "You go to schul and take a few exams, we consider something. Young people need to marry."

It was a relief, especially for Ruthie.

The Rabbi said to Harry, "What religion are you?"

"Well. None," Harry said.

"Do you believe in a God?"

"Not exactly."

Harry didn't have any feelings one way or another about God. God had not seemed to be the issue when the Mama had suggested a conversion to Judaism.

"What will you convert from, then?" the Rabbi asked. He had a warm, intelligent face, a kind old Spencer Tracy look. His face waited, smiling encouragement.

"Protestant," Harry blurted, protesting.

Harry hadn't thought of conversion as requiring a religion to convert from. Jews, he knew, had been forced to pledge devotion to Jesus Christ for centuries. Somehow many such Jews still remained Jewish. Conversos. They kept secret rituals despite the threat of rack and screw, stake burning, various Inquisitions. Most Christians, except for a few saints such as Joan of Arc, converted to whatever was necessary for survival. Many Muslims converted to Hinduism or Christianity. Buddhists converted to Jainism. Anyone could convert to any damned thing. But Jews faked it, or so Ruthie's Jewish friends told Harry. Once a Jew always a Jew. The culture, the food at Saul's, the look. Still, Harry imagined he might sneak in and convert for the parents but secretly remain completely unsaved. He could be pretend Protestant and turn pretend Jew.

In fact he once had been a Protestant. In Harry's innocent years before Ruth, when he'd joined the Navy as an Ensign fresh out of college, a tight-lipped, stout, forty-year-old, overworked WAVE secretary had told him he had to choose a religion to put on a dogtag in case they had to bury him. Harry tried to charm her out of any such erroneous definitions, but she'd heard too many flip young officers make the same jokes.

"I thought the Navy just fed you to the sharks," Harry told her, but her plain, bored face wrinkled up and hardened even more.

"Sir," she said. "The Navy requires you to state your religion."

"Buddhist," Harry finally blurted. "I'm Buddhist." He'd been twenty-two and had little idea what Buddhism meant, but didn't expect to die, and if he did, he'd at least make someone in the Navy wonder what in hell to do with a dead Buddhist.

"The only choices are Hebrew, Catholic, or Protestant. H, P or C." Her flat, matter-of-fact voice told Harry she knew fools like him. She wasn't interested in his childish sense of humor. He began to mutter.

"I resent this. I'm not anything." His face had flushed with anger.

She stamped P for Protestant on his official dog tag. Shades of Martin Luther, Harry thought. When he left the Navy he threw away his dog tag and converted back to N for nothing.

Conversion to a belief such as Judaism, which was more than two thousand years old, older than Catholicism, weighed on Harry more as he attended various classes in Judaism for dummies. He was surrounded by serious wannabe Jews. They discussed the big fish, Leviathan. Jonah. Harry thought these were Christian myths, but Jews claimed them first in the Old Testament. Noah and the Ark. Plenty of battles and smiting. Joshua the great warrior blowing his ram's horn at the gates of Jericho. Job. Lot's wife turning to salt. A good man going to waste. Some sex-starved incestuous daughters.

Harry learned something, and that felt good, but also a little terrifying. Every lecture was filled with assumptions that the audience was there to dredge up latent religious fervor. Harry was there to please the woman of his dreams, that is, to please her mother. He didn't give a damn that a prehistoric whale had supposedly swallowed an idiot someone. How could a whale swallow a human being without choking to death, anyway? A whale might swallow a grapefruit or a squid tentacle.

And a God that brought on boils and destroyed families to win a bet with the Devil made Harry feel itchy. He didn't want to spend any time at all in the same building with such a God. Whirlwinds. Whirlpools. Phooey.

God was unknowable, as well as unpronounceable, Harry learned. YHVH. God brought plagues to whole civilizations. Locusts. Black Death. The God of the Old Testament seemed more of a fearsome mass murderer than someone to worship. Still, He parted the Red Sea and let Moses and the Jews escape Egypt and not get their feet wet.

Pretty soon Harry knew more Jewish stories than Ruth. She'd ceased feeling Orthodox and had stopped learning about the wrathful God of the Old Testament somewhere in the Sixth Grade.

"You're setting a bad example here," Harry said. "Pretty soon I'll be the only Jew in the family."

He found himself trying to convince Ruth of the metaphorical beauty of Judaism. But she wouldn't go to schul with him. She had physical therapy classes to attend. Besides, she was already Jewish.

Somewhere in the midst of a droning lecture on an opaque Talmudic debate, Harry fell asleep and nearly slipped to the floor. The lecturer, an intense skinny young Rabbi, was furious.

He poked Harry on the shoulder and laughed harshly. He said, "It's a little embarrassing if the audience falls asleep and snores in the middle of the lecture." He was about Harry's age and wore a yarmulke above a nice Italian suit. Harry shook himself, said he was a teacher himself and understood, and walked out.

For the time being that was it for Harry's religious conversion. He told Ruth his brain was temporarily full up with Judaism. He longed for a good cleansing story about cherry trees. *Give me liberty or give me death*, he wanted to say. *To be or not to be*. Later, after resting his brain, he might go back to schul, he told her.

Ruth missed her period. Her mother pried it out of her even before she told Harry, and he felt betrayed.

"Mama just phoned before I could tell you," Ruth said, placing her hand on his cheek. "Besides, it's not for sure." Harry felt a pang of panic. Ruth was pregnant and the Mama was headed up in a week to check it out. Ayy yay yayyy…

"Go back to schul, just a little more," she pled. "Until Mama's come and gone."

But Harry was too irritated by schul, though, in all fairness, schul was more interesting than the half dozen Sunday School classes he'd attended as a ten-year-old.

And he was anxious about teaching. What was he taking on? Marriage. Responsibility. Suddenly, fatherhood. Schul. Lesson plans. Way too many worries all at once. Couldn't Ruthie understand?

She did. She did.

During a Berkeley heat wave the Mama arrived in a rented car. All in black she strode in and claimed a space for herself, spreading out her coat and purse and gifts of pickles and bagels and home made cheese cake in a semicircle around her chair, the only chair, really, since the front room was also bedroom and kitchen nook, too. Ruth had spent two days cleaning, though, while Harry had worked on the garden outside.

He stayed out of Ruth's way. Judith wasn't *his* mother. He'd wanted to say something funny about the Mama to break the ice, but Ruth was especially touchy and so they didn't talk about anything. Their sex life had cooled too, and Harry felt their closeness oozing away.

When at last they made love again Harry vowed to Ruth he would be hers forever. He could overcome any obstacle, any Mama to keep Ruth's love, and all the early passion flooded back into his heart. Ruth too vowed she would be his forever. They would find salvation in each other's arms, and it didn't matter what the world thought of them.

'It's not fair, though," she said. "You don't have parents."

The purple bougainvillea that covered the arbor over their little garden cottage in their landlord's neat, flower-filled back yard made the entrance seem like a wilderness grotto. They had a rock wall swelling with nasturtiums, a bed of Johnny jump ups as well as pansies, and explosions of African daisies. Harry had carefully nurtured a watermelon patch with six little green watermelons just reaching the quarter-pound stage. He tended the garden every evening, very soothing. Caring for flowers was easier than trying to talk things over. When the Mama had walked up, Harry had been watering the African daisies.

He'd said the normal things. "We could have picked you up." The Mama preferred renting her own car. She smiled and gave him a hug. This was the friendliest he'd ever found her, and his heart began to open a bit.

They sat and talked. Mama drank from a bottle of water she brought with her and she sweated through the armpits of her shiny black suit jacket that she refused to take off. The parents' house in L.A. had air conditioning and she hadn't expected this 95 degree heat. It was unusual. They chatted about her plane ride, the bronze color of the sky in L.A. compared to the blue sky in Berkeley, and an uneventful hour slipped by. Ruth served tea. She had some wonderful blessed cookies from a local kosher bakery. They laughed and got friendly. Mama took her jacket off.

Maybe the Mama *wasn't* here to judge them or put the pressure on. Maybe if Harry just smiled and was his normal charming self, made a joke or two and let things slide past, they'd have a decent time and nothing at all would happen. They could go to Saul's.

Mama said, "How's the schul going?"

"I don't know if they'll let me convert," Harry said, after a moment's reflection. He wanted to trust her, and hoped for some practical advice. "I don't have anything to convert from." He looked at her and smiled his most charming smile.

Her face froze hard as if he'd slapped her. Ruth's lovely mouth fell open. She dropped a plate of salad she'd been balancing on her knees, and it broke in half and the greens and shattered bits of plate scattered over the floor. A dictionary fell from a shelf. The mother stood up heavily, grunting with the effort, spread her arms wide from her hips, and, looking upward to the Unnameable, cried out in defense of all Jews, *"What about the Children?"*

Children? Jesus Christ! It was clear she included in this number Ruth's child, Ruth and *his* child, which might arrive sooner than planned. But these great masses of coming children would be his children too, Harry wished to say. His face burned. He wanted to slap her. She'd set him up by talking sweetly to him, by removing her jacket, and pretending to be friendly.

"What do you know of our struggle?" she said, her voice breaking. "What do you know of the Diaspora. The Holocaust! Our struggle to make a homeland free of anti-semitism? Do you even know how Jewish children were torn from their mother's breasts by the Nazis?" Her arms raised and lowered, her hands shot toward Harry, clutched at Ruth. Tears streamed down her cheeks.

"I'm sorry," Harry said. Millions of displaced and murdered Jews trudged toward him through the blood of pogroms and holocausts ancient as Egypt, ancient as the grinning desert. A huge wind seemed to blow him backward.

Now it came, a torrent of accusations. She built her case against him, against all goys, charge after charge.

She said, voice booming, "People live in *sin* today, and never think about their *children*." She remained standing, enormous as history, and eyed Harry haughtily, side to side, up and down. He felt he was the worst of sinners, he'd led Ruth down into Hell or whatever there was for Jews, down into the ovens of Hades, and had given no thought whatsoever to the child they were about to produce. Harry thought, she sure throws her big tits around.

"I'm sorry. I'm sorry." He couldn't find anything else to say to show his sorrow for all the suffering of the Jews.

He was going to be a teacher, Harry tried to say in his defense. He loved children. He was cut off by Mama's sobs and groans.

"I thought we were friendly," Harry said at last, but she was too busy with her own words to hear him. In a rage, he banged his back hard against the wall behind the bed, aware that something might fall on him from a shelf. Caught between anger at Judith and his love for Ruth, trying to maintain some remnant of pride, he couldn't walk out or swear. He was paralyzed as the Mama raged on. He imagined picking her up by her belt and giving her and Judaism and every religion he'd ever heard of the bum's rush right out the door, but he held back for love's sake, paralyzed. Yet, after a particularly biting insult from the Mama, who condemned his parents for not teaching him better, Harry at last pounded his fist on the table, knocking a coffee cup over and spilling coffee all over their rug. Ruthie's trick. It didn't work.

"I'm not like that!" he shouted. "You can't talk to me like that!"

"You see? No one can talk to him," the Mama said, turning to Ruth. "Can't you see he's just another angry meshuggeneh!"

Then she broke down completely and fell back into her chair and began to shake in surges. Ruth ran to her and cried softly, hugging her.

The part of Harry that was sane and not filled with hatred stood back and admired the dramatic performance of the Mama. She was outrageous, someone out of a Nineteenth Century melodrama.

With great, slow, pained dignity and a withering glance at Harry, the Mama gathered her jacket and left, Ruth holding her up by her waist as they limped to her Hertz rent-a-car. Harry watched Ruth and the Mama, feeling as if he himself had been crucified. His stomach hurt.

Ruth stayed by the car for a half hour, embracing the Mama again and again, both crying. From the garden Harry watched them. He'd failed all the tests, an unredeemable Job. At the end he had no easy repartee ready, no saving jokes, none of his normal charm, just a tipped coffee cup. He was a non-Jew, probably an anti-semite. He was a seducer, a womanizer. He'd been married before, an irresponsible shlemiel like most goy males. He had a child. He was a bad father. He didn't believe in anything. He'd been living on unemployment. It all came out. He was dirt, a shnorrer, a shlemazel, a regular putz. Harry didn't know the meaning of all the words, but he caught the intonation. Judith was expert in changing the inflection of a common word so it became an insult. The word "father" slid off into a sneer.

"You! A father!" Judith spit the word out on to the rug. "What else can you do!"

After she left, Ruth tried to look into Harry's eyes and hug him, but he couldn't respond. He was still angry, and doubly so because she had gone to her mother first.

"It's all right, it's all right," she said, rubbing Harry's shoulders. He tried to hug her but was unable to connect his arms to his brain. His hands fell to his sides. He was a shadow, left behind, drained of profane flesh.

Ruth stood back and lifted her palms toward him as if she wished to make an offering, "I'm probably not pregnant." She smiled hopefully. "They called just before Mama came in. I explained it to her outside as she was leaving."

Harry took it in as if it were long distance news, a telegram announcing the death of an unknown cousin. It was mildly disappointing.

"Aren't you happy?" she said. She smiled and took his slumped shoulders and shook him.

"I don't know," he said. "I think I'm shit."

"Oh, don't…" she said. "I love you. You have to be strong." Her voice drooped with dismay. She pressed her arms around him tight enough to squeeze any possible response from his heart. She was powerful. He couldn't say a word. He thought of the little bed, their nights together, how they compressed themselves into each other, how his knees fitted perfectly into the backs of hers, the smoothness of her breasts on his palms, her nipples as they hardened. But how the hours had lately dragged on in silence, how their lives had become divided by work and mama and religion and desires beyond their understanding. There was a queasy scream rising up from Harry's slugged belly into his heart.

He slipped out of Ruth's arms and went back to the garden and turned on the hose. What else could he do? He could water plants. He watched the silvery water spray into a rainbow laden mist in the sunlight over the watermelons. It was hard to overwater watermelons. Water was soothing, almost as necessary as air.

They didn't talk seriously for a week. It was his fault, he knew. Time slipped away like steam from a cup of coffee. Harry was very quiet. Ruth was busy memorizing her charts of human muscles and circulation. Harry thought it really amazing how she could look at a complex illustration of human anatomy and within a quarter hour or so be able to reproduce it almost perfectly. They didn't make love.

When he walked out he couldn't say anything. He packed his clothes and left while Ruth was in class. It was cruel, but he didn't mean it to be cruel. He hadn't planned it. He couldn't do anything else. He took his clothes and books and placed his key on the pillow. He didn't leave a note, though he almost wrote how he just needed time and would return, but he didn't know if that was true. He was crazy. He wanted to die. He wanted to return to the nothing he'd been.

Three days later Ruth found him sitting at the wheel of his car two blocks from the little studio. He'd been sleeping in the back seat, in this familiar neighborhood, hoping for a miracle.

She stormed in beside him and screamed, "I thought we were okay! Why did you leave? *Why*?" Harry had no words for her, not for himself either. They hadn't been okay. Hadn't she noticed the dead silence? He sat there stiff, unable to touch her. But she deserved this opportunity to explode on him. And this had been love, was all Harry could think. He'd been longing to see her, but now all he could feel was queasiness, as if he'd had too many syrup smothered pancakes.

"What did you *think*? Why didn't you leave a note. Call? *Anything*? Did you think about me at all? God damn you! *God damn you!*" She screamed loud enough to bring the neighbors to their windows.

When Harry didn't say anything, she hammered on his chest as hard as she could. He didn't defend himself.

"Say something!" she screamed. But he was far away. He leaned back from her and held his hands over his face while she howled and pounded at him until she was exhausted. She hit him with the balls of her fists everywhere she could, on his hands on his chest and arms and shoulders, on his hands over his face, and she hit hard, a big woman, like her mother. When her rage cooled, she left suddenly, slamming the passenger door open and back onto its hinges. All the maps and papers in the side pocket of the door flew out and danced away in a light breeze over the street. The car radio blared on and Willy Nelson sang, *Georgia. Georgia. Just an old sweet song…*

"Sorry about the door!" she spit out angrily as she left. Harry had never defended himself. He agreed with her accusations. What was wrong with his vocal cords, he thought, as she ran down the street crying, an ever smaller figure stumbling down a long block until she turned sharply and forever and forever gone around that corner. Some immense force glued his mouth shut, froze his arms and legs, a breathless pause just before darkness, a terrible game. He'd loved her so much. Where could love go? For a moment it was there, racing around the corner, just out of sight, the afterimage of it in his mind, a thing of feathers and tar and flying pots and pans. If he didn't run after her and call her back he knew he'd never touch or see her again, but he could see nothing but darkness and a sense of his having been lost and found and abandoned forever, but by what, by himself, by Harry himself, protesting in his soul, neither Buddhist, Christian nor Jew, a seeker of failed love…

Lab Experiment with Cats

They chastised Pearl, until she escaped. Earl had invited tiny, blonde Helen and sweet, darkly curled Marlene into the lab where Pearl, his white lab mouse, had been in training. He'd named all his mice Pearl.

"I like it," Helen said. "Earl and Pearl. A regular hillbilly band."

This Pearl was a fast learner. The experiment centered on a nationwide series of mazes, thousands of mice, fMRI's, and hundreds of Ph.D. candidates, everyone exchanging statistical information automatically. Mice were run through various puzzling mazes until they couldn't go any faster, overall times averaged, learning rates recorded, brains examined and all of the data divided into male v. female statistics. They chose the best mice and bred them. What hundreds of doctoral candidates might discover working together was unknown. Smarter and faster mice, perhaps. Mice that might run for President.

It was 1988. Earl and Marlene were just coming on to ecstasy and in love with every hair and blemish on each other's bodies, while Helen had taken acid because there were only two hits of ecstasy. Helen was tripping about a Chinese Garden she'd seen on the way in. Really, as Earl had pointed out while still capable of pointing out anything, the bush was an ordinary red and green fuchsia climbing a splintery trellis back lit by a dim light on a small street behind campus.

"Didn't you see how beautiful the little red and white dancers were?" Helen insisted. "And the purple? The purple…fuchsias… little perfect dancing Chinese ladies, their little legs too…" She couldn't explain the depths of her feelings. Everything was little. She was trying to think of a better way to express her love for everything. Little. Delicate. Beautiful. Nothing defined the flood that raced through her heart into her soul and out her fingertips to the touched world. Her hands went through twisty motions as she attempted to describe the way the flowers and leaves drooped and yet leapt higher at the same time. Earl was falling in love with Marlene, and with Helen too. He hugged Helen in tight to his chest as she kept explaining, but he held his other arm around Marlene's waist. He'd lost all his shyness. If this were drug induced delight, so what? Skin mattered, the silky touch of it, the electricity of his bare arm on Helen's shoulder and Marlene's hip. It wasn't sex, or if it was —he couldn't deny it —it was more than that, a twinning, or tripling, in this case. He, still a virgin, now holding two lovely women and not a question of making love. They were beyond that, on some intimate cloud, pressed together, laughing.

"They had light inside them," Helen continued to insist as she inhaled Earl's delicious sweat. "The light in the red dancers made them Chinese." She said this in a flat, decisive tone. "Chinese."

Marlene and Earl kissed Helen's hair and breasts and cheeks and neck. She was somewhere else, but Earl was now so in love with both of them that he could experience everything they experienced, their own bodies rubbing against his, and his lips on Marlene's mouth kissed on to Helen's mouth by Marlene, all perfect, even if Helen was obviously feeling a bit twisted. It must be that acid created a different experience than ecstasy.

He wanted to impress them with Pearl, to show them his immense love for Pearl too, his love rising and resting and rising again step by step on sculpted terraces on some green island mountain, a vision coming back to him from a book he'd read, a color photograph with Polynesian women carrying baskets on their heads. But when he opened Pearl's cage to time her, she wouldn't go into her maze. He gave each girl a wheat straw to stick through the wire mesh to gently push and get Pearl started. But she turned on Earl's straw and bit right through it and wouldn't leave. Earl, stopwatch in hand, slapped the remnants of his straw on the top of the cage and encouraged the girls to lash at the cage also. Pearl cowered miserably.

"Poor Pearl," Marlene said. "Poor scared little mousy. We love you, baby." She bent over, her heart filled with warmth, and kissed the top of the cage whereupon Pearl dashed out frantically, made an impossible leap over the high glass walls of the maze, and darted out of the open lab door into the vast darkness of the building. Zip! Just like that! Earl's heart leapt with her. The leap was perfectly timed. Everything perfect. Everything. She'd done it, what no other mouse in his experiment had ever done. But how could he report this to his colleagues? It wasn't what they were looking for.

"Little mousy didn't like my kiss," Marlene said. She looked at Earl, her eyes liquid and questioning. She wanted to be forgiven.

Helen's head was boiling over. "They'll eat it," she said, her voice raspy.

"Who?" Earl said. "Eat what?"

"The cats. Pearl."

"All the cats are in their cages," he said to reassure her. "Locked up."

Marlene was pressing her left hand on Earl's buttocks but gently rubbing Helen's palm with her right thumb. "Don't feel baddy," she said to Helen. She meant to say badly. "Very smart mouse."

"Locked up?" Pearl's escape had broken Helen's glowing introspection on the Chinese Garden. Her mind worked slowly, swamped by brilliant images. Cold steel wire replaced red lanterns. Images of imprisoned cats began to claw at her. Earl had showed them to her on the way in, each in its little cage, some with antennae inserted into various areas of their brains, some looking perfectly normal, many mewing and begging to be petted or released or fed. It had disgusted her, yes, but she'd had red and purple and blue and green Chinese images flooding her mind at the time. Now the pain of being enclosed and experimented on began to grow around her like a cage and she could feel the fear of the kittens. The Fear of the Kittens.

And while Marlene and Earl unbuttoned each other and sank to the lab floor, Helen raised her arms and began to fly. Helen, the Bird Girl, saviour of things caged. She flew like an angel, arms out, into the hall and into the Cat Lab. What were these bad cat people doing to all these cats? Cats were lovely, sweet creatures. They merely needed a new name, not the short ugliness of the word, cat. Kats. Katz. Kittens was a better name, but these were adult cats imprisoned and tortured. They might eat a mouse like Pearl, of course, starving as they were, deprived of their nature, but they deserved their freedom. What was one sweet beautiful mousie versus the freedom of all these cats? This was a question of Cat Liberation. A mouse heroine would liberate these poor cats. Mighty Pearl Mouse and Helen, Queen of Cats, to the rescue.

She could hear Marlene and Earl giggling next door in the Mouse Lab. She opened cages, and slowly, reluctantly, cats stretched, or licked their fur and a few leapt softly down, as if escaping were what they always did.

Earl and Marlene could hear the clatter of the cages opening but were far more interested in rubbing against themselves until cats also began rubbing against them.

There were nearly 100 stacked up cages to be opened. Helen raced from one to the other. Some were merely hooked shut by wire, but some were locked. She broke these open with a hammer. At first, many, even most of the cats, stayed in their cages. Others wandered the room or just nosed out the door into the hallway. They meowed, hissed, and swiped at each other. It was a great moment in the history of cats. They were multi-colored and multi-racial, everything from mongrel to Maltese, some grey, some almost pink, black, yellow orange, striped, some white and fluffy as down pillows. Many had been carefully weighed and measured since birth. Most had spent their entire lives in their cages. Still, they were living, breathing, God's own soul-filled creatures. Cats! Even if newborn in a sense, with a God granted instinct to leap casually on to the floor, up on to the surgical tables, across the desks, scattering papers, hunting things. Hunting Pearl.

They oozed out the lab door, a multicolored feline flood into the hall, Angora cats, Siamese cats, alien cats with little plugs protruding from their heads, cats with special collars that could be attached to electronic recorders. No doubt thousands of hours of scientific data had been collected on these cats, but Helen felt good releasing them and her shoulders lifted defiantly. Cats were not experiments but God's precious creatures, even if she were a little frightened because, after all, there were so many of them.

They rubbed against her legs. She, the Holy Mother of Cats, pitied her tiny beasts and stood, left hand raised among them, banging, unlocking, opening, caressing. Her fear and pity seemed the best emotions she'd ever felt, a loving sadness that made her weep. What kind of world was this that tortured Nature's sweet creatures so?

Earl came in naked, aroused. He wanted to tell Helen to come back, that he and Marlene were waiting for her so they could all roll around together on the cushions Earl had laid out in Pearl's lab.

But what was she doing with the cats?

Helen had never seen Earl naked before, with his thin muscular arms and flat chest, a light down of dark hair on pale skin, his raised penis, which amused her even as she continued to open the cages.

Earl looked away from Helen to the mass of open cages and said, "Uhhmmfff," and his penis drooped. Cats darted everywhere. Many had disappeared into the various rooms and floors and mysteries of the building. First Pearl, now this. But when he took Helen's arm to stop her from opening any more cages his hand slid around a firm breast, and he caressed her shoulders and hips as she set the last cats free, a matter of first things first. Helen felt so good to Earl's hand.

She tried to explain how she'd had some reluctance about releasing those cats with wires in their brains, that she couldn't decide which deserved freedom and which didn't, so she'd released them all in shifts ranging from most apparently normal to most surgically debilitated. Her words flooded together and even still couldn't keep up with her thoughts, so she led Earl from cage to cage by holding on to his reviving penis with her left hand while freeing the last cat, a tortoise shell that had wires not only in its head but tiny rubber electrical plugs down its spine.

"Poor. Poor. Poor," she said, almost purring herself.

For just a moment, at first, she'd been confused about her purpose here. Was she anti-science or was she pro-cat? But the heart was all, freedom for all beings. These cats had hearts too, and dear little minds that thought cat thoughts. She remembered her childhood kitten, Speedy, a mischievous, intelligent devil, the first creature she'd ever loved more than her mother and father. Cats were not that much different than people. She would lay it all out it to Earl and Marlene later and they'd agree.

Some of the cats hissed at her, and some still refused to leave their cages. They should all leave. That was important. But Earl's erection was important too.

After she opened the last cage she pulled Earl back into Pearl's lab, shooed out some cats, and sank down on the cushions with Marlene. Marlene and Earl began to kiss Helen and slowly peel off the last of her underwear. She had never felt so loved, so warm, so silky smooth.

Earl felt like he could make love all night, even though it wasn't so important to actually penetrate or have sex, though he did, in periodic swells of pleasure. He'd never done anything like this before, never even taken drugs, never made love, but it was so natural it felt as if he had always done it, had lived forever next to these two girls, feeling with his palms and fingers their sweat, the thick tenderness of their skin, burying his nose in their smells.

When he fell back, Helen and Marlene caressed each other and then again him, even with cats purring against them, even if Helen did wonder about Pearl.

"Pearl's okay," Earl said when he could talk again. "We'll find her. We'll clean up. No one will know about her. Anyway, I can get another." He'd briefly forgotten about the cats.

"Another Pearl?" Helen said. Somehow that was horrifying. She drew back. But then they kissed. They made love again and fell exhausted on the floor. They napped and made love, twining in and out, and slept again. They didn't care about anything except each other.

But when he woke in the early morning, Earl found that he did care about the cats. In the drug-clear light of new morning flooding through the windows, he could see there was no way to clean anything, no way to place cats back where they belonged, or even find them.

Cats in particular. Cats in general. Cats had roamed the lab, into the building, and out by small passages or doors into the unknown night world. A cat with wires in its spine was stuck, mewling pitifully behind a couch. Another had jammed its head into some slats and its wires had kept it from drawing out again. It meowed hoarsely as it tried to free itself. These sounds had awakened him.

Some cats screamed far away in agony. Others silently watched, grooming themselves. Three cats, two tortoise shells, one blue with a leather collar, slept on the buttocks of the entwined girls, whose bare limbs shone seductively beneath a messy pile of jeans and shirts.

"My God, what have we done?" Earl said, looking at the neon light on the ceiling. His mind flew back over the night to the release of the cats, to his ecstasy fueled indifference to all but the girls, their touching, their complete devouring abandon. He'd had no idea how passionate girls could be.

He thought of the experiment, and back before the experiment when he was a child collecting lizards and frogs, or swimming in the surf in Long Beach, out to the horizon past the sun, a child's world of wonders, a small intense ball seen blue from space, great teeming cities, lights at night around the world, everywhere scientists trying to discover things, studying cats, mice, whatever, and he'd been a tiny part of this process, connected, and important, but now.

The first pale light of morning had peered into the Mouse Lab. Years of statistics and hard work had gone up in a mix of sperm and sweat and cats. The lab was a shambles of scattered papers and clothes. Earl groaned and rose and explored. In the Cat Lab, equipment lay shattered on the tile floor, the room reeking of acrid cat piss and shit. A half dozen cats had climbed back into their familiar cages to sleep. Earl's career had blown away. Any chance he'd had at a Ph.D. was over. He'd be jailed.

His stomach held a familiar tight lump, though he had flashes of the love making, which, after all, had been, at the time, of far greater importance. Could he have resisted? Up to this night he'd been an innocent young scientist who dreamed fantasies, now all in one night he'd lived out most of them in an explosion of drugs and fur, and here were Helen and Marlene still exquisitely glowing under their scattering of clothes and cats. Could he blame it all on drugs? So what if he did? So what if it had been Helen's idea. He was the guilty one no matter how he might excuse it.

Earl shook them awake. "We gotta leave." He pulled on his jockey shorts and handed the girls their pink panties and pale bras. The girls were so fragile, their nipples so helplessly naked, their hips so round and defenseless. He would have to protect them. His wristwatch had disappeared somewhere. By the soft light through the windows, it might be six in the morning, and doctoral students would be here in an hour or so. They had to get out.

"Let's go. Let's go."

Helen and Marlene tried to sort out their clothes and wake up at the same time. They wore identical Ralph Lauren jeans except for size and got them wrong. Their systems had shut down almost completely during the night's sleep, and each movement seemed mired in the mud of half remembered dreams.

"Christ!" Helen said, hopping about from foot to foot as she pulled on her panties. They'd been sleeping dangerously close to some broken coffee cups. "What's all this?"

"About two thousand years of scientific destruction," Earl said in a soft, crushed voice. He shook the fingers of his right hand around in a circle.

"Oh, but you have to admit it was worth it," Marlene said, her face glowing, questioning. She stretched out on the floor and wriggled her hips into her jeans. Helen and Earl each took a hand and pulled her up.

"Kaput," Earl said. "My whole life will be digging ditches."

"A good unexplored subject for a dissertation," Helen said in her professional voice. "Ditches. Digging of." She shook her head at the lab. "We should do something. Clean up, maybe."

"We have to leave!" Earl took her arm and began to anxiously lead her toward the door.

"No! I've got it," she said, pulling away. She began to tip over tables.

"Jesus!" Earl said. He stood back holding his fingers up to his lips. "You're going nuts. This place is already a wreck. Mother of God. "

"No need for praise," Helen said, shoving a stack of empty cages to the floor. "I'm trying to save your dear little rear end."

"Good idea. A raid," Marlene said. She hopped across on one sneaker and pushed over a chair.

"Yah. What do they call themselves?" Helen said.

"The Society for the Prevention of Cruelty to Animals," Marlene said.

"Oh, that's ridiculous," Earl moaned. "Anyway, they're not the ones. It's a bunch of Christian do-gooders."

"So are we," Helen said. She sang softly, chin raised: "Onward kitten soldiers..." and then, "Set... our... kittens... free...ee... ee." In lipstick on the wall she wrote in block letters: SET OUR KITTENS FREE.

Marlene wrote, "FREE HUEY."

"That's very silly," Earl said. "He's not only free, he's dead."

"It's what my parents used to say," said Marlene.

They rubbed it out and Marlene wrote, "CHRIST LOVES CATS."

"My parents used to say that Christ loves all creatures," Helen said. "But I can tell you first hand it just ain't so. Cows and chickens for example. Ants. Chiggers." As the girls stuffed their shirts in and admired their work, Earl took them firmly by their wrists and pulled them forth onto the cold, still deserted campus. They hurried past familiar pines, a grove of eucalyptus, the old, bronze statue of a mother bear and two cubs. He was surprised the conventional world hadn't turned upside down.

In the Village, they stopped at Espresso Profeta for coffee. Helen and Marlene giggled while Earl moaned. The coffee smelled so ordinary, so good. Five young people in jeans and tee shirts stood at the counter and ordered lattes or cappuccinos, and munched on croissants. Earl hesitated to look closely at anyone, for fear they would be fellow research students who might notice him and say hello.

Softly, Marlene said, "At least there are plenty of poor cats and mice still being examined in the world." She wanted to make Earl feel better.

"Too many," Helen said, giggling. "We have a purpose in life now."

"This night has given us Holy Mission," Marlene said, pulling Earl's face up by his chin and looking directly into his eyes. "We've been born again. Right?"

"I'll drink to that," Helen said, raising her coffee cup. "Come on Earl."

But Earl was still feeling down. What would he do with his last few free hours? For the past two years he'd been a research student. He'd have a hard time giving up his normal pattern of analyzing data and getting a PhD, though he wasn't nearly so worried about that as he was about lying to his fellow research graduates. All their work was shot too, and they didn't even have a good time. They'd be really pissed.

He would get sued. His colleagues and professors would want to kill him. Maybe his parents could be sued. Hadn't they signed for his loans? Weren't they responsible for him? He'd have to pretend to be one of the outraged, but the others would know. Jerry would know for sure. And Ed, and Doctor Fredericksheim. They knew him too well. Or he'd slip up. He couldn't stand it. He wasn't a good liar. His fingerprints would be everywhere, and Helen's, and Marlene's. There'd be prints on the cat cages, even on the floor. The lab was a trap he'd set for himself, a maze from which he couldn't escape. It had started so innocently, a mouse, sex and drugs. A helluva lot of cats.

Was his life over? Could he just leave forever? Could he live hidden under an assumed name on a commune in Europe, or Alaska? Could he now join the Animal Liberation Front and be a hero? He had to be serious and think. If he still had a brain, he should try to use it.

"The Animal Liberation Front," he said to Marlene and Helen. "Not the Society for the Prevention of Cruelty to Animals. The SPCA mostly cremates lost dogs and cats."

"Right. Right. I forgot," Marlene said. "The killers."

"Anyway, let's don't talk about it here." He looked around to see if anybody he knew had come in.

He'd been a Dean's List student too, and precocious as a PhD Candidate at 19. But what kind of scientist destroyed data carefully collected over years? He knew what had been lost, a whole laboratory. Pearl. His parents would be horrified. All that money, years of study, his father's reputation shot. Overnight the world had turned bleak and there was humbling darkness all around him. Profeta's tables dissolved into planar levels and angles intersecting with the skeletal lines of the chairs.

Holy Mary, Mother of God. He was regressing back into Catholicism.

"Hott verdammer!" he said fervently, remembering a Dutch friend.

"C'mon Earl," Marlene said, placing her hand on his cheek. "Don't be sad. We gave you everything we had. Think freedom. Be born again for us."

Born again, yes, as someone entirely new, a new name, a new identity. He'd have to run for it. Disappear forever. Leave everything in his apartment, his guitar, the autographed outfielder's mitt signed by Willy Mays. Pretend he'd been so discouraged by the loss of his experiment that he'd gone mad, or pretend he'd been captured. Send a letter: "WE HAVE PEARL. AND EARL."

Helen caressed Earl's forehead, spit on her hands and ran them over his disheveled hair. Her fingers were soft and loving. "We know you were a virgin."

"What? Oh. How did you know?"

"Oh, women know. Anyway, only virgin males can make love so many times in one night."

Was that true, he thought. Was it drugs? Was it a stored up libidinous energy, too much sperm bottled up over too many years of fantasy?

"And think what you'll get," Marlene added. "Few people have the chance at such fame."

"Fame! As a criminal? What are you saying?" He thought about the three of them on the floor.

"Blessed art thou among cats," Helen said. "You didn't know I was once a Catholic, did you?"

"Me too," Earl said, after a moment's silence. "But I'm really fallen."

"Shocking," Marlene said.

"A cat-ass-trophy," Helen said, She laughed at her simple joke.

Earl imagined going into his childhood confessional and saying, "Bless me Father, for I have sinned among cats. I took MDMA, made love with two women on the floor and released 100 cats and a mouse." And Father Crosby or Father Flanahan would say, as usual, "Repeat five Hail Marys, and three Our Fathers." And the shutter would slam. And he would still be out there in the real world with real professors and graduate students waiting to lynch him.

He looked into Helen's exquisite blue eyes, and then into Marlene's brown, caring eyes. The love he'd felt for both of them was beginning to return. He imagined their lovely, slim bodies as he'd seen them on the cushions at the lab, the exquisite sex. Was that real enough to hang on to, something permanent? Would it ever happen again? Could he trust the girls to carry him through? Marlene loved him, he was pretty sure. Helen had loved him for this one night, but she was far too attractive to too many men. Marlene loved Helen too, but Helen loved animals more. An equation in too many unknowns. If Marlene loved him and Helen, did Helen also love Marlene and him? Was that all enough? Surely love ought to be enough, with great sex, but was it as stable as statistics? No. Some things lasted. Some didn't.

Aaaghhh! His head was filled with cat fuzz. The girls would go on with their lives while he would have to change entirely. The FBI would trace him. In previous times when there used to be wilderness with places to hide he could have taken a new name and started a new career. It wasn't fair. A man's freedom would be lost, and crimes such as his were easily uncovered. And punished. He didn't mean to do it! He hadn't planned it! He wanted to cry out in Profeta's. *I am innocent!* If only he could set out defiantly, accept his fate, and move on, be courageous, be a sailor on unknown seas, an adventurous captain of men, and keep the love and adoration of Marlene and Helen, but no, he had to feel depressed. He would lose them both. He was a coward.

He knew his moods. He would have to wait to find some new hope. The girls would get sick of him. He'd be poor, or in jail for years. It wasn't all his fault; he wasn't the one who suggested drugs, who released all the cats, yet he could never turn Helen in, and what good would it do to blame her? She didn't imagine she'd done anything wrong. What was scientific research to her? No, no. He was the instigator. His drugs, his key to the lab, his desire to show off, he the pervert, sex, drugs, cats. International headlines. Photos of the wronged girls. Helen would become famous, a model or a star. Marlene's soft eyes would gain the sympathy of the world. He, the sex criminal who drugged young women, would be led off in handcuffs to be beaten and buggered in a dank cell.

But they might not suspect him at all. He sipped his bitter but good coffee. The shop was cold and there was a little steam. A new life lurked just beyond his understanding. His failure or success in these unknown shadows would probably depend on how daring he could be.

The Engimatic Smile of George Brooks

"Sit down, George!" The teacher's voice had a sorrowful sound, an old bell ringing. George had arrived late, as usual. He'd been warned, but he'd been stopped by two friends in the hall and they had messed around and the bell had rung and it was already too late, so he told a quick joke and danced as he told it, and then ran to class out of breath. There was a little ripple of applause as he came in.

"They…" George began to explain, but Mr. Selke said, "Never mind, George. Talk to me after class." And George couldn't think for all the worry that gave him, and he had to pop up and smile around at the class to see who might still be his friend. Mr. Selke put out a slow hand, palm down, and motioned at George's seat with it. It was smart how Mr. Selke could keep talking and wave at the same time. Did he smile just a little at him, George wondered. Was he mad at him?

He'd been in School of the Arts for a year and he was doing pretty well, his counselor Mr. B. said, and if he kept on he might graduate. Mr. B. was going to help. He'd been helping right along, telling him when he was dreaming.

The school was small, only 425 students this year. George had come in from McAteer as part of a racial balancing quota required by law, and he had special needs. But he could draw, and could be mainlined and taught in regular classes with his friends. Ten percent of the school had to be Black, ten percent Latino, the rest could be anything, white or Asian or Native American. Some people thought George might be Native American, but he was Black. From the Gold Coast, his mother, Helene, told him. He could see it, sunny and shining.

Mr. B. had told them that the highest judges in the land, The Supreme Court, had stated that racial diversity formed a compelling interest in higher education. It was a law. George's mom was pleased as anyone could be when she'd found out her boy had been chosen for such a fine school. George could draw funny cartoons of people with big heads and big smiles. He might get some excellent training, and maybe even learn enough to get a job as an artist. George hoped that was true.

Otherwise, his mom just didn't know what she would do. She had so little money. George cried when he thought how hard she worked at Lucky's and all the homes she cleaned, working hard sixty or more hours a week, and sometimes she had to come in and talk to the school about his behavior. And she always made meals for him too. How did she do it? He never wanted to cause trouble, he just wanted to have fun and please everyone, especially his mom. And now he could feel the anger of Mr. Selke, who he liked.

Mr. Selke was talking about a story, The White Heron, that George was supposed to have read for homework. It was about a little girl who lost her cow and a huge white bird that nested in the top of a tree. He recalled the drawing of the girl and the cow in the book, and he'd got sidetracked trying to draw the bird, one that existed in islands in the South far away from California. George dreamed he was on that island and could see the bird and the beautiful ocean. He'd met the little girl too. He drew her with her enormous smile lighting up the whole island like the sun rising. He would help her find her cow.

It was just that he couldn't read very well. The words didn't make a lot of sense, and they shifted on the page, and he would fall asleep or his imagination would take him somewhere surprising.

Mr. Selke was saying, "This is the first boy that Sylvy ever knew who was a stranger, and he's handsome, and kind, and offers to pay the family ten dollars if they will help him find a white heron so he can shoot it and stuff it and put it on display at his home with dozens of other birds. He's an amateur bird watcher and collector. And in those days, ten dollars is the same as two hundred dollars today. What would you do if you were poor and were offered two hundred dollars to lead someone to a bird so he could shoot it?" No one but Lance raised a hand. Groaning, Mr. Selke said, "Lance?"

Lance had been waving excitedly. What he said was, "I'd go to the bathroom."

The class guffawed. George knew it was Lance's joke. The class always waited for it, and Mr. Selke fell for it every time.

"Take the pass," Mr. Selke said, unperturbed. "Danielle?"

"I think the girl likes the boy a lot," Danielle said. "She's very lonely. All she has for company is an old grandmother and a cow, and this cute boy comes along, so she wants to please him. I would, myself."

"Sure you would," Christopher said. "You'd want to please anybody in pants."

The whole class broke down in waves of laughter. George stood up and walked past Mr. Selke across the class to Danielle, who was blushing, and put his arm around her. It was a gallant gesture. Danielle was a round faced Chinese girl, a pianist, while George's arm around her looked black as licorice. They'd known each other since Junipero Serra Elementary. Both had been the object of many jokes, but both had their own ways of dealing with them.

Danielle had just this year grown into a beautiful girl, when she wore the right clothes, while George always had a smile and a joke. You couldn't put him down, *diss* him, as everyone said. He'd laugh at himself right along with you. He was happy if he was the center of anyone's laughter. But this time he understood from Danielle's face that Christopher was being mean to her so he just had to give her a hug. He loved her, she was so smart and pretty.

Mr. Selke said, "Umm… Christopher. Stop by at the end of class, okay. And George, thank you, but sit down."

Most of the class had not read the story, it turned out. What could Mr. Selke do? He talked about it then he gave a quiz. A pop quiz. What was the main character's name? She has two conflicting interests. What are they? In what state does the story take place? What point or idea or theme is the story trying to get across to you?

Well, George hadn't really listened. He hadn't a clue. He couldn't remember things like that. People in the class were a lot smarter, and he accepted that. All could play some instrument, or dance, or act, but he could really draw. People loved his drawings. His teachers at McAteer had told him he had great talent. Now he had a lot of friends at SOTA, who laughed at him and with him, and a couple like Danielle and Timothy, who were his true friends, who he'd known since Sunset Elementary.

He loved SOTA too. The outside walls had been painted over by spray can artists, kids who were fine graffiti artists. On the outside wall facing Font Avenue an elaborate green ivy vine had been painted, with faces of students peering through the leaves. You had to look hard. There was Danielle. There was George. Aya. Jenny, too. Makeda. Sal. Kat. Kaela. The real kids of the school hiding behind the leaves. Some of the teachers, too. Elvia dancing. Mr. Selke with his grey beard and Mr. Rosenblatt who looked like a friendly, overripe fig. Judy Garland Davis in her wheelchair waving her cane. You couldn't see them from the road. You had to go right up and look. George sometimes stood next to his own face on the wall, the same two smiles gleaming out at the world from the walls of SOTA.

Every school day his mom brought him to school and parked in front and walked with him up to the big glass doors, where she would kiss him one last time and send him right in through the doors. She made sure he went in, otherwise he might drift off and get lost. He often amazed himself with the funny places he woke up in.

San Francisco State was only a few steps away, a very interesting place. George had somehow wandered over to the State Film Department one day during school and fallen asleep in a seat in a huge auditorium. A janitor had found him that evening. George had no memory of how he got there, couldn't explain it, though the janitor yelled at him and wanted to know.

George apologized, saying, "I'm sorry, sorry, sorry," and smiled as wide as he could. It was okay for the janitor to get angry. It was his job, and George felt bad for him to have to put up with someone asleep where he shouldn't be at all.

He recalled standing on a stage amid hundreds of graduating students, with girls dancing like cheerleaders and a man who he thought was the President of the United States handing him a beautiful ivory handled knife. It was a pretty dream. Soon the janitor's voice faded away, and then George found himself home with his mother who made him some chicken soup.

It was just that he was forgetful, his mother explained to Mr. B., the head counselor. He was not a bad boy, not at all. The very opposite. He wanted to please everyone and anyone. His father was gone, no one knew where, and George had never met him, and she always tried to be the best mother possible, and George was so loving and sweet towards her. The father had been a sweet, dreamy man, too, his mother said. He'd wandered off one day when she was pregnant and got lost, or he might be in jail or dead. She didn't know how to find out. And it was so hard to keep everything going, getting George to school, picking him up, working so hard and leaving George too much alone.

She broke down as she explained all this to the district counselor, Jennie. The school was thinking of sending him away. George held his arm around his mom's shoulders. He had all his friends here, and he knew his mother wouldn't like it if he left.

"He's doing his best," Helene explained. And Jennie put her big white hand over Helene's tiny, coal black hand, and they both cried.

"Fine counselor I am," Jennie said, sniffling. She was a tall, woman with a flame of blonde hair, while Helene Brooks was so dark you had to look hard to see her facial features, but she was beautiful, almost Indian looking, clean and tidy, where Jennie, also beautiful, overflowed everywhere, like a flood. "I'll put in a good word for him," she said.

"He has some particular needs," Helene explained, looking up at George, who nodded. "He daydreams, he drifts away."

But not even Helene knew where George had drifted to one Thursday afternoon, when he should have met her as usual on the street in front of the school. Helene waited for him in her faded blue Honda Civic as she always had, and when students quit coming out, she went right in, despite leaving the car parked in a red zone. She asked two boys in the hall if they knew George Brooks, and they laughed.

One said, "Everyone knows George. He wanders into every class."

The other said, "He doesn't always know which class he's in."

"You have to ask the teachers. They make him go to the right class whenever he shows up."

"He's everywhere all at once trying to make everyone laugh."

"But where is he right now?" Helene insisted. "I'm his mother." She smiled sadly at them both. She was so small, so charming, so completely black like a black hole in the hallway.

They didn't know. So off to the Principal she went, Mr. Rosenblatt, who she knew well. A very small, round, compact, well meaning man with a very loud voice. He checked the attendance records for the day. "He wasn't in Fourth Period, or Fifth or Sixth either. I don't know what I can do more than tell you that."

"He loses track," Helene said. "He might have gone off to State with some friends. He has a very active imagination."

"I see his attendance is very spotty," Mr. Rosenblatt said. "A lot of tardies. I never really looked at his record before, but it looks like he's tardy about half the time. That's not good."

"He's a good boy. He's so sweet and kind. I just don't know where he is right now. He was supposed to meet me, and I have to go to work. Can you help me find him?"

"I… I can call the police." Rosenblatt looked at her as if she herself were a lost child. He wanted to help, but he couldn't think how.

"No," Helene said, her voice tired. "No police. I'll look for him. Maybe I know where he is."

"In the morning I'll ask in the Bulletin if anyone knows where he is. And, meanwhile, here's my home number in case you want me to call the police for you, tonight."

The school, which had seemed so safe, was now empty. It hovered over her with its dark halls and empty classrooms. The young people brought so much life that the building seemed especially ghostly without their shouts and laughter.

Later that night she did phone Mr. Rosenblatt, who called in a lost child report to 911. He identified himself to Dispatch as the Principal of School of the Arts.

"How long has George been missing?" the dispatcher said. And she added, "Is this really an emergency?"

"Missing since about eleven o'clock today," Joe said. "The mother thinks it is an emergency. She says he's a special needs kid."

"Does he need medicine? Is he dangerous to others or to himself?"

"I don't know about medicine, but he's very harmless, a very sweet boy."

She got all the relevant information, a black teen in a Giants baseball cap, a new red 49ers jacket, and jeans with red tennis shoes. One hundred and twenty-five pounds, five foot seven, natural hair cut short, almost sixteen. Not much to go on, a boy who looked like half the Black boys in San Francisco.

But three days later it turned out that George had not been in San Francisco at all when the call went out, had been in San Jose, some eighty miles south. The San Jose police found him asleep in a car in a parking lot outside a Denny's. The owner of the car, an older white woman, Brenda Goodman, a waitress, found him when she quit work at midnight. At first, when she saw him, she'd been afraid, but one look at his sweet face reassured her.

There he was sleeping, all curled up in back of her Ford Fiesta, a small, black boy with tears streaking his cheeks. She didn't take any chances, though, so she went back in to Denny's and called the police.

Two patrol cars roared up five minutes later, and four officers, Sig Sauers held ready, approached the car. One yelled, "Police! Open up! Get out of the car!"

First one dark hand tinged with pink then George's sleepy head appeared at the car window. As usual, he smiled. Two of the police, both of Latin descent, backed up a step and leveled their pistols at George. The two other police took positions, guns pointed, next to their patrol car.

"Both hands on the window, sir!"

George looked at them in amazement. This was some kind of dream. He couldn't quite make out what they were saying. He put his second hand on the window by pure chance. Then he reached down and tried to open the door.

"Don't move, sir!"

George brought his hand up and cupped it to his ear. What did they want him to do? Were they talking to him, calling him a Sir? He wasn't old enough to be a Sir. Made him giggle a little. He wanted to tell them he was happy they'd found him. He was hungry.

They didn't want him to do anything, certainly not drop his hand below their vision. Too many policemen and too many civilians had been shot in San Jose recently. The four policemen understood it was their job to bring in this boy alive, if possible, but this was a high crime area, with much gang activity, Black and Latino, so they took as few risks as possible. They were trained to hold their guns in front of them when they approached a potentially dangerous situation, to make a wide swing around any corners, to stay ready.

It took a moment for them to realize that they'd given him two mutually contradictory orders. He couldn't open the door and keep his hands visible at the same time.

"Hands on the window, Sir!"

That they were ready to shoot would have been all too clear to anyone but George. He didn't know if he was imagining this or not. One of the policemen, the youngest, yanked the door handle and leapt back gun still raised. When they saw how small George was, and how dreamy his face, they looked at each other and relaxed.

Nevertheless, one policeman spun him around and pressed George's hands and face and chest forcefully down on the chill hood of the car. It was not his imagination then, George decided, feeling the icy metal against his face. The hood smelled rusty.

The police soon found he'd been reported missing, another runaway black teen with a call out on him. George Brooks, missing from San Francisco. But he could have been shot if he'd made a wrong move. You never knew what to expect. There were so many angry black men, afraid for their lives, and ready to kill. O.J. had come and gone, but anger in the Black communities throughout the United States was boiling hot. A little incident might set off national outcry. There had been the Rodney King riots.

The police were angry, too. They had to hold the line, not give in to violence, not be violent themselves, not make things worse, but keep order. A terrible dilemma. You might get shot if you relaxed one little shiver, and you might kill someone if you got too aggressive. It was a heartbreaking job at times, but it paid well and it was exciting. When would people realize it was a very tough job? You had to be careful, but you had to take as few risks as possible. It paid well, that was the main thing.

What George told his mother was wild. He'd gone with some friends to Chinatown to buy a present for some one's mother. He couldn't remember the names of the boys. If he saw them in the halls at SOTA he would ask their names. While they were walking down Grant Avenue, a truck pulled alongside them and a Chinese boy reached over and pulled George's new red jacket right off his back, Or tried to. George held on to one sleeve. He wasn't going to let go of an expensive jacket that his mother had given him for his birthday. He raced along and jumped in the back of the truck as it moved away. He held on to one sleeve of the jacket with all his might. And the next thing he knew, he woke up in San Jose in the back seat of a car with a bunch of policemen pointing guns at him. He tried to explain to them that his jacket had been stolen, but they weren't interested.

What had he done for three days? Where had he been? What did he eat? Why didn't he phone home?

"There was a tunnel, ma." The jacket was gone, he didn't know where. "Some Chinese boys got it."

He'd been afraid to come home without the new jacket, so, maybe, he had walked all over San Jose looking for it. "You just bought it for me, ma." A new red jacket with 49ers printed on it. But really, he didn't remember. People kept telling him he was in San Jose, but he didn't know anything about San Jose, or how to call home from San Jose. Maybe he would know next time.

Helene cried in relief for a long time. Three days gone and she'd feared the worst. George was so defenseless. His smile was his only protection.

"Go to the police next time," she told him. "They will help." But George wasn't so sure they would help him. Many of his friends disliked the police, and told him the police were more likely to shoot him. Hadn't they pointed their guns at him in San Jose? Not that he ever thought they would really shoot him, but still they were not very nice. They'd put handcuffs on him so tight they hurt. They threw him around, and didn't feed him or even give him any water for a long time. One of them pushed him hard with his boot into a cell. No, he couldn't say he thought of police as helpful.

He promised her he'd never get in this situation again, and his smile lit up Helene's heart. The whole sky brightened when George was truly happy, and here he was back with his mother and she was holding him tight to her side, no longer able to lift him as she had when he was small, but here she was so warm, his own dear mother.

"Ma, I love you," he said, with his big smile. He was so glad to be home. He'd never been so happy. Or he couldn't remember. It was a foggy swirl, unknown places, trees, barking dogs, restaurants, hunger, a terrible sense of no one there, a dark underground space with big white men.

"He just spaces out," Helene told Mr. Rosenblatt. "He never means any harm. He forgets."

It was one of the problems of being a Principal, Rosenblatt figured, when to keep someone, when to drop them from the school. He could have dropped George from the program, and would have done so in a gnat's twitch if George had been defiant or mean. But this… this smiling boy, this sweet black mother, her tears…

Rosenblatt gave Helene forty dollars. "I expect to see George's new 49er jacket next week," he said when she drew her hand back. She smiled her tiny, pebbly smile and accepted the money and bought George a better jacket than the one he'd lost.

About that story, no one at school believed George. It was too weird. How could he ride all the way to San Jose in the back of some stranger's truck holding on to a jacket? How could someone steal a jacket right off his back? Not likely. Chinese? Three days in San Jose? What was he really up to? Did he have a hot girl in San Jose? Hah! That was a laugh. Imagine George running off with a girlfriend.

"C'mon, George, tell the truth!" What a dude!

All went well, until late May, when George disappeared again. The whole school was put on alert and told to report any information to Mr. Rosenblatt. George's San Jose girl, some jokers said. He's only sixteen, but he gets around. They didn't believe this, but they didn't know what to believe. George was too soft, too sweet to have a girlfriend. But why go off without telling his mother or anyone else? Did he go to San Jose again?

He disappeared on a Friday, and stayed gone over the weekend. What probably happened in that time, no one knew for sure, but what was known eventually was that on Sunday George had found himself walking along some train tracks in south San Jose, and a train had come up behind him and he had looked around at the conductor who was leaning out of the cab wildly blowing the train whistle, shouting, and George probably saw a huge cartoon of a black train like the one in Loony Tunes, big puffs of white smoke, with Bugs Bunny leaning out of the cab shouting, "What's up," and it was rushing toward him, would run right over him, maybe squash him flat and he would have to puff himself up into roundness again, and he laughed.

The conductor said. "I couldn't stop in time. He'd climbed the fence. He wouldn't get out of the way. He must have seen me. He heard the whistle. All he did was smile. Stupid! Stupid! Stupid!"

And that's how it was. George Brooks, a boy whose smile hung in the halls of the school, whose smile lit up the universe, who didn't know much about school or real trains, whose mother was broken in half, after so much love.

Delta

From the back wall of Room 23 of The San Francisco High School of the Arts, SOTA, there stares a five-foot-high spray-can face of a glum, fat-cheeked, heavy-lidded man, a portrait done in unleavened tones of navy blue, purple, brown and pink. It looks a lot like Principal Rosen. English Teacher Harry Selke tries to admire it, but can't. Ric, a Tenth Grade, self-defined graffiti artist, admits he snuck in and painted it over the weekend. He'd just read Orwell's 1984, and this is his version of Big Brother.

Harry's lips tighten and purse forward. "When will you unpaint it?" He says.

"You don't like it?" Ric stares up at his teacher's unamused face. Ric is a ninety pound handful of weird trouble.

After a brief silence, Ric says, "I'm glad you find it ugly. I value your honest hostility."

Emily and Lana, involved in a continuous discussion since opening day of school, ignore Harry as he finishes calling roll. He stands over them and waits as they give him their traditional, half-sneering, sidelong glances. They have enrolled themselves in the "Gifted and Talented" program and are subsequently indifferent to the masses, among whom is a particularly irritating teacher, himself, Mr. Selke.

These students are, all in all, a privileged bunch, many of them having had many hours of expensive lessons in art or drama or dance. Emily, an actress, also considers herself a writer, with a short story published in Circle Magazine when she was eleven.

"I've got an English Class to teach here," Harry says directly to Emily as she chatters on despite his standing next to her so she has to peer around his pants to continue her chat with Lana.

When he speaks to her, she stares at his belt, her red, highly polished lips briefly parted in mid word, astonished, as if he were a talking duck.

Harry, heavy and square like his father, sucks in his stomach. He'd begun to feel as if he were a cement block balanced on stick legs, something like the old Irish dock workers he'd known as a child in San Pedro.

"A foine figure of a maahn," his uncle, Patrick Henry Kelly, a retired dock worker, would say of himself or anyone shaped like him as he thumped his overstuffed belly.

I was among the handsome of the world once, Harry mouths to himself. Women, even nasty school girls, listened to me. Ric, in a far corner of the room, nods and smiles as if he'd read Harry's lips.

Delta is visiting today, on tour from Intersection for the Arts. She will read from her new book of poetry, Blood White Arrow. There's a hum in the room. The kids welcome any variation. Harry has laid out two tiers of extra chairs in the back where Mr. Mully's Ninth Grade English Class can sit and listen to this authentic Native-American poet.

Harry has also invited Principal Rosen, a self-styled poetry enthusiast. Given any encouragement, Rosen will quote Rudyard Kipling's If:

If you can keep your head when

all about you are losing theirs…

Harry hopes Rosen doesn't notice his facial similarity to Ric's back-wall portrait.

Delta's a Sioux, and her poetry of the difficult life on the reservation should fit in well with Harry's Native-American section. He'd read a few of her poems and liked them, and thought she could help the class clarify just what a Native-American might be, for there was, much to Harry's surprise, some confusion in the class about who might qualify, if not a real, then a hypothetical, confusion, a confusion led by such as Emily and Ric, who both enjoyed proving that Harry was an idiot.

The class has since expanded the definition of Native American to include almost any author of any other culture than white American, including Irish, French, Chinese, German and even foreign-born English writers traveling through, because Harry's students, mostly white, with a smattering of Asian boys and girls from upper middle-class homes, had long ago decided it was politically incorrect and unfair to exclude anyone, especially those with ancestors from any place that sounded exotic, such as Alamagordo, Walla Walla or Poughkeepsie.

Just who set the rules defining an official Native American, anyway? Did all genuine Native Americans have to live in tipis and run around naked?

Harry tried to establish definitions. Native Americans, for example, had to have been born in North America and be of tribal descent. Yumi, an Asian American girl, insisted that almost anyone who wrote well in American English had to have lived here from babyhood, implying, with smiles, that this did not necessarily mean they had to have been born here. She herself had been born here, but had spoken only Mandarin until she was six. Early use of English gave others who came from English speaking families an unfair advantage. She herself had struggled hard to catch up with English speakers. Harry's definition was, in her case, unconscionable, chauvinistic, and perfidious. She smiled, holding up her Roget's Thesaurus, which Harry had assigned to the class.

"What is the difference between native-born and Native-American writers anyway?" she asked.

"Thank you for that question, Yumi," Harry said. He'd tried to follow Yumi's logic. "We're trying to understand that difference. In your case your family has not lived here long enough to qualify as Native American. It did not come from an established tribal background."

"I was born here," she said. "I belong to an ethnic minority."

"There has to be a history of living here, a history that goes back in time."

"How far back?" said Yumi.

"Before Europeans," Harry said, hoping this would end the confusion.

The class attacked. He, a white teacher, was excluding Blacks! And Puerto Ricans! And Asians? What about white mountain men and trappers who lived in tipis and married into tribes and wrote about it? Were Canadians Native Americans? Did that definition include writers who wrote about Native Americans? What about Filipinos?

"Stop. Stop," Harry cried. "One question at a time."

"How about John Steinbeck," Emily said.

"Steinbeck?" Harry said, astonished. "A Native American? When did he even write about Native Americans."

"In some dumb book about the ghost of a dead indian we were supposed to read last year in Rayher's class," Emily said.

"You must mean Faulkner," Harry said.

"I know who I mean," she said with some haughtiness. She was finished with the subject. She turned her back to Harry and blew a kiss at Manuel across the room.

Ric said to Harry, "Does your definition exclude Mexicans with Mayan heritage?" He was arguing on behalf of Manuel, who claimed to be part Mayan.

"Yes." Harry said. "You're on the right track. But Mayans and Aztecs have their own separate Native American background, separate from the Spanish who conquered Mexico. Still Mayans are Native Americans." He licked his dry lips. Such questions could go on for days.

There continued exceptions and counter exceptions, laughter, a forest of waving hands, and shouts that, Harry felt, were, overall, good, but hard to control, and mostly, he knew, meant to delay any lessons. Still, they had stayed on one subject. That was something of a victory, Harry felt.

"Say," Emily shouted above the rising noise of the class. "Isn't this an Ethnic Literature Class?"

"Yes," said Harry. He couldn't hide the weary look in his eyes.

"And Ethnic Literature can be from anyone of any ethnic background or tradition who writes about ethnic issues? Right?" Emily had a sweet if fake smile to go with her logic. "Like Oliver Lafarge?" The class had recently read LaFarge's Laughing Boy.

Harry patiently explained that while there were indeed, many ethnic cultures in America, today's poet would help clarify the position of one specific culture, the Sioux, an example of one of many large Native-American tribes. For one thing, Delta was born here, he said, of an indigenous culture that existed long before Columbus discovered the so-called New World.

"How old is she?" demanded Ric.

"She's not old," Harry said. "Her culture is old."

"Older than what? Spain? France?" Ric insisted.

"Maybe," Harry said. He held up his hand for quiet as he simultaneously took roll. "Maybe fifteen thousand years old."

Emily said, "That's not so old."

Many of his students knew they'd been lied to by Hollywood, that movie indians often turned out to be Italians or Mexicans, that indians no longer wore elaborate feather headdresses, that they could look just like anyone else, for example, take Juan Carlos, a Senior of Mayan descent, President of The Native-American Club, who was a green-eyed John Wayne look-alike and very popular with the girls.

"Not good to exclude whole races and cultures," Emily informed Harry. "That's racist!" She leaned forward and whispered loud enough for the class to hear as she emphasized racist. She was half Asian, half white, and boys thought her very cute, so she felt herself to be expert in matters of racial prejudice.

"All teachers," she said, in her sweetest tone, "who are white, are potentially racist, and the more they deny their racism, the more racist they are."

Last year, in the Ninth Grade, their beloved white teacher, Mr. Mully, had helped them understand that almost no one is pureblood Native American. Native-Americans can be partly French and Irish and German and African American, even Jewish, much like all

Americans. Everyone came from somewhere else long ago, and what was the difference between those who traveled over some ice bridge from Asia ten or twenty thousand years ago and those who were brought as slaves by boat from Canton or Africa, or those who sailed here on the Mayflower?

Harry said. "I'm not excluding anyone, nor am I racist. Native Americans have lived here fifteen thousand years, plus or minus five thousand years."

Emily jeered. "Dinosaurs lived here for a hundred million years," she said. "Are they Native Americans?

Mully had shaken his head in despair when Harry asked him about his former students' all-inclusive interpretation of Native American.

"I only meant," Mully said with dignity, "that there are many native American cultures and one ought to try to understand that there are real cultural differences even within the general category of Native American. Some real Native American writers live within and identify with their native culture, some don't." What real or unreal Native American meant to Mully, Harry failed to discover.

The class had earlier discussed The Trail of Tears versus The Holocaust. Were Jews exactly like Native Americans? Could Jewish writers be considered Native Americans? They too had been rounded up and marched along and killed.

The class was eager to explore even the most outrageous arguments, and, despite Harry's best efforts, they managed to roll pebbles of knowledge into boulders of youthful certainty. The Mayflower, the Nina, Pinta and Santa Maria, the Golden Hinde, the Endeavor and various other "slave ships" blended into a swirl of Tenth Grade myths and histories, a meshing that could, after all, have its good side, perhaps foretelling a wave of the future – equality among all cultures, love among all, yes – although Manuel, who never smiled and seldom talked, who chewed a black stick like a cigarillo, and was of Mayan descent, and a street-smart Mexican from The Mission, stood up one day and announced, "This dumb ass bunch of dumb ass racist dopes in this dumb ass class don't know their butts from a banana." This was his longest statement to present. Almost poetic. Lots of D's and B's. He was considered hot, and dangerous. The girls, mostly white and Asian, instantly agreed with him. They knew they were not racist, not in their hearts, and not at all toward cute boys like Manuel. Among friends they said things that might sound racist, but really, they were just kidding around.

Tenth Grade Ethnic Lit, was, in reality, English, a required subject, therefore resisted, and unless Harry kept his students busy, they would invariably grow distracted. It was Fourth Period, just before lunch, and they were hungry. They could sit quietly through a movie, or pay respect to a guest speaker, as today, Delta, an authentic native-American who was coming to set them all straight about Native Americans. A Sioux poet.

Discussions tended to stir them up, and it was often difficult for Harry to bring them back into focus. Or they might grow bored, no matter what Harry did to jazz up his lessons. Bored, their thoughts would invariably wander on to their tongues and the soft rainfall of private discussion would rise into a torrential roar, and Harry would find himself shouting, "Your attention, please!"

He'd taught for fifteen years, half of that among these real and would-be artists, drama queens and little kings at various stages of adolescent scorn and need, and it had never been easy. It was often amazing, delightful, outrageous, but never smooth. Exhausting, exhilarating, like surfing big waves, so many quick, creative, rebellious young minds just developing.

He told his students over the years, "Pay attention to detail, notice differences, quit stepping on your own feet, try to learn something. Education is free for the first twelve years. Most things make sense somehow," he would say, "even in public schools, if you take time to think about what's offered. Learn to learn," he would say.

But many of these particular Tenth Grade philosophers had thought enough about public schools and had reached the End of Knowledge. They knew everything they might possibly need to carry them through life.

What they demanded was entertainment. Something like the Jerry Springer reality show. Harry hated the Jerry Springer show.

Mr. Mully's class bangs in, followed by Mr. Mully who will retire at the end of the semester. He's very tall, hunched over, with jutting jaw and exploding white hair. He was relieved of his job as English Department Head at Washington High because he poked his finger into the bosom of PTA Chair, Anita Wong, a fast-talking Chinese mother who believed in Christ and wanted to know why Mully gave her son a C.

"She went through my private desk," Mully said in his defense. "She's lucky I only poked her with my finger."

Harry walks anxiously in front ot the class. Delta should be here. He reads the Daily Bulletin aloud. Poetry Day is Wednesday. All Ninth and Tenth Graders are required to line up at noon today on the front lawn for class photos. Today is half day session.

Two more Ninth Grade boys sidle in looking cool, hoping to be noticed by girls, but Tenth Grade girls never notice Ninth Grade boys. Delta is nowhere to be seen. Seventy students have now crowded into Harry's classroom and the rising level of laughter and shouts brings Mr. B. from his room next door to complain. Harry rolls his eyes and shrugs helplessly above the din as he tries to explain about Mully's class and Delta being late, but what is there to explain? If she doesn't get here, he'll have to send all Mully's kids back, and try to make up a lesson out of thin air. A big mess. Mully's kids, rowdy 13-year-old boys and girls, could, in the brief space between classes, ravage the school, Harry knows. Principal Rosen likes Harry, but Harry's classes are often problematic. The kids get too excited. They go overboard and cause bizarre trouble, like the time Ric put a closed sign on the Girl's Toilet, locked himself in, and spray painted on the back wall the Virgin Mary with enormous breasts feeding Baby Jesus. Lots of haloes. Lots of angels. Two fat red nipples. Very well done. Ric did this during class time, and Rosen wanted to know why Harry hadn't reported him absent.

"Well," Harry said. "He'd been in class last I noticed."

A note arrives from Charles, the Main Office Secretary. Delta has called and will be late. She's lost. It doesn't say how late. Harry's neck muscles tighten. He looks around the crowded, noisy room. Shouts and laughter rise once again to a boiling pitch. Two classes stuffed into one small room is potential revolution.

But, thank God, almost before he can think what to do, Delta arrives looking slightly run over and not very ethnic in a cheap pink blouse and too-tight jeans accentuating abundant haunches. She has a purple streaked flat-top with long, black side-hair, and she carries a fiber shopping-bag with a Farmworkers eagle printed on it. Harry imagined she'd be a lot more Native American looking and would offer a bit of tribal realism, but he smiles and shakes her hand, relieved she's here. He just hopes her poetry keeps their attention. Poetry is a big risk.

He calls for quiet and introduces Delta as a Sioux poet, and there's a moment of silence. She stands, arms crossed in front of her, quivering, and after a moment the first thing she says is that she's a lesbian Cherokee poet, not a "god damned Sioux" as the teacher has said, and that she's sad and pissed off because women like her have suffered oppression at the hands of "The Fucking White Man in America!"

Her husky, almost masculine voice rises to a shout on the word America. There's a stunned, silent moment among students. Harry's shoulders jerk and he thinks, Thank God the Principal isn't here, yet.

"I was a prostitute!" She points violently at the class as if they had forced her into it, and everyone jerks up, except for Mully who raises his eyebrows, sticks his jaw farther out, frowns, then slips out through the back door.

"Yeah! No shit!" she says, her intelligent, quick eyes following Mully as he exits. "A ho!" She's short and overweight and ready to attack. Her tears well up as she takes a step toward the class. She has their attention. No student here has ever seen a fat, angry, purple-haired, Native-American prostitute poet ready to cry or fight in a public school classroom or anywhere else.

"This is a racist, sexist society." She steps toward two cute, perfectly manicured Japanese girls who deflate themselves into their shared seat. "And women like me and you were fucked over and forced to prostitute themselves, and I don't mean just by selling… their… bodies… on… stre e e e e e t… corners."

Harry stands between her and the paralyzed girls and opens his mouth to tell her that these are only Tenth Grade girls, to chill out, but tears flood down her cheeks and she flushes and turns away from him to face the blackboard on which Harry has written the next day's homework: Read Buffalo Bill's Defunct by e.e. cummings. P.578, and respond with a two-page essay or 14 line poem. A good creative assignment for an Ethnic Lit class, he'd thought.

"And this is an example of the bullshit that dead poetry is, dead white man's poetry!" She erases the assignment with the palm of her hand and simultaneously writes and recites,

"Buffalobillsdefunctwhousedtorideawatersmoothsilverstallion-andshootonetwothreefourfivepigeonsjustlikethatandwhatiwantto-knowishowdoyoulikeyourblueeyedboymrdeath?"

Hands on loaded hips she scowls around the room and glares at various girls who reflect blank looks. Even Emily seems stunned.

"Do you know blue-eyed Buffalo Bill took brown-eyed Chief Sitting Bull and put him in a circus like a seal? Hmm?" She pirouettes to the board heavily but gracefully on her left foot and says, "This homework is crap! Read living writers like Leslie Marmon Silko, or Joy Harjo, or Louise Erdrich." She pounds the blackboard with the heel of her left hand and illegibly scribbles half a dozen names on the board, turns abruptly and sees some stacks of xeroxed poems on Harry's desk and reads aloud the names of William Shakespeare, William Blake, William Carlos Williams, Allen Ginsberg. She swipes them in a fluttering cloud around the class, shouting, "Dead! White! Male! Middle-class Williams!"

She picks up a copy of Howl and says, "And this! Did you know this was written by a fucking pedophile? Allen Ginsberg!" She throws a pile of homework assignments at the class where they flutter above their heads and sway to the floor. Some duck, but no one says a word.

For a few breaths there isn't a sound in the class, not a rustle, not a cough. Most do not have a clue who Allen Ginsberg is. All they know is anything they might say or do will be wrong. They've never heard an adult speaker at any school use the phrase *fucking pedophile*. Not in a classroom.

Harry has sweated through his underwear. If the Principal were to enter the room now he might not have a job tomorrow. His sweater is way too hot. He promises God never to invite an unknown poet to his class again, Intersection sponsored or not.

There's a breathless hush as the class slips past the words *fucking* and *pedophile*, but Delta senses something and turns to Harry and opens her mouth, lips moving, maybe asking for help, or maybe accusing him. Looking down she says, "Pedophiles are dirty old men who like to fuck little children!" She stares at Harry.

All eyes turn to Harry, definitely the dirty old pedophile type.

He groans and imagines wrestling Delta out into the hall. He might lose.

"What I did I did to survive," she shouts. "I have two children. Yeah. Two about as old as you, do you know what that means?" She shakes her right forefinger at the two Japanese girls. "People like me sometimes have children. It's part of the job. I won't say what I did was good, no, but there are plenty of decent housewives who are worse than ho's." She stops, perhaps puzzled by some contradiction in what she has said.

"But… ped…o…philes… are… dis…gust…ing!"

On Emily's desk she hammers home each syllable with her right fist. Emily's make-up kit bounces to the floor. With haughty, wounded dignity, Emily carefully reaches down from her seat, collects her scattered cosmetics, rises and with head held high, exits. Delta and the class watch her silently. Manuel, slung down in his desk, his legs straight out, shakes in repressed laughter, lips open, unsmiling, eyes closed, head laid back, his whole body vibrating. One of his boot heels thumps on the floor. He can't stop.

Harry tries to gently pull Delta by her sleeve backwards from the class. She shakes him off. She's short but strong. The students hardly breathe, their defiance stunned into silence. The two Japanese girls have buried their heads in their arms.

Delta points both forefingers at the two girls and bends her head down to them. "That's right! Hide! Hide from the truth, heads in the sand. Yah, I had two children just like you and my old man up and vanished. Probably murdered by the police, or couldn't take the shit an Indian has to take. Spaniards. English. Americans. Assholes. See? They taught my own husband to hate…to hate the very breasts his children suckled. See?"

She rips a button from the top of her shirt and reveals a frilly cream colored bra that holds up two huge, whitish, melon-shaped breasts. The upper edges of brown aureoles edge forth like rising suns. The class gasps and the two Asian girls hold hands and run out screaming, followed by three more girls who stare, eyes wide, at Harry as they flee.

Delta takes a deep breath and her half exposed breasts bulge upward.

"See! My old man didn't like my breasts! My own God given body!"

Who would like such balloons? Harry thinks. He steps between her and the class. He's been blitzed. It's a war with everything happening too fast. Delta crosses her arms modestly over her bra, quiet for a moment. Harry tears off his woolen sweater and stuffs it over her head. He works the sweater down over her breasts, which feel like buttered rubber. It takes a moment for her head and arms to pop out.

She pushes him aside and in a deep, solemn voice says, "Native-Americans lived here for thousands of years before the white man. I am a Native-American. A redskin. Yup. A certified injun. I am Cher o… k e e eee yee yee."

She beats her chest rhythmically with the flat of her right hand so the word Cherokee comes out in soft ululations.

"Cherokee means, The People. We were The People who lived in harmony with the land, the forests…grass prairies…birds… animals…holy deer and bear, the sacred buffalo for thousands of years. Father Sun and Mother Moon shone down on us, until Great White Father's stinking soldiers came and stole our land and killed our men and raped our children and forced us to wear sneakers.

We were left with nothing. Nothing but lies! Disease. Dead buffalo. Carcasses of rotten meat. Elvis Presley!"

She pauses to breathe deeply and she swells up until it seems she will burst through Harry's sweater and scatter bits of bra and breast flesh across the room

"Black Hills. Wounded Knee! Sand Creek! Who… now… knows… these… names?"

No one dares raise a finger or even look in her direction, except Manuel who stares at her with an adoring look and the first full scale grin Harry has ever seen from him.

"See? They don't teach you The Truth!" She points at Harry, her voice ever more metallic. For a second she stands motionless, eyes closed, face upwards, both hands stretched down stiff at her hips, as if waiting for some truth to descend from above.

"Maybe he's a good man," she says, pointing at Harry. "But few white men are interested in the truth, the truth of theft and murder, broken treaties, babies bayoneted in their mother's arms, destruction of the great buffalo, ancient herds gone, starvation, tongues cut out, hides stripped, bodies left for maggots and vultures. Death! Excrement!Skull and bones! George Bush! Dick Cheney! Hiya, ya!"

She pauses to take a breath, her unloved bosom heaving beneath Harry's sweater. "Endangered species, hah! That's us injuns, all right. Look for our endangered burial grounds plowed under corn-belt farms, under asphalt highways, under the skyscrapers of cities, under reservoirs where the waters have drowned our ancestors. Land stolen from us. Horses gone. Babies sent to Christian schools. Still we are Cherokee! Only a hundred years ago, three generations, not much more, we rode our war horses. We haven't forgotten. We shall never forget. We shall strike back! Nature shall be our weapon. The prairies are drying up. You whites poison the waters every day. And look what you have given us in place of the sacred Black Hills." She slaps her left hand over her heart and extends the other slowly palm up toward a non-existent flag near the door. She whispers almost inaudibly, "I… pledge… allegiance to the great white Bank of America, andtothecultureforwhichitstands, the holy dollar indivisible, with prison and poverty for all…"

Tears stream down her cheeks. Some of the children cry too. Delta's heavy masculine voice sinks so low the kids in the back lean forward. Harry looks at the door, willing it not to open.

"See the filth of cities, the corruption of politicians, the atom bomb, the dirty skies where the eagle has fallen. Try to drink the sour, dung-filled water of the streams. Yes. Dung! Blood! Soapsuds! Where the people once rode proud and free… you… peasant Swedes and Okies… your grandfathers and great grandfathers were welcomed as brothers and you tilled the land to dust, blown away…stolen… Poof! Into the sky." She points up at two tiny, white, wooden herons Harry had hung years ago on threads from the ceiling light, wings spread as if flying. "See here what they have given us!"

As the class looks up at the hitherto unremarkable herons, Delta pulls from her fiber bag a half gallon bottle of Thunderbird, unscrews the cap, tilts back and drinks. "Firewater!" she shouts between swallows.

Harry breaks toward her as the glug glug of the wine slips down her outstretched throat. He twists the bottle away from her grasp in a spray of red, pours it down the sink, and thrusts the empty bottle back at her. There's a shout from the class. Then silence.

Delta has attacked Harry's class and he's furious. I won't have a job tomorrow, he thinks, but I can recapture my class today. I marched to protest the victims of Wounded Knee, to free Dennis Banks and Leonard Pelletier. I supported the Farmworkers. I ran Coast Guard blockades and delivered food and water to Alcatraz when the American Indian Movement claimed it as Big Rock. But now the whole school and all the parents will hear about Delta, that she said I am a racist white man, a thief, a murderer of babies, a teacher who lost control of his class, perhaps a lying pedophile, who allows wine to be guzzled in his room.

Harry shakes his head clear, takes three deep breaths, begins to feel calm, almost liberated. He holds up his hand until the class is totally silent. They are numb. They look to him. They want to know what to do. This is better than Jerry Springer.

He takes another deep breath and holds it for a count of ten and lets it out. His heart slows and he relaxes every muscle, trying to let his anxiety slip out of his fingertips. But he can see it in the Chronicle. Front page news: "Indian Prostitute Exposes Breasts Gets Drunk in Front of Tenth Grade Class." A class he used to teach. His fifteen minutes of fame. Fifteen years down the drain. A decent record as a teacher rubbed out. He has worked hard for not much pay, amid a lot of adolescent insults, and now he is draining down the sink with Delta's wine. Maybe he can lie his way out of this, but the terrified, wooden faces of his students are undeniable. He hasn't protected them. Manitou has not been with him. He's the Great White Bad Father. All the forces of Christianity will descend on him tomorrow. The John Birch Society will scalp him.

He grasps Delta firmly by the wrist, but before he can haul her away, Head Counselor Wendy Horn respectfully tiptoes into the room, hands a note to a student in back, and leaves, as if nothing at all had ever happened. As if he still had a job.

He pulls Delta toward the door, which opens to reveal Principal Rosen just entering. Harry's white shirt is glued by sweat to his chest and shoulders. This is what he feared most, the Principal here to take his class from him, to throw him forever onto some heap of child abusers.

But Rosen says mildly, "There's going to be a fire drill in a few minutes. You can lead your class out front to the lawn."

"Fire drill? Front? Lawn!" Harry can't for a moment think what the words mean.

"They're going to take the class photos after the Fire Drill," Rosen says, a puzzled tone in his voice. "I told everyone yesterday. It's in the Bulletin." Then he looks over Harry's shoulder at the dazed class and at Delta and the eagle bag with the wine bottle sticking out and Harry shrugs his shoulders.

"Everything okay?" Rosen says. The reek of wine floats through the room and tries to escape through the door. The smell is sour. Unmistakeable.

"Fine," Harry says. Rosen's eyes drift over stupefied faces, some girls crying.

"I'm sorry that I couldn't get here for the poet," Rosen says, shifting back a step.

Harry almost feels sympathy for him. Rosen's a friend and he's going to hate what he will have to do to Harry tomorrow. But now Rosen wants Harry to translate his apology to The Poet. Rosen can't bring himself to talk to her directly, and Harry certainly doesn't want Delta to breathe on Rosen, even if it doesn't much matter any more. As she opens her mouth, Harry wrenches her wrist. "Ow!" She says.

"She's done already," Harry says. "She gave a powerful performance. Too bad you missed it." Rosen looks again at the empty wine bottle and at Delta's purple hair and disheveled sweater.

"That bottle's a prop," Harry says quickly. "Part of her act."

"Oh," Rosen says. "Give her my regrets." He says this to Harry as if he should translate, as if Delta weren't standing in front of him.

Rosen shakes his head glumly. "I can't be everywhere, you know." Harry glances at Rosen's graffiti portrait on the back wall.

"Sure," Harry says, and turns to her. "He sends regrets. He can't be everywhere. He's the Principal."

She half curtseys, a parody of humility. Her partly purple partly black butch-cut head nods over Harry's ill-fitting, wine-stained sweater to Rosen, who backs away a step, and leaves.

The fire bell rings. The class rises as if awakened. Harry tells them to go outside and stay in a group on the front lawn and fall in for photos with the other Ninth and Tenth Graders. He's imitating himself as teacher. He pulls Delta down the hall. "Let's go somewhere else fast," he says. It's a life-saving half day schedule.

She laughs. She likes being led. She skips behind him and drags against his urging, a little girl being pulled along.

"How was it?" She twists free and steps in front walking backward and looks seriously into his eyes. Her eyes have turned a sparkling grey green. She says, "Damn good performance, don't you think?"

They scurry past the Main Office desk where Rosen stands talking to a gold-braided blue uniformed Fire Marshall. Delta searches Harry's expression. "No?"

A performance. She didn't read one poem. She didn't help clarify what is Native American. If he loses his job, his wife will still have an income and they can pay the mortgage for six months or so, and get by until he's back on his feet, though he has a brief twinge as he wonders what the job market is for a 60-year-old English teacher fired for indecent classroom behavior.

Maybe he hasn't been the best teacher in the world, but he has tried not to be the worst, has worried over his kids, has stayed up late reading papers, planning lessons, has put in some of the best years of his life, and another five years to go before retirement, and now this, a native force beyond his powers to contain.

He wants to explain all this to Delta. The artist.

"Hmm," he says. He can't talk, What can he say? It's too late to strangle her.

"It wasn't boring," he says at last, the best he can do.

"Thanks. The Truth, capital T, is never boring."

"Possibly not," he says. He hurries her out of the building toward the Lake Merced Boathouse Cafe. Some of his students are already walking away from school in groups of three or four, though it's not quite lunchtime and they're supposed to line up for class photos. He motions them back to the front lawn. The students eye Harry and Delta. Some stare up at a nervous photographer as he focuses his camera on top of a ten-foot ladder from which a panoramic shot is to be taken. It's a very green lawn. Harry is supposed to line up there, too, he knows. There are kids milling everywhere and Mr. B. and Yvonne, the Vice-Principal, are yelling for some to go away and others to line up. The combination photo-shoot fire-drill is already a failure. It's a half day schedule and very warm and most kids want to go to State's cafeteria or to the beach, though some linger, eager to pose for anything.

There's a fire drill but no fire, except in Delta's purple flattop flaring up with the sun through it.

"They're sick of lies." Delta's outstretched hand rotates in the general direction of the kids on the lawn.

"Lies? What?"

"They want Reality," she says. "Capital R. The T. R. U. T. H!"

Harry corrects her. "Capital T you mean."

"Right," she says. "That too."

Over a pitcher of Miller's on tap at the boathouse they watch three real mallards swim by and Delta gets chummy and confesses that she's only one-sixteenth Cherokee. "But I'm a legal injun. I grew up on the Rez."

"I'm one-quarter Irish with a Jewish great grandmother," Harry says. "Who knows what else. Maybe Chinese."

"You might be injun," she says, slapping his right hand with a high five. "Hoka hey!"

"Ellen go blah," he says, lifting a mug of Bud with his left hand.

Stoned

"Oedipus Rex is …" Harry paused for his Fourth Period Advanced Placement English class to respond. Thirty Senior boys and girls sat in seat-desks intended for middle-school children. The room was yellowish and poorly lit, but Harry had brightened it up with posters of paintings by Chagall and Dali and Walt Disney.

"A cretin." This comment from six-foot-six-inch, bony, high-school Senior, Francis Stone, was somewhat crude, for him, but the class laughed. What he said was more a matter of timing and tone than humor, insult with a sly smile, dealt with an under-tone of *shove it*.

Francis's legs stretched like double taproots from beneath his desk far enough to force Harry to step over them as he tried to pass. Francis didn't look up and he didn't move his milk-white legs, which exceeded well past the cuffs of his jeans. He wore no socks. Black hairs grew down his ankles to his high-top sneakers.

Harry usually circled the room in an effort to get students to respond to each other rather than the teacher, but thirty heads turned like so many owls, their eyes following him. They were, in general, some of the smartest kids in school. Harry thought of himself as reasonably intelligent, capable of teaching such a class. Clearly this opinion was not shared by Francis and his acolytes.

"Not a *Cretan*," Harry said. "A *Theban*. But nice to hear from you, Francis. Go on. Tell us more." Harry smiled at him on the general theory that it was better to smile at obnoxious students than get angry when insulted. It threw them off.

Harry had been hacking his way through Francis and his gang, Karen and Bick, for the past six weeks, and the class had suffered. Francis wasn't interested in what Harry had to teach, and didn't give a damn whether others learned anything or not. Harry's job was to teach kids how to write essays, and to fill their heads with information about certain well-known literary works, such as Hamlet or Oedipus Rex. Harry was, from his own point of view, failing with this class, for many of the kids were intimidated by Francis's derision. If Harry asked a question or brought up some idea a student couldn't understand at first, well, that was the teacher's job, but If Francis made a joke of their answers, that was fatal.

Francis said in a sing-song, "You're going to tell us that Freud based his whole theory of psychology on Oedipus Rex. You told us that at the beginning of the year. You wrote it in your classroom handout."

"Why, no, Francis, I wasn't going to say anything about Freud. Anyway, I never said his whole theory…"

That was a mistake. Harry knew just as soon as it slipped out.

"His *whole* theory," Francis said with a judgmental deepening of voice on whole, the male voice of authority.

"Did he or did he not say *whole theory*?" He turned and glanced over his shoulder at Karen and Bick sitting at attention in desks just behind him. "*Did* he?"

"I distinctly heard him say Freud's Whole Theory," said Bick, a pale blonde boy, smaller and even thinner than Francis. He sat as if paralyzed, his back straight, shoulders square. He lisped. His red lips, the only moving part of him, seemed painted on, and now they poked from his thoughtful, innocent face as if sucking on a straw. Wherever Francis went, Bick was sure to go.

Francis's smile curled out and down in a wide I'm-a-lot-smarter than you grin, full lips like Bick's, but pressed bloodless. His eyes noticed everything. Harry usually held his own with students, but Francis had a way of digging immediately under Harry's skin so the discussion ceased to be about the subject at hand and more about whether Harry, clearly a fool, had anything worth saying at that moment.

One morning, as Francis engaged in his usual on-going conversation with Karen, Harry asked him if he might like to share his views with the rest of the class.

"Sir. If you were my age I wouldn't be required to talk to you at all," Francis said. His eyes narrowed. His tone said, fuck off.

"Wow! What a damned *relief* that would be," Harry replied. The class laughed, for a change, at Francis, who went home that evening and complained about the use of the word "damned" to his mother, a Professor of English at California City College.

She called her friend, Arlene, the School District Superintendent who phoned Joe, the generally kindhearted school Principal, who pulled Harry in out of class and asked, "What did you actually say to Francis Stone? The Super tells me Francis's mother is threatening legal action."

Harry shifted warily in front of Joe's desk. Apparently Francis was building a case, so the Principal, Harry's friend Joe, would be required by Human Resources to investigate and write a report. Joe could have done nothing, of course, and merely *said* he investigated, but they both knew Bernice Stone, Doctor Stone, accuser of erring teachers. She had complained about her son's treatment to Joe or the Superintendent's office several times over the past two years. She and the Superintendent belonged to the same church, and she knew how to plunge past protective secretaries with a tone of outraged motherhood. Still, Bernice Stone lived far away at the other end of a phone, while Joe, his old drinking pal, his boss, a man he generally respected, was right there staring at him.

Harry shook his head, irritated at being called forth to defend himself against Francis. "This is a big nothing, Joe. A joke. If there's any abuse it's coming from Francis. I called on him and he told me he didn't have to talk to me and I told him that was a damned relief."

"You're right there," Joe boomed. "But you knew better than to swear." He was a compact, stout, broad-shouldered man, maybe five-six at most, but he made up for lack of size with a thunderous voice. The kids laughed at him and called him, affectionately, The Bullfrog Cheerleader. He seldom punished, but when he got excited you could hear him shouting up and down the halls. He'd spent much of his adult life playing the tuba in a marching band, a short tubby man marching with a huge tubby tuba, puffing his way to success.

"Whatever you do, try to keep him happy," Joe said. "I know he's a problem. His mother calls me or the Super if someone accidentally sneezes on him."

Francis was no ordinary student. He had a perfect score on his SAT. He was also Student Body President, and president of three clubs. He was, in most people's opinions, especially his own, a genius. He claimed he once, by accident, handed in a homework assignment, which was good for a classroom laugh. Whenever he took a test, he got A's, apparently without listening or studying. If Harry made a mistake of any kind, Francis landed on him claws spread, lips quivering. Karen was his girlfriend, Bick his sergeant. He thoroughly enjoyed his school power. He was in Drama, and with his intelligence and height, generally took a leading part. You couldn't avoid him. Beneath the fuzzy, teenaged glow of his pimpled face lay an intense need for attention. A terrible loneliness, Harry felt.

Harry had tried the old ploys. He'd tried to talk to Francis on some non-lethal level in his best, most honest, serious, good-guy teacher voice. *I'm okay, you're okay.* But Francis wanted to control things, and he was good at it, his wit and verbal staying power mowing down any opposition. Even Manuel, a tough Mission Street kid who took shit from no one, would shake his head and stand clear of Francis's barbs. But with Manuel, Francis walked a careful line. If he ever directly insulted Manuel, Francis would receive a street lesson in manners. Even with Harry he walked the line between wit and direct insult.

Maybe Francis' craziness lay in the restless white corners of his eyes, or maybe it was an act, but if he were acting, it was the best performance of his youthful career, Harry thought. Francis's eyes rolled. His head shook. His wooden stare said, *Stay away. Amuse me. You're a fool. I'm crazy.*

Harry had taught other brilliant kids, kids that were clearly off the scale, often living in some Bosch like reality, and he could sometimes touch them, but with Francis, no chance. Other teachers had differing opinions of Francis, some liked him, some hated him.

Just outside Harry's room stood a partly broken down ten-by-ten greenhouse left over from the days when the building had been a primary school. Denise and a half dozen kids in the Ecology Club had asked Harry, their likeable Mr. S., to help them repair the drip system.

In a tight pack they stood just outside the greenhouse door straining to understand as Harry read out instructions on the timing mechanism.

Francis flew by, arms stretched low like wings, fingers stiff, palms parallel to the ground, lips buzzing. Harry had watched him flying across the parking lot and was glad when he disappeared around the corner of a building. Then he was back, still buzzing, not a jet plane, a B-24, Francis declared.

"That *nut*," Denise, a determined little environmentalist, said, shaking her head and half smiling. They all waved at Francis who dipped his arms in response.

After the second roaring pass Harry said, "Ahoy, Captain Stone. Can you fly somewhere else?"

"Plane's too big," he said. "Need space to maneuver." He circled around the little group. Two of the girls smiled and preened at Francis.

"We're trying to learn how to repair this greenhouse here," Harry said.

"Stand by."

"Right. But Francis, could you *please* fly somewhere else?" Harry let his irritation slip into his voice.

"Free world," Francis said, performing his famous shoulder shrug I-got-you grin for the admiring world. "I'm under orders from Mr. Redburn. Practicing a part for Drama, sir. I'm a B-24 that's lost one engine over the ocean. Have to dump bombs." He shook his butt and grunted and pretended to take a dump. "Got to have a place to splash down, help the crew into survival suits and all that rot. Have to practice. Can't lose anyone. Right? *Sir?*"

Harry didn't answer.

"*Sir?*"

Harry waved vaguely. Francis flapped his arms and buzzed. The Ecology Club girls giggled.

Harry herded his kids inside where small, cracked pots held shrunken wads of dry dirt and faded black stalks of desiccated plants. Ceramic shards littered the floor. The afternoon heat filtered through broken panes. When Harry opened the door, Francis increased his engine noise, a high-pitched irritating hum. It was hard to explain the timing system above Francis' engine noise.

Francis spent another ten minutes zooming around just outside the greenhouse, then popped in to say, "Headed back to the hangar, folks, one motor gone. But don't worry, I'll be right back after repairs. Otherwise, all's well. Bye bye. Captain Stone out."

By some miracle, they got the drip system working before Francis returned.

A few days later, Harry opened his class to find that Francis and Bick, late the previous afternoon, had hung an old-fashioned, black, high-heeled woman's shoe on some monofilament they'd tacked to the ceiling. The shoe dangled just beyond the highest jump of the tallest kids. He considered that Francis might be making a peace offering. Probably not.

A little friendly foolery, fine. What got Harry was Francis's patronizing attitude. Francis would smile facetiously. He'd lick his lips and shrug his expressive shoulders. He used Harry as a straight man, talking around him to the class, adding Sir as an insult. His sly grin said, I'm smarter than you. *Sir.*

Francis's lower lip would quiver and his expression take on a strained tension, as if in fear, whenever Harry spoke to him. If Harry turned his back, laughter erupted behind him.

Harry knew he, himself, was no genius. He was a decent fellow, helpful, knowledgeable. He had twenty years of more or less successful teaching, and he loved it when it went well. He felt that teachers, especially, have to think they are capable or go hang themselves. He had a background in Psychology and taught a bit of Freudian Theory along with Oedipus Rex and Shakespeare and and Kafka and Emily Dickinson, good works from brilliant writers for smart seniors. Like a good parent, Harry tried to like all his students, to find something in each to encourage. But if he complimented Francis, Francis made a joke of it. Who was this clod teacher anyway, to compliment *him?*

"What's on the shoe?" Manuel asked Francis. Harry could see some small white letters above the stiletto heel.

"A poem," Francis said.

"What does it say?"

Bick pursed his lips and started to respond but Francis shushed him. "For all to find out," Francis said. He smiled at Manuel then at Harry. "What's the hot news for today, dearest profe*sor?* Has Dr. Freud answered your post cards yet?"

Grades, of course, were a major issue. Since Francis didn't do homework, and since he spent much precious classroom time talking and joking with Bick and Karen, Harry docked him a grade on his first report card. He gave him a B. Harry didn't grade on tests alone, but also on work done, total points as well as grades on exams. Francis scored A's in four major exams, missed another, asked for a make-up, which he didn't show for, and piled up zeroes on homework.

In class, as he read out grades, Harry told Francis he had to do more than pass tests, that he wrote so well a teacher couldn't challenge him on written exams, but that he could at least challenge himself on some of the homework. Bick and Karen stood at attention behind Francis.

"What makes you think I *don't* challenge myself?" Francis's face glowed with his down-curled smile. He knew something no one else knew. "I challenge myself all the time, *sir.*"

"He challenges himself very hard. Sir," Bick said. "We all do."

"Well, everyone has to turn in homework and participate in class in a positive manner."

"Not good reasons for a B," Francis said, looking down at Harry. 'You give homework and then test us on it…"

"I'm not testing you merely on homework. It's an important part of the learning process in itself. Hopefully, it makes you think. It teaches you to focus, to do research, to prepare for college. I spelled out my grading system when I handed you my AP Requirements sheet. I asked those who didn't like the requirements to drop out then if they didn't like how I set up the class. You had a chance to drop right at the beginning if you wished."

"At the beginning of what?" Francis insisted. "The *Universe?*"

Karen and Bick applauded softly.

Harry held back. Control, he repeated to himself.

"The beginning?" Harry said. "Of *class*. The first day you signed in to class I said that I graded everyone equally on points gained for exams, homework, and general participation. Theoretically, everyone could get an A if they did the work and helped the class run smoothly. It's in the handout. Did you read the Points and Grades handout?"

"I was not here the first week of class. I was in Spain, and my mother is a witness. And you can't grade me down for your opinion of *my* classroom behavior. It's not allowed, *sir.*"

"No, but I can refuse to *give* you points for participation when you don't participate."

"I always participate."

"By participation I mean that you add something *positive* to classroom discussion, that you help others learn."

Francis stood, waggled his shoulders, pumped up his chest and grinned, turning the glow of his smile back and forth between Bick on one side and Karen on the other. They remained stiff as soldiers, standing as he did, hands flat to their sides, their feet spread. The class always laughed, a performance that grew better with repetition. Francis was a great admirer of comic Steve Martin. Repetition is the soul of wit, Francis had once explained to the class.

"Sir," Francis said much too loudly, eyes focused over Harry's head, "can you explain the difference between classroom behavior and classroom participation?"

"Sure," Harry said. "In *participation* you help out, you answer questions, you help others learn how to write their essays, and so on. You help. With poor *behavior*, you make jokes, you try to stop the class from focusing in on schoolwork, you generally try to make a fool of the teacher. In classroom participation you participate. The word implies that you help out. In poor classroom behavior, you behave like a teen clown. For example, you might stop saying sir."

"Excellent, sir. I will relay that message." Francis turned to Karen and Bick and said. "No one here is to call him sir."

"Yes, sir," Bick said. "May we address him as *Master*?"

Francis turned to Harry, gave him a sad, serious look, and said, "I hesitate to transmit this request to you, but some of our crowd want to call you Master."

Harry waggled his head grimly. He threw up his hands. The whole class laughed.

Francis understood there was no real difference at all between the terms classroom behavior and classroom participation, and he knew from his mother that School District policy prevented teachers from docking any student a letter grade because of disruptive classroom behavior, otherwise called Poor Citizenship. Behavior was the key word, so Harry changed the word behavior to participation and doled out points or took them back according to *participation*.

Francis's one weakness was that he wanted an A, or preferably, an A plus. Harry's system threatened to force him to do two things he hated, be quiet in class and turn in homework. Top students got into the best colleges, as Francis and his mother well knew, and many of the best universities required better than an A average, especially for scholarships.

If a kid went over the line, acted out, ran around the room, or threatened anyone, a teacher could call the Vice Principal or the Principal or 911, or, with enormous trouble, create a "paper trail" and suspend the kid, or give him or her a U for Unsatisfactory Citizenship, but a poor Citizenship mark meant nothing to a troubled teen, and a kid tossed out one day could well reappear in class the next. In reality, it was almost impossible to suspend anyone. The District was opposed to suspensions. They lost money for one thing. And it could look bad if the suspended student were from a minority, which Irish Francis was not.

With Harry, Francis stayed just this side of suspension. In that, he was a true genius. If Harry caught up with Francis and his pals outside and tried to explain that he had a hard time teaching while Francis opposed him, Francis would say, "Who's opposing you, sir?"

"C'mon, Francis. You talk while I'm trying to teach. You make jokes at my expense. You're an intimidating presence here. I'm just an ordinary guy with a whole class to teach. Lay off. Your grade will improve."

Francis winked at Harry and ran his tongue over his lips. "Sure thing. In other words, I'll get an A if I behave in class." Karen and Bick stood, as always, at Francis's side.

"If you help us learn, yes. If you participate helpfully."

"If I *behave* nicely, I get an A?"

"If you *participate* by helping out, by not disrupting the class, you'll easily get your A."

"Disrupting?" Francis said. "You hear that comrades? I'll get an A if I just don't bother him? Take that down Chief Commissar Karen. It smacks of capitalist blackmail to me."

"Wrong," Harry said, a familiar sinking pressure in his stomach. He'd tried to be honest with him just a little, in front of witnesses. "You get your A if you do your homework, participate positively, and continue to get A's on your exams. But right now, your classroom participation is holding you back, not to mention your lack of homework."

They went round and around. For one test Harry assigned the class a sonnet to memorize. Most of the class memorized it overnight. Francis refused. He said he had a learning disorder.

"You're in Drama," Harry said. "What happens when you have a part to memorize?"

"That's different."

"How?"

"That's Drama. This is English."

"Touché, Francis." Harry fed him a wan smile.

Still, Harry wasn't ready to touché up Francis's grade. When, after the second grading period, Francis still had a B, his mother, the redoubtable Bernice Stone, Ph.D., Professor of English at California City College, rolled in for a visit.

She smiled. She nodded at a chair. She sat down in class next to Francis. "You have some extra room for an observer, I see."

She was, indeed, imposing, a woman almost as tall as Francis, dressed in a fashionable navy blue suit, a white frilly almost see-through silk blouse cut low to emphasize her impressive, somewhat wrinkled cleavage, still seductive, her breasts pushed forward like Colt revolvers. Her face was stern but attractive, something like a cat's, her round eyes gleaming, eyebrows plucked and lifted quizzically, a faint mustache. When she'd been young she might have been considered beautiful. A big, full-figured woman. But deep frown lines had made her face more manly than feminine. There was, Harry thought, something wrong with her, some unhealthy glow inside her. He couldn't say exactly. Or maybe it was just his own prejudices he saw. Maybe Francis was really all right, Student Body President that he was, a leader. Or, perhaps, Francis and Harry had descended from some ancient warring tribes and were, thousands of years ago, sworn enemies. Maybe Mrs. Stone was merely being motherly, worried about her child's future, sitting upright next to Francis in class, waiting.

Maybe Harry was the crazy one. Depended on your viewpoint, Harry thought. After all, being a teacher was, in many ways, insane. What was *he* doing, well past sixty, still in high school undergoing a high school hazing? He was sure that being a teacher for so long had stunted him in unconscious ways. Still, he generally liked teaching and could hardly imagine any other job quite as challenging.

Being around Francis was painful. Harry, as a rule, tried to avoid direct conflict, but Francis stalked forward, slyly insulting, always ready to pounce on any perceived weakness. Loss of points was no deterrent, only another argument.

In the past, Harry had loved teaching Advanced Placement. He'd been able to talk about the great writers. But face to face with brilliant, hostile Francis, Harry felt his joy ebbing. Now he was glad when AP was over. Francis and his pals posed an unsolvable problem, an equation with far too many variables and no apparent solution. He couldn't get rid of them. He couldn't get along with them. Trapped.

The class was studying Hamlet, and the day's lesson was the relationship between Hamlet and Gertrude. An ironic choice for this son and this visiting mother.

Harry called roll, collected homework. The class, normally loud, seemed particularly subdued. There was an adult visitor. The kids glanced at her warily. Some knew who she was.

After a few polite words about how honored the class was to have Francis's mother observing class today, and a quick, plaster smile from Mrs. Stone herself, Harry plunged into his notes. Harry had battled to a standstill with the son, now the mother had arrived in reserve.

On the back wall a framed poster of Mickey Mouse, three-foot-high in his best brass buttoned stars and stripes shorts, brown clodhopper shoes, and two pancake black ears, waited and smiled in his hopeful, innocent way. You can think of yourself as wise or foolish, Mickey's expression implied, it's all how you look at it.

A naive era, Harry felt, when a cartoon mouse became the international symbol of hope, before and during the most destructive war to that date. After the war a bad-boy duck replaced him.

On the wall behind Harry's desk an oversized Bart Simpson aimed a slingshot into the room. The caption read, *Eat My Shorts*. Even a teacher, Harry wanted to imply, might be rebellious.

What Harry said about Hamlet and Freudian theory was, "We all marry someone somehow similar to our opposite gender parent, and struggle with the parent of the same gender." That was a lot less concise and less powerful than Freud's original, "Men want to have sex with their mothers and kill their fathers." But teachers had been warned by the Superintendent to remain gender neutral in classroom discussion. Nor were public school teachers allowed to discuss sex, certainly not incest. The Superintendent was an Assistant Minister at Ocean Avenue Presbyterian Church.

It used to be, ten years or so ago when Harry first got the idea he could discuss Freudian theory in a high school, that some students might be actually shocked to be told they could be attracted to someone who reminded them of their father or mother. Who was this Freud? And now, since the rise of the Religious Right, Harry had to be careful how he phrased anything, though Oedipal Theory was pretty much old stuff to the more sophisticated kids.

Even The Simpsons had run a program devoted to Freud. Many in the adult world had rebelled against what now seemed to them to be Freud's too obvious insights, wishing to force psychological interpretation back into the Nineteenth Century, to an era just before Freud published his first major work, The Interpretation of Dreams.

Hell, Harry thought. Most of these kids have already seen every kind of pornography on line.

Harry glanced at the Stones. They both frowned. He gave them a friendly smile. They flashed him a mirrored dose of quick smile parodies, lips snarling down over brilliant white teeth for an instant, eyes cold as snakes.

Harry pointed out to the class the father/daughter relationship between Hamlet and Ophelia, and Ophelia and her father, Polonius. "Hamlet kills Polonius, his father-in-law to be, thinking it is his existing stepfather, Claudius, who he suspects of having killed his father. Claudius has not only taken over the Kingdom, but has snuck into Gertrude's bed. This is completely unacceptable to Hamlet, who, though young, knows he should take his father's place as king. Gertrude and Ophelia are described in familial terms, one a mother, the other a daughter, and Hamlet is described in intimate terms as being a young man deeply, sensually attached to his mother Gertrude. He may love Ophelia, who some think is a mother substitute, but in a jealous rage Hamlet rejects her when she spies on him for her father, to whom she has remained deeply attached. The term is libidinal attachment," Harry said. "In some way or another, according to Freud, we all are attracted to the parent of the opposite sex, the boy to the mother, the girl to the father. According to Freud, this is human nature."

"Wow! I hate my father," said Denise. She shrank away in mock horror from her boyfriend, Carlos, in the seat next to her. She was Chinese. He was Mexican. He stared back at her in amazement and opened his arms.

"Bay *beeee*," he said. "Mama*ceeeta.*"

The class laughed. But not Mrs. Stone. She frowned, a dark cloud of judgment on her face. She and Francis began to argue in whispers. Harry shifted from one foot to the other and waited patiently. When they stopped, they gave him their lip down smiles, a family trait Harry decided, not always a scornful grimace.

"My apologies," Mrs. Stone said, as Harry waited for class whispers to die out. Francis looked at Karen and bounced his eyebrows.

Harry said, "When Laertes returns to find both his father and sister dead because of Hamlet, which of the deaths most affect him?"

"Ophelia's," Denise said.

"And how does Laertes behave towards Ophelia?"

The class was quiet. But Francis, who had been suspiciously still, couldn't resist. Splayed out in his undersized desk he said, "You're not asking us to think. You're asking us to parrot back what you think. You want us to say that Laertes has become Ophelia's father. But that's no truer than saying Ophelia is behaving like his mother. It says nothing and everything all at once. Patently B.S., *Sir.*"

He grinned triumphantly at his mother, and then again at Karen. Karen did not look at all like Francis's mother. Karen was tiny, half the size of Mrs. Stone. Her face was thin, almost foxlike, her features fine rather than broad. She was compact, a tidy bosom on a slim body, lovely really, but hardly the centerfold type. Without clothes, she would nearly disappear. But she was a lead dancer in the school's Dance Program.

Of course, Harry was old enough to be Karen's father, even her grandfather. He had tried hard to befriend her, to show he was sympathetic despite her steady support of Francis. She was, unlike Francis, quite friendly when Harry had a chance to talk to her alone. By himself, Bick was more friendly too, or at least polite.

Harry had once asked Karen what she felt he ought to do to get Francis to allow class to move on peacefully.

She shook her head. "*Peacefully?* Good luck with that."

Two Stones, Harry thought as he watched mother and son in their too small seats, but where was the father? Buried. Stoned to death. An offstage ghost. Probably, at some level, Francis and his mother didn't like each other, making any simplistic analogies with Freudian theory difficult. But Freud was hard to argue against. If you hated your mate, it was because you hated your parents. Or you were in denial. That's a nice one. If you were a son who hated your mother, you'd be acting out a disappointment in your desire to have a better mother. Trapped by Freudian logic.

"Anyway," Harry told them, "it's not necessarily a physical resemblance Freud was discussing, but any resemblance, especially in personality. We're always judging people in terms of how we related to our parents. We take the familiar, what we learn as infants, and paste the new over it so we can understand what the new is all about. It's a starting point."

Harry waited, walking from one side of the room to the other, nearer the Disney posters. No one responded or nodded or took notes. Denise and Manuel whispered to each other. Some doodled on their desks. After a few moments, Sam, a Pakistani, raised his hand, and Harry said hopefully, "Yes?"

"I got to go to the toilet."

The class giggled. It was a tired old joke, but well timed.

Mrs. Stone raised her hand and asked if she could say a word or two. Harry said yes, but asked her to wait until he completed this part of his lesson. He paused to explain to the class that Dr. Stone taught English at City College. Then she rose and stood before the class, as if she hadn't heard Harry ask her to wait.

Harry shrugged. He smiled politely. He sat.

She began, "It's dangerous when an untrained teacher spouts unfamiliar theories as if they were the whole truth. In the first place, Freudian theory has been debunked. No one believes in it any more. The very idea that there's a libidinal attachment between sons and mothers and daughters and fathers was based on Nineteenth Century misinformation and dreams and lies. We've lived through the worst of Freudian hypocrisy, and it's a shame to bring it up again as if it were a religious creed. Basically, Freud says that we are the victims of our instincts and early parental training, but others know we have individual minds capable of freedom of choice and the ability to control ourselves."

Throughout all this she half smiled the same all-knowing irritating smile that Francis had. She occasionally turned to Harry as if for agreement. His face reddened. He could imagine how flushed he must appear to the class. If he'd expected any polite phrases from her, her first words crushed that. He wanted to take Bernice Stone by the collar and heave her violently through the door. He might as well keep going out the door with her then, but the pleasure of hurting her might be worth it. Patience is a virtue, he thought. Also a weakness.

"It's noble of you to try to introduce something such as Freudian theory at this age, but you have to be more balanced and let your class know that the theories are just that, theories mostly based on case studies, not on scientific experimentation. You might benefit from reading someone like Frederick Crews, The Pooh Perplex, for example, or the Madness of Crowds."

God in Heaven, Harry said to himself. Will this period ever fucking *end!*

"Thank you, Doctor Stone," he said aloud, rising as if to dismiss her. Great. He had been exposed as a phony. He looked down at his scuffed, worn shoes as he gathered his thoughts, though he couldn't talk for a moment. If he had spoken it would be in curses, not even curses expressly for Bernice Stone, but for the world, for himself too, for allowing her to take over the class. What right had this woman to come uninvited and undercut a teacher in front of his students? How would she like it? Harry thought.

What right had she to set him up as an ignorant fanatic who believed so deeply in some perverted form of Freudian theory that his teaching was dangerous? She'd cut Harry off in mid argument. She'd just done it. She'd implied he was a teacher who not only didn't know what he was talking about, but who spread perverted lies. And he'd let her take over. He was passive, a fool easily run over. He had to say something. He tried to see the humor in his situation. Why couldn't he?

"Freudian theory," Harry bent forward and spoke slowly, "is something I studied for four years as a candidate for a PhD in Clinical Psychology. I don't think it is the absolute truth…"

"In that case," she interrupted, "you should not present it as if it were. You might wish to return to your clinical studies and refresh your ideas, and until you do, I would appreciate it if you didn't try to teach such garbage to my son." The edge in her voice was razor thin. There was a soft intake of breath among students.

Only a few minutes until lunchtime. When Mrs. Stone sat down, Harry asked the class to exchange notes and begin to prepare an essay on today's lecture, pro and con. He sat and looked at his grade book, though he was too angry to concentrate. He shook his head clear. Bernice Stone had condemned psychological interpretation as faulty. A work of art such as Hamlet should not be limited to some absurd psychological approach she'd said, and he agreed. A Freudian interpretation was only one approach. But Bernice had interrupted him in mid argument and set him up as a fanatic Freudian who taught trash.

The bell rang. He imagined his hands around Mrs. Stone's throat, his thumbs dug deep into her larynx.

It took a moment to relax his clenched fists. If he wanted to keep teaching he had to watch himself.

He collected homework papers and fiddled at his desk hoping she would leave, but she waited at the door. It was time to eat, to relax for a moment and prepare for the last two classes of the day. He took a breath. Why should anyone try to teach anything to anyone?

"I hope you didn't find my ideas too intrusive." She moved next to him, her voice seductive, whisper soft, coming at him as if she were inside his right ear. He shuddered.

"Oh," Harry said with his most indifferent tone, repeating, "Oh," lying in word and body language. "Different points of view."

"Yes," she said. "An alternative view. And thank you for being so hospitable. But now I have something else to discuss with you."

He grunted. *I wonder how my life would change if I just hit her in the fucking stomach?* But he merely spoke a pleasant, questioning, "Yes." Better to listen and not argue, let it all go, and then escape quickly. One probably shouldn't kill a parent.

She smelled like gardenias, and her perfume filled the room now that all the students had gone. Her earrings were gold inlaid with three tiny diamonds. She'd put on her power. It occurred to Harry that she might have feared this confrontation. He'd thought that she might phone in to question Francis's grade, but so few parents ever came to school that Harry had been surprised when she appeared. An apparition. *I am thy mother's spirit.* What could he have done today anyway? Not teach Oedipal theory, for one thing. Or they could have gone to the zoo and discussed the feeding habits of lions. She must be an expert on beasts of prey.

She was an inch or two taller than Harry. She leaned against the desk and looked down at him. Her frilled bosom slid toward his throat.

"You gave Francis a B."

"Yes." Francis kept his voice friendly. "He didn't do the required homework. He didn't take an exam."

"He says he got A's on your other exams."

"All but the one he didn't take."

"He wanted to take it."

"I gave him a chance and he didn't show."

"He clearly understands the material. I know because I home tutor him. And I also hire the best tutors in all subjects."

"Yes. He's always at the top of any exam."

"I'd like to look at your grade book."

He hesitated. "Fine," he said.

Harry's elaborate grading system, a series of points added or subtracted from a total that led to a letter grade, reflected everything a student might do in class. It was his "capitalistic" grading system, as Francis had said. It was available for all students to see. He tried to explain it to Mrs. Stone, but she held a peremptory right index finger up for silence. She laid her left breast against his right arm for a moment, nudging him aside. She leaned directly over the grade book, her palms flattened over the scattered papers on his desk, wrists cocked, elbows out pushing him even farther away.

"This grade book seems very elaborate. I see here that Karen and Bick have more points than Francis."

"Well. They participate somewhat more in classroom discussions. It's not a big part of the grade, but it can knock a student down a notch. And they do their homework."

"Francis says you don't like him, that you grade him down for what you say is his classroom behavior. That's not appropriate. I thought I'd come and see if you were doing that, and I see you are." She moved back triumphantly.

"No, it's not his behavior but his positive participation in the activities of the class that I find difficult. Anyway, I don't dislike Francis." That wasn't exactly a lie. Dislike wasn't the right word. He more than disliked Francis, and this woman. Two birds, one filthy nest.

"Your own grades tell a different story. I suggest you change that system."

"Yes. We see this differently. At any rate, another thing that held Francis back this grading period was his failure to take the sonnet memorization test."

"Your *yes* means you will change your policy on behavior?"

"As I said, we differ. I've explained my grading to Francis."

"And he explained it to me, so I do understand how clever you think you are."

Harry moved without comment to the doorway, gesturing with his shoulders for her to leave, leaning on the frame so that a hinge dug hard into his back. Mrs. Stone followed, took a step beyond him into the hall, and blocked his way. Students wandered by. Some smiled and waved at Harry, trapped inside his little space, his own classroom. He thought of a line from a Stevie Smith poem that went, "And not waving, but drowning."

He counted slowly to himself, and thought of being out on the beautiful blue ocean on a calm day. Childhood at the beach. Fishing. He would fish for his peace of mind, for a peaceful, vibrant world starting right here in his classroom, right now. He took a deep breath. Held it. Let it go. For an instant he relaxed. One brief moment.

"Francis told me about the sonnet memorization," she said. "I was utterly astounded that a supposedly intelligent man like yourself should require Advanced Placement students to memorize something as archaic as a sonnet by Shakespeare. What in God's name were you thinking?"

Whatever she said, he thought, let it go by. Answer her rationally. Get out. Go eat.

"I was thinking my students would have something to refer to when they needed a quote or two for an Advanced Placement essay. Also, that a memorized sonnet might stay with them for the rest of their lives."

"Umm. Yes. Francis has a problem memorizing. Did he tell you that?"

"Yes. Still, that's the assignment. If he were interested I'm sure he could memorize it. He is in Drama, after all."

"And did you know he suffers from migraines, that he's Student Body President, the president of three school clubs, and is taking two other AP classes, and two college level classes at State?" Her eyes filled with tears. She took a deep breath. Her chest heaved passionately toward Harry, who tried to back up further into the doorframe. When she exhaled her breath smelled of stale coffee and cigarettes.

No wonder he has migraines, Harry nearly said. But he looked at Mrs. Stone's aging face and for a second saw her not as his personal enemy, but as an eccentric mother trying to protect her son. Perhaps she was going to all Francis's teachers, pleading for mercy. It would be hell to live with her, but she cared about Francis, and Harry's heart softened an ounce, though he desperately wanted to get away from her and have lunch. He was exhausted. He needed time and space and enough food to take him through the afternoon. This knot between Francis and Bernice Stone could take a lifetime to unravel, and he didn't want to get tangled into it any longer than necessary. He had two more classes. He wanted to sit at his desk and put his head down and close his eyes. Perhaps he could tell Joe he was too sick to teach the rest of the day. But he would stick it out, not out of pride, but because it was something he'd planned to do, the lessons all laid out, and only twenty minutes left for lunch. *Twenty minutes!*

"I know about his clubs," Harry said. "I didn't know about the migraines or the other classes." Despite himself, he felt a tinge of sympathy for Bernice. She was a mother. For a moment he wondered what she would do if he reached over and wiped away her tears. She might sue him.

"I'm sorry," Harry said. He couldn't say sorry for what. For everything, for his dislike of Francis, for his dislike of Mrs. Stone. Bernice. He wanted to like her, it would be easier to be helpful, his true, cowardly, liberal nature oozing out to comfort Bernice Stone who didn't want any comfort at all and might have screamed rape if Harry had so much as leaned toward her.

"And why are you teaching Shakespeare at all at this time and age?" she said, suddenly. She banged down her right heel on the floor as she emphasized her words. "Today's *students* want something *relevant*, like Richard *Wright*. Did you ever *hear* of Richard *Wright*? Of Native *Son*? Of Ntozake Shange? "

Harry did know about them. He'd taught Native Son in American Literature. He'd attended one of the first Berkeley performances of Ntosake Shange's *For Colored Girls Who Have Considered Suicide When the Rainbow Is Enuf*. But before he could respond, Mrs. Stone, her black heel striking hard again, said, "No, of course you haven't! You don't know anything about Black Literature. That's the sad situation. Most high school teachers are caught in the past teaching things that kids no longer find relevant to their lives, such as

Shakespeare. Try Leroi Jones. James Baldwin. *For God's Sake!* Don't you even know who James Baldwin is? Or Zora Neale Hurston? *Their Eyes Were Watching God?* Of course not. Of course not. You should make up you own lessons, find your own books. Young people need to read books relevant to their lives. My God, it's thirty years since the Civil Rights Movement. *Where... Were... You?"*

Harry was boiling again. She had no idea what he knew or didn't know or what he'd done in the past. He'd fought for Black Literature in the Sixties at Oakland Tech, in the center of the Black Power Movement where Huey Newton and the Black Panthers had demanded relevant works. He'd bought books by Black authors with his own salary. He knew Bobby Seale and Huey Newton. David Hilliard had spoken in this very class. Harry had been at the eye of a whirlwind, demanding that African Americans have books they could relate to. He'd fought against the John Birch Society. He could tell her so much, but he was seething. He knew James Baldwin. He'd had a luncheon conversation with him long ago at Kay Boyle's. Ridiculous, if he said it. He looked down, avoiding her eyes.

Lunch.

He was paying attention to her, though, noticing how her mind worked, one that didn't wait for answers or knowledge beyond what it already knew. He watched her huge earrings glitter under the overhead lights of the room. Food. He wanted to sleep even for five minutes, to lie on the couch in the Teacher's Lounge. He wanted her to go away. Her earrings jingled as she chopped her hands up and down and rebuilt her case against Freud and ignorance and against Shakespeare and teacher indifference, reminding Harry again that Francis was not only taking all these outside classes, but was lead actor in Marat/Sade, a very complex part.

"I will ask your Principal if we can keep Francis enrolled in Advanced Placement English and just take the exam. I want him to attend English classes at the college level. The college classes are a much better test of his abilities. So what you should do is take all this into account and give Francis his much deserved A." Her heel tapped softly.

Harry absorbed her words and said nothing at all, merely leaned against the doorframe against the all too real hinge digging into his left shoulder blade, reminding him of the outside world where the steaming pleasures of the San Francisco State Cafeteria curled up from pizza or rice and beef stew.

But the hallways were crowding up. It was nearly time for the next bell for the next class. No lunch today, a crushing realization. He'd thought, for a brief moment, to make friends with Mrs. Stone. She'd squashed him before he could make even a small gesture, a crude, bitter, self important woman. Once again, she condemned his teaching, even the subject matter, even poor old Hamlet, which he was required to teach in English Literature. *Shakespeare*. He loved Shakespeare.

His stomach growled and he felt a bit queasy. If he defended himself, if he told her that he'd been something of a pioneer in black literature, the confrontation would drone on, the situation worsen. Anyway, this discussion involved only one student. He had a whole class to consider, five classes in fact, a hundred and eighty kids. A job. Patience was something he'd had to learn step by step over the years. He didn't want to argue with Francis or his mother or anyone. With such a mother, Francis had made himself invulnerable. Let mother and son work out their affairs themselves. He had something valuable to teach to other kids, and if Francis didn't want to learn it, fine. Maybe Mrs. Stone was right and Francis was an exception to all the rules. Who could say this particular information, Harry's so-called teaching, was important, that it could add even the least bit to Francis' life. Of course Harry's teaching wasn't important in Francis' mind, for he would never miss what he didn't let in. He'd learn what his mother wanted him to learn, or whatever his own prideful, isolated mind found. *He was a genius!* Why should Harry try to get genius Francis to understand his ideas of Hamlet or Freud when Francis had all the answers already, with an important mother as back-up army. Francis' brilliant mind could easily lead to success, whereas he, Harry Selke, was simply a high school teacher, someone to step past, a road sign. Harry didn't like to think of himself that way, but he tried to understand when anger or opposition or failure was not in the best interests of a student. He was a teacher, not a dictator. He took a deep breath and held it, then let it out fast.

Now Mrs. Stone reiterated carefully and logically how *she* taught, what books *she* used. He could learn from her, she said. She would send him her book list. He could take college courses. Harry nodded. He was bored with her arguments. He was finished with them. He leaned back. Anything now. Francis could drop the class, Harry suggested. *No*, she'd said. That wasn't what she wanted for Francis, not an option. That would show how prejudiced Harry was toward Francis. She wanted Harry to give him credit for AP. But Francis could concentrate on his college classes and not have to actually *attend* Advanced Placement. He was going on to university, and needed a scholarship. He must have credit. A grade of B just would not do.

"Yes," Harry said. Some students were waiting to come in for Fifth Period. It was too late to eat. Take Francis out of class, please. Get this woman away from me. Let him drop the class, and I'll give him credit. I'll even pay him to stay away.

"Certainly," Harry said. "He can take the AP Exam. Fill out a request form in the office, that's all."

Harry's body itched all over… his scalp, his back and arms, even his legs. He rubbed the small of his back against the comforting door hinge. He'd never last in a prisoner of war camp. His skin would fall off, his teeth rot, he would reveal anything, and Mrs. Stone would be commandant. He took her by her fleshy upper right arm, squeezed hard, feeling the bone, and turned her forcibly toward the hall.

"I have a class," he said. "Please excuse me." His shove was firm.

She stumbled, and for a moment Harry imagined her spread out on the floor. That would be satisfying but hard to explain. He caught her by her belt. "So sorry," he said.

"Thank you," she said in a very angry voice. Her heels clicked down the hall as three students from the next class filed in.

Harry gave his class some reading to do and he sat down and breathed. Maybe it was a good thing not to eat lunch. He could lose weight. He felt his empty stomach rise and fall, and wondered how old he would be when he died, how long he would last. Eighty two, he had once predicted, and twenty years to go. He didn't want to hold himself to that prediction. He might live longer. Or, if more Stones showed up and he stayed in this bloody job, he might die right away. Patience, as a defense, went just so far. Thirty to forty students per class, five classes a day. One day an angry mother, the next a sorrowful pregnant teen looking for salvation. He could take minimum retirement. Then what? He needed a job and he was pretty old to find another. He sometimes loved teaching. It was always interesting, if often overwhelming. Some kids he helped, some he fought with. Sometimes he had a great day, and other days were depressing, as with Bernice Stone. And Francis. A little flash of energy surged through him as he thought of class without Francis. He'd believe it when it happened. What would Francis's troops do? The odd thing was, he liked Bick and Karen. They were, in some ways, just like Harry. Alone, they spoke to him openly. Karen had hinted at a secret she'd wanted to tell him, and tears had come to her eyes when she came to class one lunch time. It seemed she wanted to trust him, but couldn't say.

"Go on," Harry said, his heart warming. "I'm here." But her tears stopped her.

Bick, too, had come in angry with Francis one time and had almost explained why, but when Francis called from the door, Bick's eyes lit up and his full red lips pursed thoughtfully and he told Harry, "Later."

After the last students of the last class of the day filed out, Harry got the janitor's fifteen-foot stepladder and wrestled it under the hanging shoe in the middle of the room. It was probably Bernice Stone's shoe. He climbed up and turned the shoe in his hand and read Francis and Bick's poem written in White-Out above the scuffed black heel:

Snow in Springtime.
Shoe fills with snow.

Poor souls. High heels.

Poor souls everywhere. He left it swaying slowly, and there it stayed motionless for another ten years. Once or twice a month he looked up and noticed it, and sometimes smiled, and once a year or so he explained where it came from to a new class. For a couple of years some students recalled Francis and Bick and Karen. Then, for another few years the shoe with its sharp, black heel was just a familiar oddity glistening under the lights, dangling, with all its energy melted away.

When he retired it was still there.

At the Border

Usually we drive right through, and if there is a question it's from the American border guards re-entering San Diego, but this time my Subaru Outback gets pulled over by a Mexican Customs Officer as we cross in to Tijuana. He's a skinny geek older than me with what looks like chicken bones stuck in his throat. His uniform is dark brown and grease spotted and the under arms of his jacket are a moldy green. He's a poor representative of the noble Nation of Mexico. His grey jaws work slowly side to side across a wad of tobacco. I've let my grandson Joe drive, and he's not much for kissing the ass of anyone in authority, especially someone with green armpits, though this sad looking Federale also packs a shiny 45-caliber pistol in a shiny black holster.

"What you declare, *senores?*" He's sweating in the dry heat, a hot Santa Ana wind blowing down off the mountains, very unusual for early October. I'd heard the border was tightening up, both sides, that tourists were sometimes being harassed by Mexican Customs, but this is the first time I'd ever been stopped and asked even one question on my way in. I don't like it, but it's undoubtedly retribution against Americans, who many Mexicans see as obnoxious and superior. What can a humble Mexican do to complain, though? Americans are rich and Mexicans are poor, and most of Latin America wants to live in California del Norte, where a laborer can pick up a job and send money home to his family. It is as it is.

El Norte. Home of the arrogant and the rich.

I understand these feelings, as far as I understand anything, but it's all confusing because there are so many Mexicans that want to live and work here that the American way of life and culture could be overwhelmed. What do they know of George Washington and his cherry tree, or Mother Jones, or Jack Benny?

The Mexican Customs Agent grows a bit irritated at Joe's silent stare out the windshield.

Completely sensitive to the situation as usual, Joe answers at last, using his flat, western hero voice, his imitation of dead pan humor, saying, "We got enough dreams stashed here to sink a battleship." It's a paraphrase of the ending of a Juan Ramon Jimenez story I used to read to him when he was little. It amazes me that he remembers it.

I quiver at his answer. I imagine that all the Customs Officer hears is "stash… sink a battleship." He gives us the *ahah!* eye, stares at the four of us, three hopelessly young people, my twenty-year-old grandson, my twenty-two year-old granddaughter and dark-eyed, twelve-year-old Angela, who we call "Bacon." And me. A grandfather.

El Agente de Aduana curls one forefinger at Joe to get out of the car.

Without really intending to antagonize anyone, Joe's tone of voice had an edge to it, sort of a what-kind-of-shit-is-this tone. It echoed from way deep in his chest. Hollow. bored.

"Oh, hey *dude*…" Joe starts to say, but stops suddenly as he looks carefully into the face of the dude customs guy, who stares back at him hard and puts his hand on his 45.

"Joe," I say. "This is the man's job. He's gotta ask these questions."

All we'd wanted to do was go swimming. Now it looks like we're going to be stuck here while we get searched. This old guy is going to shake us down. We must look like suckers, hot dollars ready to drop into his shaky fingers.

Joe used to be a little shit who irritated people by following them around and tugging on them as if he were about to ask a question. He'd say, "Ahhh…" and you'd wait for him to finish his thought, but he never would. Now he's a big shit, and while he can be very funny if you take time to understand his humor, most people who don't know him only hear the sharp edge of his words. If he'd lived in the Old West, he'd have had to develop a fast gun. He's tall and muscular from hard work, and pretends he doesn't give a good goddam about anything, but is innocent and gullible as an Easter bunny, and given any reason to do so, would trust a rabid coyote.

"Amigos," says the Customs Officer in a worn, raspy voice, "park el Subaru over there while we check you up." He indicates what looks like a junkyard of autos, some old, some new, some squashed this way or that. The Customs guy looks at Joe's license. He looks at mine. He says to Joe, "You got the papers for the car?"

I do. I fumble through a side pocket and show the registration to him. He says to Joe, "How about you, muchacho?"

Joe doesn't know what to make of this. "I'm the owner," I say, trying to guess what he wants. "He's my grandson. He's just driving for me."

"Gramson?" the officer says. "Ah... su nieto." He collects the registration and our drivers licenses. Angela is too young to have I.D. so when he reaches toward her she shrinks back in terror. "You got no papers?" he says to her. She squirms and looks at me hopelessly from the corners of her wet eyes. Her upper lip curls up flat against her nose; she's about to cry. I'm supposed to save her.

"She's our friend from San Diego," I say to the Officer. "She's only twelve. We're just headed for a swim at Rosarito Beach. We're returning to San Diego this afternoon, around three."

"A las trece," he says.

He waits, his foot on the bottom of the open door frame. He pushes down and lets up several times, rocking the car. The lump of tobacco in his cheek shifts rapidly one side to another. I see from his frown that he doesn't like Joe.

Maybe I should offer him a little gift. I know how this works. But he motions with the flat of his hand for us to stay in the car, says something to himself in Spanish, and, shaking his head, disappears into a cement building.

I say, "Jesus, Joe. Don't joke around with these Mexican border cops. "

"Right," Joe says in a dead voice. He always says right to everything. Tania punches the back of his head hard with the palm of her right hand.

"Hey! What did I do?" His voice rises in an oppressed, younger brother wail.

"You said something the cop didn't understand, dude, and you said it in a way that sounded like you were hostile. *Your tone of voice*, you know what I mean? *Tone?*" Tania calls it as she sees it. She's the elder sister, after all.

"Right…yeh…"

We park next to the little cement office. Sweating in the hot car, air conditioning full blast, we wait and stare at the building. The smell of our bodies mixes with a deeper stench of unseen garbage.

We wait. A half hour passes. Nothing. Nada.

Frowning, but trying to smile, Tania says to me, "Dude, I'm fried." She gets up and starts to walk toward a shady spot behind the cement building. She's an attractive girl with a flirty hip and a homemade white skirt of something flimsy that slips down far enough to reveal a butterfly tattoo over her butt. Not exactly a sexpot, but attractive, with enough family features to prove she belongs to us. She usually has a guy or two chasing after her.

Joe too, looks like me a little, his nose small but shapely, a silly-sweet smile from ear to flapping ear when he's not trying to look tough. We've been explaining to him how he got us in trouble by the way he said what he said, and he finally gets tired of answering "Right," or "Right on," and gets royally pissed. "Okay. Now fuck you all," is the sullen variation he offers.

I regret this trip now, but it was my idea, so I have to try to smile and be patient and keep up everyone's spirits. I am responsible for these two grandchildren staying the summer, and for Angela, my neighbor's daughter, so I thought I'd give them a special trip, a little excitement in Mexico, as if Rosarito Beach were significantly different than the strand in San Diego, thirty miles north. Same waves, same sandcrabs, same everything, all the illusions of travel to a foreign country rolled into a day, the cultures being so close to each other on the border that only the language and the greater poverty of Tijuana contrasts Baja California to California del Norte. And no special visa or passport needed, a driver's license and an American accent enough to get you in and out, to at least Rosarito, ordinarily no hassle, except for today. You just never know what's next when you leave the safety of the familiar. Could be death, love, a shakedown, a bargain in woolen blankets woven by Tarahumara women, a ceramic pink and purple pig, a virgin sister.

"My seester," young Mexican men say to men in cars waiting to return across the border. "She a voorgin."

At last the old geek comes out of the building with a short, bow-legged, indian looking officer, a man you might find in a blanket selling turquoise jewelry at an Arizona road stand. His black bangs hang low over a glistening, brown, moon-shaped face. He's so young, his face so eager that it's difficult to take him seriously, but he has an automatic rifle strapped to his back, and his eyes over a white smile are hard obsidian pebbles.

The young officer says, "We looking on the computer, and this car got a hold on it. So, *vamanos, amigos*, get out and stand against that side the building. We check him out." He stares at Tania's butt suspiciously, while his eyes travel up and down her figure as if she were a ripe mango. Under her fluffy skirt she has on her white short-shorts above which is a white tank top, and a lot of skin shows through, including her ringed belly button, the style these days. I hate the cold way this man looks at her.

We stand in the shade nest to the Aduano sign.

"A hold?" I say to the three young people. It slowly hits me as the two men dig into the car and start throwing things out. "That can't be."

But I catch Joe's guilty expression and see that it is. "Jo… eee…" I say, my voice rising. He's been borrowing my car a lot lately, chasing after girls, the ordinary thing for an eighteen year old boy. I'm a replacement for his dad, who accidentally blew his house and himself up with some stored dynamite.

"Did you…*do* something with this car I don't know about, Joe?"

"Nothing serious," he says, ever so slowly. "We hit somebody's dog. It wasn't nobody's fault, man. It was just an old dog. Dude, the dog ran out in the street."

"A dog?" I'm completely puzzled. Why is he telling me about this dog? "Then what?"

"Nothing. I gave the owner all the money I had."

"All the money you had? What was that?"

"Ten bucks."

"Then?"

"Nothing. I split."

"And you reported it to the police and these Mexican border patrol guys got hold of it?"

All this is said quietly as we stand in the bleached hot sun while the Mexican Customs Agents go through the car, tearing out everything and throwing it out in a pile. They take our picnic lunch from our cooler and place it on the hot asphalt where the wicker basket begins to sink in.

"I just split," Joe says. He grins. "You know."

"Split! Where'd you leave the car?"

"Well, I wasn't driving. I was sort of stoned. I got out to look at the dog, see?"

I'm trying to picture all this. Joey was in this car somewhere when it probably got into a hit and run on a dog and the whole thing is somehow on the computer here in Tijuana. I stare at him, my face hard.

He squirms for a moment and tries to hide his discomfort. "See, what I didn't tell you there was a bunch of angry dudes running up, so I threw ten bucks down on the dog and hauled my sorry ass away and jumped in the car."

Tania screams and laughs loud enough to make the two Customs Officers look our way. They hold up two Budweiser beer bottles, my lunch beer.

"*What we got here?*" the young one shouts over at us.

I have to think. But right now I want to strangle Joe. Little Joey. I used to throw him up in the air. Now he can throw *me* in the air. Angela is afraid and sniffling. I shrug and push my hands palms up at the Aduaneros. "Lunch," I shout.

"You hit a dog," I say quietly to Joe. "Threw ten dollars on its carcass, and jumped in the car, which you let some jerky buddy of yours drive… *my car!*… and drove off as a hit-and-run. And they have a hold on us here at the border for something you did where? In…San Diego?" I take a deep breath. "Something doesn't make sense, dear Joe…eee." I see the worst flying toward us.

"Right." Joe says. "Errr… Well…"

"What, then?"

"Well. The angry dudes were Mexican."

"And you were here, in Tijuana," I say, hoping it's not true.

I had to hear it from him. To get out of this I must know exactly what happened. If only a little prayer worked, I could pray us out of here, just rise up and fly away. *Holy Mary, Madre de Dios, take us back to our safe little home in Los Estados Unidos del Norte.*

"*Here*, then?" I insist.

"Umm… here."

"Tijuana?"

"Right."

"You drove here on your own, crossed into Mexico, in my car? You didn't *tell* me?"

"It's no big deal," he says, his voice lifting half in anger. "My buds do it all the time."

"Your buds? *My* car!?" I say stupidly. Memories flit like an old film badly edited, Joe in the back yard with chocolate and mud smeared over his mouth, the time he fell asleep at the wheel of his buddy's pickup and slammed into a ditch, the filthy cast he wore for six months on his right ankle, the surprised zero on his face as he tripped into the chilly waters of The Feather River, me slapping his three-year-old wrist as he tried to grab the steering wheel out of my hands while I was driving. My grandson. His lovely smile. Age four, a frog squirms in his hand. Six years old, his feet kick up dust at a Doc Watson concert and he crows like a rooster as two girls walk by ignoring him. Ten, a seagull at the zoo swoops down and steals his hamburger right from the paper plate in his hands and he jumps and flaps his arms trying to fly as he chases it.

After a few moments I add, "Is that all, Joe. The whole story?"

"Ummm…" Joe leaves me hanging anxiously. "Not exactly…"

"Well, *exactly what?*"

Joe looks over at the Customs Officers. "I think the old guy is the dude who owned the dog."

"What do you mean, *think?*"

"I'm pretty sure. I seen him holding the dog. Pretty sure he saw me too."

We're silent for a long time. I want to pound him. He's too big. I can send him back to his mother, my daughter, if I can ever drag him back across the border. One thing I can't do is leave him to rot in a Mexican jail. Maybe for a week…

The Customs Officers hold up objects from time to time. They smile at us. They waggle a box of Trojan prophylactics. *My own grandson*, old enough to use rubbers, so how old does that make me?

The old one holds up a baggie and yells gleefully, "*Marijuana!*" That hits me. This is dangerous. I can't look at Joe.

He says, "Hey…"

I hiss, "*Shut the fuck up!*"

They take out the seats and slice them open with a knife, and then rip open the door upholstery, and ask me politely for my keys so they can search the luggage compartment. They search the engine compartment too. After a while the car looks like it's been bombed, everything piled up next to it, a stack of picnic food and blankets and clothes all tumbled together, the upholstery all ripped to shreds. All in all they find, besides the beer, some rubbers, a matchbox of joints, and a baggie of marijuana.

"That's evil, dude," Joe says. "I wasn't even carrying no weed. That's not mine."

Tania and I nod uh-huh at each other. Angela wears a brave, smiling face, but tears ooze out of her eyes. What she thinks I can only guess, but she must feel the tension. I want to swear, but I try to hide my anger.

"No, man," Joe says, nodding his head, standing his ground. "Even I wouldn't carry no dope *into* Mexico. What for?"

"Even you…" Tania says sarcastically.

"I want to go home," Angela says. "Mom's gonna be worried."

Tania puts her arm around Angela and hugs her. "Grampa will get us out of here soon."

But this Grampa is not so sure.

We're far away on the wrong side of the border, on the wrong side of everybody's law. One moment your world is fine, you're home with a glass of beer and a ballgame on TV, and suddenly, you step outside, and your life changes in a flick. Strike three.

I imagine dingy little Mexican jails. Beatings. Tania…

My mind kicks in. I tell Joe not to mention the dog, even if the old man accuses him. "Just pretend to be as stupid as you are!"

I walk, smiling grimly, over to the two officials, "Senores. Es necessario hablar."

"Si," the young one says, but the old one shakes his head no. He throws some old road maps on the melting asphalt.

"We got a what you say, the warrant for this car," the old one says. "And this marijuana. No es possible."

I'm getting the Tijuana version of good cop, bad cop.

"Senores. Hay un problemo." I smile with a friendly intake of breath. "A mistake of youth. Tengo muchos amigos en Tijuana, and tengo mucho dinero en mi casa en San Diego. Claro, es posible encontrar uno acuerdo."

"Tal vez," the young one says. "Pero esta muy dificile. Es mucho dinero para el fraccion."

"We got to arrest you, now, senor. No later. And," says the old guy, "Conozco a su nieto. No?"

I raise the palms of my hands and shrug, my heart sinking. I wave Joe over, and he strides up. He makes an effort. He smiles.

"Don' I know you, amigo?" says the old one.

"Uhhh… No sir. I never seen you before." His tone is respectful.

"But a little case of un perro, a dog, muchacho?"

"Dog?" Joe says. He says it with a soft rising tone, smiling. He can look right at you and tell you the most outrageous lie.

"Mi perrito run over en la calle la semana pasada, and you car and you there. Es verdad?"

"No, sir. This is the first time I been to Tijuana in my life. And this is my grampa's car here."

"We check on la computadora, hokay?"

"Wait," I say, desperately. "Por favor. Before everything es muy complicado, no? Es necessario hablar." I'm cursing myself for my baby Spanish. It's not at all clear what I have to do, offer a bribe, yes, take a chance on being arrested for offering a bribe, but make it a good thing to accept and a bad thing to refuse, but how to do it without insulting Los Federales, Christ, come on great mother of invention, kick in, invent up. Let the juices flow. Let the story unroll itself.

The young one nods to the old bony one. The young guy is clearly in charge, so I look at him only. Clearly he understands English very well. His facial responses are quick, outlined in furrowed brow and hard lips, then just as suddenly a tight smile, lightning, a brilliant flash of his too white teeth in his smooth, dark brown face. I send the kids back behind to the building.

"Go to the other side," I say in a deep grandfatherly voice. I've spoken to my gang firmly and established control. The guards must think I have some authority. I own a new Subaru, after all. Compared to them I must look like a millionaire. All Americans are rich.

"Senores. I am very sorry about el perro. I know my grandson, and he is not a person to hurt a dog. The car was here, yes, but my grandson was not driving. But I would like to give you both some little gift for all this inconvenience. Un regalo for el perro, senor," I say to the older man, "and a gift for you, too, for your own efforts in controlling crime here in Tijuana," I say to the younger. "Soy un amigo con El Jefe de Policia, Colonel de la Fuentes, and with Ernest Grimes, el patrón of the San Diego Tribune, and they have many muy importante amigos in Tijuana on newspapers and in la policia, no?"

I let that sink in. They look at each other but say nothing.

"You are lucky to have met me, senores. This is a serious matter, the car all torn apart, the mystery of the marijuana. "

I shake my head at them and frown a bit.

"But my friends can help you, if you want them to. And I can help you with some dinero for your efforts here. But this little incident must not go too far, for I am an honorable man, and so are you both. This could become muy serioso, muy malo. Pero, no es necesário." I reach for my wallet. "Tengo aqui dos ciento dolares, US, and I am going to give este dinero to you, amigoes, un regalo, so you may clear this up." I say this to the youngest, his quick eyes flashing, "un regalo para la policia, to do as you wish." I keep talking to the younger as the old one tries to break in.

"But you see, senor, esta muy serioso, porque mucho marijuana," the old one says, at last, his voice harsh. He struggles with his words. "Mucho mas dinero. Si?"

"Ah, si," I say. "Esta muy serioso por todos. But for the good of the police force, and for you and for all of us, it may be best to personally keep la marijuana as evidence. Pruebas, no?" I point at it. "When you need it in case of an even more serious crime, si?"

I hold my hands forward, and slowly move a fist full of twenties slowly towards the youngest officer. "You do not have much to gain if you arrest us," I say. I speak very carefully, looking him right in his dark eyes, waiting for him to think about what I've said. The old one won't shoot me, but the possibility that the young one might crosses my mind. "Si ustedes detene las personas aqui entonces obtene nada, for surely the marijuana will be taken into custody by otro policia para evidencia, as well as the two hundred dollars. Aqui esta uno ciente dolares Americano por cada uno. No problema, si? And then my friend who owns the big San Diego newspaper would not have to write about how some policia are arresting honest American grandfathers, their whole families, even a little innocent girl, and this would make mi amigo, El Jefe de la Fuentes muy triste, no? For this is all a mistake, es verdad?"

The old man's frown turns to worry as the younger speaks rapidly. If they believe me about the non-existent Ernest Grimes, or my non-existent friendship with Senor Police Chief, Rafael de la Fuentes, whose name I happen to know from an article in the Tribune, or if they have even the smallest feeling that my story might be true, their best bet would be to accept the two hundred dollars. That's good money for a border guard in Tijuana.

There's a lot of hot Spanish exchanged. I catch the words " perro…culo…chinge… periodico… jefe. "

We have driven to this spot on a simple journey to cross a border, a hundred yards wide at most, and now we find ourselve quite out of reach of our own laws. Though I have personally cursed these laws dozens of times when given some ridiculous traffic ticket for a seat belt unfastened or a license plate light out, or when face to face on an anti-war line with black helmeted officers, now, when I need them, our police are a world away. Sure, I could wave for help, but it wouldn't come, and if it did, it would probably spit us out, me, caught in a web of marijuana and dead dogs, the grandfather, the owner of the getaway car.

Damn Joey!

What else has he done? I hope it's not something big that might land us in jail for a long time or be very expensive.

Only a few weeks ago an influential American businessman and his young wife had been robbed by two Mexicans next to a Tijuana Customs Office, and the Tribune made much of it, and three Customs agents were fired. Senor de la Fuentes picture was printed as he made an official apology. Since then, continuing exposés about corruption in Tijuana have made life miserable for the Mexican police at the border. Tourism, the life blood of Tijuana, has diminished. If we were to be arrested by these Border Police, and if they were to find I really do have important friends it could be the end of a sweet little job. Or I could be bluffing. But money in hand comes first, and duty comes next, and the two hundred dollars are real, while the next step remains unknown.

"One must be too much careful," says the younger, and maybe I have him. Or he has me. The sticky Mexican legal system can be very costly, I know from friends. Bribes upon bribes. And Mexican jails are hell. Napoleonic law allows los federales to beat the crap out of someone first and take confessions second. To torture them.

"Si," say I. "Especialmente ahora." The younger officer reaches for the money with both hands, but I pull one hand back slowly, smiling. "Por favor, senor," I say, giving him half the money with a little nod. "I know it is your desire as bueno policia y amigos to put the poor car back together, no?" Which they do somewhat, the old man sullenly, leaving torn seats and upholstery, and I hand over the rest of the money to them and I've won this one tiny battle, not without some serioso losses, however, as I won't be able to set foot in Mexico for a long time, for who knows what information may be slyly kept on the computer, the laws in Mexico archaic at best, and arbitrary, and liable to strike without warning years from now.

The border remains intact, a demarcation that beckons and separates Mexico from a land stolen long ago by los gringos. The armed might of the rich stands on the northern side, while on the other side the poor and hungry are governed by a few vicious rich, a nation of 100 million Mexicans waiting behind a line in air and sand and raw earth stretching from far out in the Pacific Ocean east for 300 miles, the line arbitrary as wind, but real as the .45 on the old Customs Agent hip, and surely, from the scowl on his face, he would like to shoot us, at least Joe. He spits a long, brown chew of tobacco towards the left front tire of my Subaru as the younger officer waves us into our seats.

"Safe," I whisper to Angela as we drive out in the car. I try to give her a hug, but she leans away from me. She still has tears on her cheeks. It's my fault. I took her for a scarey ride to Mexico.

We zip through American Customs fast, nothing to declare, not even sand from the beach, nothing Mexican at all, thank God! The American agent looks in at our torn seats suspiciously. I explain that we got a shakedown by Mexican Customs. He looks at my driver's license, hears my accent, asks Angela where she was born, and when her upper lip curls over her teeth up to her nose and she says Philadelphia, he laughs and waves us on. I slowly relax as we breeze north along Pacific Coast Highway, and I tell Joe he got us into this mess, and that he has some making up to do.

"Right," he says.

The wind off the sea through the car window is cool and very nice.

"The next time you run over a dog in Mexico, you will have to do it in your own car."

"Right."

"And you owe me a new upholstery job, plus four hundred dollars."

"Aww," he says. "Right." His voice is not quite so fuck off now.

"Ri… *I*..ight," I say, imitating the falling note in his voice. "And until all that is done, I will not loan you my car for any reason, and never never never for Mexico. And if you ever again take it to Mexico, I will call the Mexican border police and say you stole it and to keep you in that filthy prison there until you are too buggered up and too old and feeble to drive. Entiendes?"

The harshness of my voice stings him. "Aww, Dude," he says.

Tania digs her left elbow hard into his ribs. "Aww, Dude," she says, her voice falling to a sarcastic snarl.

"What's more," I say, "I want you both to know that I am not a 'dude.' I'm a god damned grandpa. *You're* the dudes!"

Angela for some reason thinks that's very funny. She starts to giggle and can't stop for many minutes.

Childhood Revisited

Charlie, known as Joe, stood waiting for the J bus. He'd been taken by his Aunt Maxine to visit his mother at the hospital, and now he was headed home.

Maxine, over six feet tall, and heavy as a whale, had found him and talked him into the car.

"I don't want to go," he'd pleaded.

"Sit down," she said. He was polite, so he sat down. That was his mistake. When he heard her out he tried to open the door and run for it, but she grabbed him by the shirt collar and dragged him back onto the seat. Hell, he thought. She was too strong. If he could get away, he could easily hide from her, as he'd done before. But she held on like fire.

"Your mother is dying. This is your last chance."

"She's not dying," he said, his voice edging down. He really hated to listen to Maxine's high pitched whining voice. Mom couldn't be dying now, for she'd been dying so long he'd almost forgotten when she had been his loving mother, had taken him to the movies, or even to the barber shop where she bet on the horses in the back room while Conrad clipped his hair… which fell in greasy blonde clumps around him on the polished floor. He didn't want to remember.

Maxine held him firmly by his arm and marched him through the hospital. Okay. He'd come this far, and he'd have to go through with it, if not now then later. It wasn't that he didn't love his mother, he loved her too much and now she was, once again, leaving him. He'd long ago thought of her as dead. He couldn't think about it any more. It was over as far as he was concerned.

In his mother's room there was a terrible smell of alcohol and something else, sweat or electrical connections, like burning flesh.

There was a plastic oxygen tent, inside of which the skeletal image of his mother lay propped up on pillows, and where a nurse sat brushing his mother's still beautiful movie star black hair. It was as if mist surrounded them, obscuring them, making their outlines blend into the bed.

From beneath the tent his pale mother, eyes ringed with black circles, reached her thin hand and held his. She squeezed hard for a moment, but her fingers relaxed. She was all bone.

"I'm glad you came," she said, her voice muffled. "This is not easy for you, I know." She smiled at him. Her normally white teeth were stained brown, some darker than others.

"Hi, mom."

"Before you leave here," she said, her words breathless and uneven, "I want you know how much I love you." It felt like there was glue in his throat. He'd never said the words before, and they came from him in a strained grunt. "I love you too."

He couldn't look at her when he said it. Then he broke down completely, bending over sobbing on his cold metal chair, his mother's hand holding his again, then caressing his hair as she had when he was very little, before she'd left him with his grandparents.

He'd half understood why she'd had to leave him with Mama Lou and Daddy Lewis. He blamed his father, who wasn't there to help her, to keep them together, as a regular father ought to do. Then, later, he blamed The Great Depression too, and he began to understand that she hadn't left him so much as she'd been torn from him by something big, as a tornado might whirl off with a house. But he was angry with her any way. She could have kept him with her somehow.

Ever so softly she rubbed his shoulder and he looked up with a jolt. Before he could slip away she tugged at his sleeve and said, "How's school?" It was so ordinary a question that his tears welled up again.

"Good," he said. He stared down at his hands. School wasn't good. He hadn't gone for weeks, but he was afraid his father would find out and he didn't want to hear about it. He hadn't felt like going, that was all, though he'd poured himself into homework before that, running as fast as possible and holding his breath, but he hadn't lasted. And now he was in the room with her, and she was beautiful and dying, and his breath was giving out. He knew too much death already, his grandmother Momma Lou, his beloved uncle Pat, his cousins, and now his mother. Why was he being punished?

He hadn't eaten his peas. When she had enrolled him in nursery school, he hadn't eaten the canned peas they fed him for lunch, instead he threw them all over the room, one at a time, in every corner and hidden crack of the room where he sat alone, his diminishing scoop of sick green peas on a white plate before him.

"We don't waste food here, people are starving," an enormous woman in a shiny black dress had told him as he sat there his peas in a pile on his plate. Charlie wasn't used to being forced to eat something he hated, and he hated canned peas almost as much as lima beans or buttermilk or cottage cheese. When the fat lady found the peas everywhere, she shook him and called his mother and she came and took him out of school, and that was the end of that school for him, though, five or six years later, he saw the same playground again in the alley behind Bobby Miller's house, where the boys played stickball. It was a surprise to see the same slide, the same backyard monkey bars. Did nothing ever go away?

He hadn't understood it at the time, but looking back he could see that if he had been able to eat those peas, he could have stayed in that nursery school. He could have stayed with his mother. But that was a long time later when he figured that out. At age six, things just happen, he recalled, and had no connection to anything else. People came and went from his life. He'd suddenly found himself living at his grandmother's in Long Beach, while his mother stayed in Los Angeles. She became an occasional visitor, though, at first, he waited for her every weekend. Then she was hardly there at all, except when he had measles or whooping cough. Then she came and fed him and touched his forehead and told him stories even more exciting than those Uncle Pat told.

His father Louie was nowhere. Momma Lou and Ethel called his father Babe. Baby. His father, their baby. It was hard to believe.

She reached to touch his hand again, and tried to lift the oxygen tent, but as she turned her shoulders toward him the nurse doing her hair, gently pulled her back. "She needs to sleep now. She's been awake waiting for you, and it's been too long." She waved her pencil-thin fingers at Charlie, but she wasn't angry, she was sad and loving. He felt like he was in a Christmas play where all the children had to perform some few lines, say the right things. The rest of the play he forgot. The pressure wouldn't let him go, and he couldn't recall what he might do next. Go home, sleep, go back to school. Go to Claudette's. It wasn't a memory anymore, just a weight. His father was waiting for him.

He'd wanted to run, had been avoiding the whole thing, had been playing as hard as he could with Bill Ruch and Doug Harb and Dick Goff, running the streets, chasing girls, sneaking into miniature golf. He'd put his mother far at the back of his mind, had kept her there for two years in fact, because his father had told him not to tell her she was dying, that she didn't know and what she didn't know would help her get through the last few months. But the so-called last few months had lingered into two years, and Charlie's seventeenth birthday was coming up and he quit thinking about the impending loss, the real loss of his mother, who had lain in bed reading or under sedation, or slept under frozen eye masks, whatever they called them, for months and now years.

For fear of blurting out that she was dying, he'd stopped going into her bedroom, unless she called for water or some little thing, not trying to forget her exactly, but trying to live a normal life. He wanted to run and read and hide out from everyone except when he was with Dick or Doug. He had buried himself in homework, but that wasn't enough to keep him going, for he had to keep running, keep on the go, not spend a boring moment alone with himself, had to be really tired when he finally climbed into bed, though his dreams were bad. He'd dreamed of being old, his hands as thin as his mother's. Waiting. He looked at them now. They looked old. Thin. Filled with knotty veins.

Waiting. His dad was home waiting, but mostly drunk, so there was no real hurry to go there. The only hurry was to get away from the Home. At first, when Charlie was four or five, his dad played with him, though he smelled always of beer or wine. But when they wrestled and his dad allowed him to climb up on his back, and would shake his shoulders and trumpet like the elephant Hathi carrying Mowgli, and mother would cheer or sometimes say, "That's enough rough house now, you two," O then he would quiver with excitement. And they would go to Clifton's Restaurant, where the gypsy violinist played Tzigainer, an odd name with a tz in it, and on the way he would hold their hands and swing between them, and he could fly like Tarzan over puddles over curbs so he would love and love and love them both. But they didn't love each other and there was no money.

Now his father was distant, smelling of wine and grease. He went to work unshaven, and returned covered in grease with a bottle of Gallo to sit in his chair and watch TV. Baseball, or football, or I Love Lucy. And his Aunt Ethel had come to stay with them, and she liked her whiskey, and talked and talked, boring him with the same old stories he'd loved when he was small, Gyp and Cub and the family of rattlesnakes in the back yard, or the cries of the men who drowned in the flooded mine in Great Grandma Mauzy McNeil's backyard in Placerville.

Just the name, Placerville, brought back the actual mine, a hole in barren ground that passed for a yard. Mauzy, or Miser. A peculiar name. Women were all mothers, except for Aunt Nita, who had no children because Uncle Art had been sick. This mother of grandmothers, Mauzy, had given him a jagged red rock she said was gold ore. It didn't look much different than all the other rocks in the back yard. It had been Hallowe'en, with grinning Jack O' Lanterns all over the yard and back porch, their eyes and noses and jagged grins alight from candles inside, and the masses of excited children coming by holding paper bags filled with candy. He'd been too young to go Trick or Treat, and he didn't want to go up to people's doors alone either, though he'd felt the electricity in the chill night air as he dug holes and stacked rocks in the back yard, surrounded by dark trees, as unknown children came by and looked at him. He meant to go when he was older. A long time ago. He'd been four, maybe five…

It was all strange, his father and mother together, his bent over great grandmother in her flowered house coat and slippers holding him, smiling, feeding him marble cake. He couldn't say he'd loved her, no. He didn't know her. She was so old, like a twisted wire. They said she'd traveled west in a covered wagon. There was a great grandfather too, Whitt, who whittled, who himself seemed made of wood, or knotty branches twined together. He never spoke.

The J was late. There were other buses, but he'd used this one for so long that he always took it. Oh, he thought, it's Sunday, and they don't come as often. The bus schedule on the bus stop sign was obscured by dirt and faded. He'd wait it out. That was all he could do. Wait.

He was sad about his mother, yes, but he had a great girlfriend, Claudette, and they spent as much time as possible at her house while her parents worked at their French Hand Laundry. And Claudette was more exciting than anything, better than his childhood on the shoulders of his father, even more exciting than fishing off Catalina.

A soft white breast. Kissing. Petting, the old folks called it, or necking. Silly names for what was so pleasurable it almost caused him to faint. And Claudette was so eager. She would have gone all the way, but Charlie hadn't wanted to. Something held him back, possibly the fact that she was Catholic, and he would have to marry her, he knew, if they had sex. They did everything else, and if there had been more to do, he didn't know what it was. Everything about Claudette was deliciously hidden, her bra, her underpants which she allowed him to slip off. It was inevitable that they would go all the way, and get married. But he'd been sixteen. Jesus! He was too young for a family, to be a father. His own father was no help at all. Nor would he in his worst nightmare ever reveal to his father that he even had a girl friend, not her address, not her name, not a bit of information. His father. His enemy. Claudette was his own personal business.

The three of them, mom and dad and he used to go to Yee Hung Louie Chinese Restaurant in China Town, for his father's name was Louie, and so that was a joke. Usually late at night his father and sometimes his friends from work and his mom would head for China Town deep in the heart of Los Angeles, in the old days, when they'd lived in Los Angeles. Now it was San Francisco, and he had a hard time thinking San Francisco when he'd lived almost all his childhood in L.A., City of the Queen of the Angels. El Pueblo de Nuestra Senora la Reina de Los Angeles de la Porciuncula, and now Saint Francis' city.

How did he get here?

Thousands of child years ago, when he was 12, he'd traveled all by himself at 1:00 in the morning on the Red Car to the sport-fishing boats in San Pedro, hauling his 12-foot fishing pole all the way. The conductor wasn't going to allow him on with the pole, but Charlie had begged and had told him how he could lay it flat behind the seats. And the driver had let him go. And then Charlie got lost but determined in the dark streets of San Pedro where he'd carried his pole over his shoulder, worried about being late for the boat after all this effort, stopping an occasional man to ask directions, and a policeman who wanted to know why he was out this early.

"I'm going on the Alalunga, for albacore," he'd said. He was friendly with policemen, though he'd been chased by them before. "I've been doing this since I was eight," he said proudly. He was smart, the policeman must have seen. "I made this pole myself."

"Well… I don't know…" the policeman said, admiring the bamboo pole. But there was no law against a twelve-year-old going fishing early in the morning.

The policeman said, "I'm a fisherman. I'll take you. You're only five blocks away."

So instead of arriving too late, he arrived a little early, like royalty, in a police car lights flashing red, the long pole stuck out the window like a lance, the men already there giving him the best spot on the stern of the lighted boat, the dark night around, the harbor full of salt sea smells, seaweed, thumping hum of an idling diesel engine beneath the deck, a huge live-bait well full of sparkling anchovies swimming lively as bees. He was a regular little fisherman himself, they said on the boat.

And the fishing was so good, he'd caught ten albacore, so many his thin arms gave out. Still, as long as they were out on the ocean, he couldn't stop fishing. He gave six albacore to the men, sold three for a dollar each to some Italian housewives waiting at the dock, and got a ride home all the way to L.A. with his one fish in a gunny sack, for which his mother and father praised him, and his friend Bobby's family, too, praised him for the fresh tuna, Chicken of the Sea albacore tuna. A victory, a great adventure, a long long day across the Channel to Catalina and back with fish. And he'd paid for it himself with money from his paper corner.

He had a bad feeling about the bus. Was it coming? He did feel a little faint. Would he have a fainting spell and couldn't remember? Was he sick again? He'd nearly died when he was seven from whooping cough and measles and a painful left ear infection that left him increasingly deaf in that ear. Still, he had two ears. That was when his mother had come to stay in the back bedroom in Long Beach and he'd had to sleep on the couch, and she had taken good care of him, and loved him, and he had recovered. And had gone back to school.

He leaned against the bus stop pole. He hung his weight on it. The J would come any minute now. What had happened to Maxine? She had been with him in the hospital and had vanished, and here he was, as usual, waiting for the bus on his own.

One of the big nurses from the Home came puffing down the sidewalk. He knew her name, for some reason, *Rose Marie. Rose Marie, I love you.* Light opera. He didn't like heavy opera. He surely didn't love this Rose Marie.

"What on earth are you doing here, Joe," Rose Marie said. It was an accusation. She was too heavy to be moving so fast, not as fat as Aunt Maxine though. A black man in white came running a half block behind her. Rose Marie's face was far too red. Bad circulation, Charlie knew. She could just keel over with a sudden stroke.

"You better not strain your heart," Charlie said. He wasn't going to let go of the bus stop pole.

"Come on Joe," she said. "You can't be running around in your pajamas."

That's right, he thought. *Now I'm called Joe. It's my secret name.*

The male nurse, Mitch, came up and pulled on his arm, but Charlie held on tight as he could, saying, "I'm waiting for the J." J for Joe. His knuckles swelled with strain. There were brown spots on his hands, one of them open and bleeding. Blue veins like tiny mountain ranges.

"Right," Mitch said. And Rose Marie said, "It's supper time, Joe. Time for meds." And his arms, suddenly frail as dead flower stems, flowed into Mitch's hands which were licorice black, and they held him up, with Rose Marie, still breathing heavy as a harbor seal, saying, "Be careful. He's been out in the sun a while."

"But it's time to catch the bus," Charlie explained, his feet dragging along. "My father's waiting."

"Yes," said Rose Marie in her lying voice. "He's waiting for you now. Back at the Home."

About James M. LeCuyer

Mr. LeCuyer holds three Master's Degrees, in Education from UC Berkeley, in Creative Writing from San Francisco State University, and in Psychology from The Graduate School of Psychology. He was, for three years, a junior officer, USN. He was a technical editor and writer for the Physics Department of the University of California. For some twenty-five years he taught high school English in the San Francisco Bay Area, in Albany, Oakland, and San Francisco. He worked for some fifteen years as a commercial halibut and herring fisherman out of Tomales Bay and Sausalito.

Among other jobs, he has been a taxi driver, a beer truck driver, and a report writer for the Berkeley Police Department. He managed a coffee shop on Telegraph in Berkeley. He was an anti-war activist during the Vietnam era. He was married once, has a daughter, Camille Alfred, and two grandchildren, Joseph Varga, and Tania Varga, and three great grandchildren, Tezla Williams, Sophie Varga, and James Varga. He presently lives in Fremont with poet Florence Miller. He loves them immensely.

Other books by James M. LeCuyer

A Brick for Offissa Pupp, poetry, published by Floating Island Press, 1979, reprint Fall, 2018, Darkhouse Books. *Threnody for Sturgeon*, stories, published by Outskirts Press, 2016, available through Amazon.

About This Book

The typeface in this book is 11.5 Garamond and Helvetica (for the headings). It was laid out using Adobe InDesign software and converted to PDF for uploading to the printing facility.

About Darkhouse Books

Darkhouse Books is dedicated to publishing entertaining fiction, primarily in the mystery and science fiction field. Darkhouse Books is located in Niles, California, an inadvertently-preserved, 120 year old one-sided railtown, forty miles from San Francisco. Further information may be obtained by visiting our website at www.darkhousebooks.com.

Also from Darkhouse Books